A PERILOUS POWER

By E. Rose Sabin from Tom Doherty Associates

A School for Sorcery
A Perilous Power

A Perilous Power

E. ROSE SABIN

TOR®

A Tom Doherty Associates Book
New York

A PERILOUS POWER

This book is printed on acid-free paper.

Map illustration by Jackie Aher.

A Tor Book
Published by Tom Doherty Associates, LLC
175 Fifth Avenue
New York, NY 10010

www.tor.com

Tor® is a registered trademark of Tom Doherty Associates, LLC.

Library of Congress Cataloging-in-Publication Data

Sabin, E. Rose.
    A perilous power / E. Rose Sabin.—1st ed.
      p.   cm.
    "A Tom Doherty Associates book."
    ISBN 0-765-30859-2 (acid-free paper)
    1. Wizards—Fiction.   2. Mentoring—Fiction.   3. Male friendship—
Fiction.   I. Title.

PS3619.A27P47 2004
816'.3—dc22
                                                                    2003057057

First Edition: January 2004

Printed in the United States of America

0   9   8   7   6   5   4   3   2   1

For Diane,
in gratitude

Acknowledgments

This book has been a long time in the writing, and I have received guidance and inspiration from many people along the way, from my first creative writing teachers, Marvelle Lightfields (then Marvette Carter) and Fred. W. Wright, Jr., through all the kind and discerning people of PINAWOR (the Pinellas Authors and Writers Organization), to the small critiquing group of Betty DeBate, Linda Harrell, Joyce Levesque, and Louise Miller, whose advice and encouragement sustained me over many years. Especially, I thank my good friends and fellow writers Diane Marcou and Barbara Harrington for their help in getting me through the editing and revision process. Special thanks go to Janice Strand for sharing her knowledge of marketing strategies and to C. J. Jeffers and Susan Adger for their help in setting up my Web site.

I will always be deeply grateful to my agent, Jack Byrne, for his willingness to take a chance on a new and inexperienced writer. And, above all, I thank my editor, Jonathan Schmidt, whose incisive comments and patient explanations have made this book so much better than it would have been.

A PERILOUS POWER

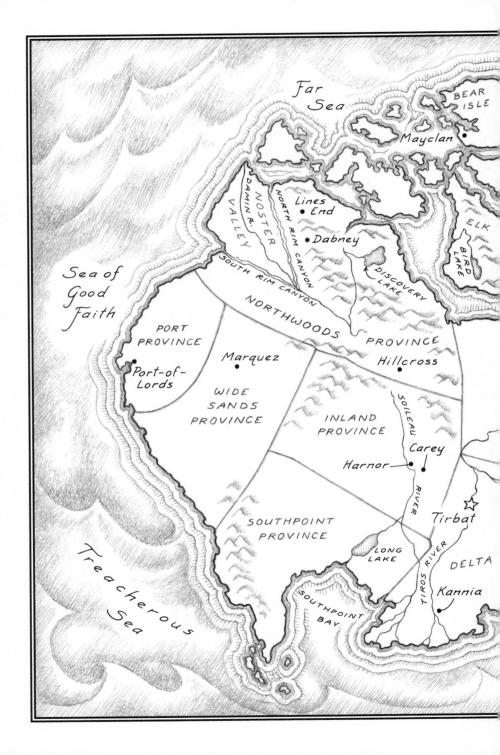

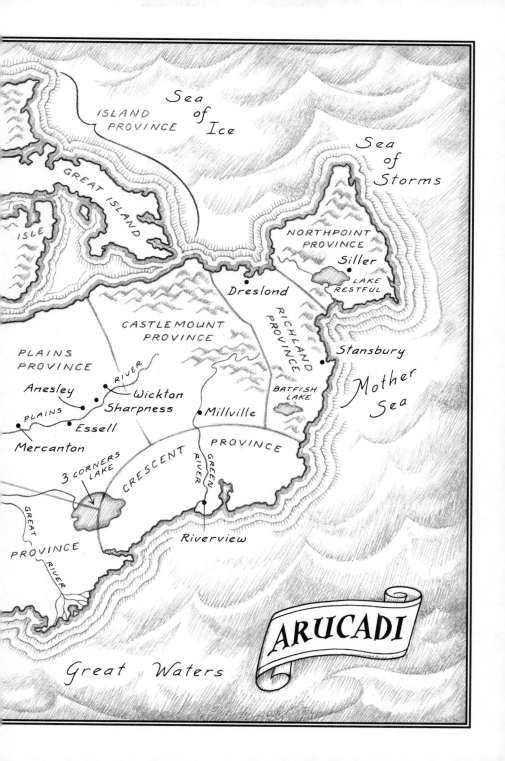

1

A Change of Direction

Trevor Blake leaned against the kitchen wall, watching his mother slice beef and fit it into rolls hot from the oven. The yeasty aroma of the fresh-baked rolls, the spicy scent of cinnamon-laden pear tarts, the savory odor of the roast all conspired to distract him from his mother's lecture.

"Trevor, are you listening to me?" she asked as she slipped the beef rolls into a box and held it out to him.

"Yes, Mom." Grinning, he accepted the box. "You said to hurry, don't miss the bus, and be careful with my money." He hadn't heard any of that, but it was a safe guess.

"And be sure to get good, practical clothing. I know you want citified things so you won't stand out when you get to the university, but it's more important to get good material that will hold up and keep you warm through the winter."

"I'll remember."

"I doubt it." With a sigh, she wiped her hands on her apron. "I wish I could go with you, but your father needs me here. Do try to be sensible for once."

He laughed, knowing well what really kept her from coming with him. His father could have spared her for a day, but she was terrified of the "newfangled" buses, which had replaced horse-drawn coaches less than two years ago and which did indeed break down with alarming frequency. Planting a kiss on her cheek, he said, "I'd better get going."

"Lands, yes." She glanced at the kitchen clock. "It's getting late. You don't want to miss the bus."

No, he didn't, but it rarely arrived on time, so he didn't hurry. The soft buzz of the bees in the honeysuckle and the rich scent of the blossoms hanging in the still air infected him with laziness, so that he strolled slowly down the dusty lane. The sun-baked sand burned his feet through the soles of his shoes. The heat of late summer had driven most folks indoors or at least into a shady part of their fields. In spite of the cloudless sky, a rain dove cooed a distant prophecy of rain. Trevor felt so much a part of this familiar summer scene that he was struck by the sudden impression that the lane and the whole village would vanish when he left.

He had long dreamed of leaving, but now the nearness of that day filled him with sadness. When he was gone, the village would not be what it had been. It was as much a product of his making as he was of it. Up ahead was the Widow Marsh's gate and fence he and his friend Les had painted and repaired last fall. Over the fence on the other side of the lane he could see the row of young poplars he and his father had helped Farmer Croftley plant for a wind-break a few years ago. If he looked behind him he could see in the distance the belfry of the old schoolhouse where he and Les had learned to read and write and do sums and coax a tale from the teacher and smuggle a fat toad into the desk of the giddiest girl and stop up the chimney with rags on a cold day so the smoke would pour back into the room and the pupils would have to be sent home until the damage could be repaired. He had often felt the sharp sting of a birch

E. ROSE SABIN

switch and known the tiresomeness of writing two thousand times, "I will not . . ."

Despite the mischief he'd done, he had graduated at the top of his class, well above Les and, to everyone's surprise, above Maribeth Hanley. When the lot fell on the village of Amesley that year to be privileged to send its top scholar to the university, he, not Maribeth, had received the grant from the provincial government. His parents had never been so proud of him as on that day last spring when the president of the village council had placed in his hands the precious certificate entitling him to enroll in the National University of Tirbat. Maribeth cried, and her mother, Mistress Hanley, glowered throughout the presentation. But Les looked as thrilled as if *he* had won, though he would be left behind when Trevor boarded the train to travel south to the great city. Simple farm folk did not travel far from home and could not afford the high cost of the university for their sons and daughters. Trevor would take the marvelous journey alone in two more weeks.

Today's bus trip was only to Essell, the county seat, to buy clothes suitable for university wear. But even that short journey seemed an irrevocable commitment to a totally new life, a life that would cut him off from Les, his chum from early childhood. His steps lagged as he thought about that loss.

He paused at the cemetery where two years ago Grandfather Blake had been buried, the latest of five Blake generations laid to rest among the spreading oaks. The cemetery was not large, and the graves were arranged in even rows and topped with headstones that for the most part were similarly shaped and no more than knee-high. Near the Blake graves, however, was a single tall stone column on a square

A PERILOUS POWER

base with the words NEVER AGAIN inscribed on the column and names and dates carved on each side of the stone base. One of the names was Oma Blake. He had asked his father who Oma Blake was and what the monument represented, and was surprised when his father scowled, said, "That's a question you need to ask your Uncle Matt," and refused to give any further explanation. A short time later his mother took him aside and said, "Don't ever ask your father about that monument again. Oma Blake was his sister, and she died tragically. I don't know the whole story myself, but I think your Uncle Matthew was somehow responsible for her death, though it was an accident. Your father was deeply affected by it and doesn't like to be reminded."

Trevor gazed at the monument for several minutes, still curious, wondering whether he would ever learn the story.

He walked on but, in need of more pleasant memories, stopped briefly on the creaky wooden bridge over the little stream that had provided him and Les with a few fish and many long, dreamy hours lazing on its banks with cane poles in hand.

A short distance past the bridge he came to the pear tree he and Les had climbed to rescue old Mrs. Darby's cat. Recalling how they had claimed their reward in pears, he looked hopefully at the tree. Most of the pears had been picked or had fallen, but a juicy-looking pear still hung from a top limb. Trevor's mouth watered. He hadn't forgotten the promise he'd made to his parents long ago, but at age seventeen, ready to leave home, he no longer felt bound by it.

Fixing his gaze firmly on the pear, he stretched one hand toward it. The power still came easily despite years of disuse. The stem snapped and the pear floated gently into the air and sailed down to his waiting hand.

E. ROSE SABIN

Only after the deed was done did it occur to him to look carefully up and down the lane and peer at Mrs. Darby's house to make sure that no one had seen. He thought he saw a hand release a curtain in a window, letting it fall back into place after being pulled aside. Holding his prize, he waited to see whether anyone would come out of the house to confront him. When no one did, he decided that he had seen nothing more than the curtain blowing in the breeze.

He bit into the pear and ate slowly, relishing every mouthful of its sweet-tart goodness. Tossing away the core, he went on his way singing.

The song died when he reached the crossroads in time to see the bus to Essell disappear in a cloud of dust. He ran after it, yelling, but it sped away.

His mother would be furious. She was always berating him for his carelessness. He kicked at the dirt until an idea popped into his head.

In a few minutes a bus should come from the other direction on its way to the towns of Sharpness and Wickton. His Uncle Matt and Aunt Ellen lived in Sharpness, only a little more than an hour's bus ride from Amesley, but he hadn't visited them since the summer he was seven years old. He'd spent two wonderful weeks with them then in the big, drafty farmhouse where, as far as he knew, they still lived.

His use of power to bring down the pear brought back memories of that visit, when he had discovered his special abilities. Oak trees surrounded the house, and on the second day of his visit he had climbed one of them, a branch had broken beneath his weight, and as he was falling, he'd caught himself and floated gently to the ground.

For the rest of that visit, although his uncle urged caution, he used his power often. Uncle Matt praised his growing skill but warned him to use the power sparingly, and never in the presence of his father. As usual, he hadn't listened, distracted when Aunt Ellen brought in a plate of sugar cookies hot from the oven.

When his father came to pick him up, he brought Les along. It was Les's first trip away from their home village, and he'd bounded off the wagon, a red-haired, freckle-faced whirlwind. Trevor and Les raced around the farm together until Aunt Ellen called them in for dinner. Asked to pass a dish of peas and eager to show off his newfound powers, Trevor lifted the dish and floated it above the table to his uncle.

Instead of being pleased, his father shouted and smacked him across the face. His father and Uncle Matt quarreled violently when Uncle Matt defended that use of power. Trevor had been glad for Les's comforting presence when his father, declaring that no son of his was going to be trained as a sorcerer, stormed from the house with the boys in tow and forbade Trevor ever to visit his aunt and uncle again. Later he had appealed to his mother for help, but she had staunchly supported the prohibition. Not only that, but his parents had forced from him the unwilling promise not to use his power again but to hide it and forget it.

He broke that promise many times in his younger years. His power was too much a part of him to be cast aside. Several times he'd slipped and used it without thinking, and sometimes he'd used it at school to show off. From time to time at Les's urging he performed some feat just to fascinate his friend or to help him with his chores. But after his father lashed him with a horsewhip when he caught him using his power instead of the pitchfork to lift hay from the loft into the horse stalls, he'd kept it suppressed. Until today.

Today he was of age and no longer bound by his parents' restrictions. He could do as he pleased. He'd pay his aunt and uncle a farewell visit before leaving for the university. He'd never had the chance to ask Uncle Matt about the monument in the cemetery; at last he could.

The bus chugged and clattered into view. He waved it to a stop and jumped on, handed the driver two small copper coins, and took a seat. As he watched the countryside jog past, he thought about how much Les, too, would enjoy a trip to Sharpness. What fun if they could share this final adventure before their paths parted, perhaps forever.

He'd used his power once today; he could do it again.

He closed his eyes and drew pictures in his mind: first, Uncle Matt and Aunt Ellen's house as he had seen it last, a rambling frame farmhouse of three stories. Painted a dark brown, it had a high-peaked, wooden-shingled roof with three tall chimneys. And lots of windows. He remembered Les saying that those windows looked like eyes watching everywhere so nobody could ever sneak up on the house. To Trevor that had seemed an odd notion.

Then Les as he was today, his fiery red hair as unruly as ever, his boyhood freckles melded into an even tan, his body tall and strong from working in his father's fields.

He pictured Les walking along the lane as he had, waiting at the crossroads where he had waited, and, like him, boarding the bus—the afternoon bus this time—to Sharpness and Wickton. He pictured Les taking this same ride, feeling the same monotonous jiggling and rocking all the way to Sharpness.

Trevor smiled a satisfied smile as he stepped off the bus. It was almost noon. He strode through town and on down

A PERILOUS POWER

the curving country road that led to his uncle's house.

His heart leaped as the house came into view up ahead on the rise, the oak trees on either side of it as full and magnificent as he remembered. The house itself had changed little. He hurried toward it. Aunt Ellen opened the door before he reached it. She looked older than he remembered. Drawing him into a warm embrace, she said, "At last you've come back."

"I wasn't sure you'd recognize me," he said. "You haven't seen me since I was seven."

She laughed. "You've grown up, right enough. But you still have the same straight, shiny brown hair and thrust-out chin. And the famous Blake nose that you're all blessed with."

He laughed, too, and hugged her harder. As a kid he'd hated that "Blake nose" with its bump in the center, but now he had to admit that it was distinctive.

Over her shoulder he saw his uncle beaming at him. "Trevor, my boy," he boomed. "Of course we recognized you. We've been expecting you."

Released from his aunt's arms, he received a hearty hug from his uncle and allowed himself to be drawn into the comfortable parlor and installed in an overstuffed wing chair.

"How could you have been expecting me?" he asked. "I only decided to come on impulse after I missed the bus to Essell."

His uncle's hearty chuckle jiggled his muttonchops. "I know, I know. And on the way you decided your friend Les should join you here. You broadcast the suggestion so loud and strong, no sensitive within forty miles could've missed it. Be interestin' to see who turns up along with Les. We might have us quite a party."

E. ROSE SABIN

"A dangerous one." A worried frown creased Aunt Ellen's kindly face. "Most gifted folks stick together, but there are a few bad apples, and if one of them gets the message . . ."

"Now, now, Ellen. Won't be nothin' we can't handle. Don't worry the boy."

But his uncle stroked the fringe of beard that outlined his jutting chin, and Trevor knew the gesture meant that his uncle was worried, too.

His rash act might bring trouble to this house.

2

Too-Loud Summons

The bus was late, and Trevor paced impatiently in front of the Sharpness general store where it would stop. Through the glass storefront, he could see Uncle Matt leaning against the counter talking to the storekeeper. Aunt Ellen had remained at home to prepare dinner, and Trevor's mouth watered at the thought of the feast he knew she'd set out to celebrate his and Les's arrival.

For what must have been the hundredth time he walked out into the street, shaded his eyes, and peered into the distance, hoping to sight the bus, but the road was empty.

"Hurry!" Trevor muttered. Squeezing his eyes shut, he sent the thought soaring. *Hurry, Les. It's getting late. Tell the driver to go faster.*

Uncle Matt burst out of the store, a bottle of lemon soda in one hand. "Stop that!" He thrust the bottle at Trevor. "Drink this and cool down. The bus'll be here in a few minutes."

Trevor held the cold drink to his forehead for a few seconds before drinking. After taking a long swallow, he looked sheepishly at his uncle. "I'm sorry. It came out without thinking."

His uncle clapped him on the shoulder. "No harm done, I reckon."

"No more than I've already done, you mean."

"We don't know that you've done any. Don't worry about it. What've you got back from Les? I haven't picked up any sendings of his."

"Les can't send," Trevor said, startled. "He's not gifted."

His uncle's brow furrowed. "Of course he is. How else could he receive?"

Trevor shrugged. "We've been so close. I guess it's 'cause we know each other so well."

Uncle Matt shook his head. "I'm sure Les has the power. I sensed it when I met him all those years ago. Figgered that was what drew you two together. Mean to tell me all this time you never knew?"

Again Trevor pressed the cold pop bottle to his temple. Les, gifted? Impossible. "If he'd had the gift, he'd have told me. Several times he asked me to do some little thing—sometimes just for fun, sometimes to help him out. Like once when he dropped his dad's good hedge clippers into the well, he asked me to raise them for him, and I did. He used to try to do the things I could do, but he couldn't. I'd try to help him—push him a bit. But I found nothing to push, no power to spark on. After a while he accepted the idea, and it didn't bother him anymore."

Uncle Matt stroked his beard. "Never heard of a person without the power being able to receive mind-to-mind. It takes a sense normals don't have. But the power comes in many different forms. He may be gifted in a way you've never recognized.

"Ahh! Yonder comes the bus. We'll know soon."

Trevor heard the rattle of the bus's motor, saw the blue

vehicle bounce down the dirt street. Jubilantly he raised his pop bottle high, then swigged the remaining soda before the bus rumbled to a halt in front of them.

The doors opened with a squeal, and Les bounded off.

Trevor grabbed his hand, drew him close, and pounded his shoulders. "I knew you'd come!"

"Did you leave me any choice?" Les's wide grin robbed the words of reproach. "Dad's probably still scratching his head over the excuse I gave for taking off during rye harvest. You might have given some thought to how hard it could have been for me to get away. Lucky Dad had plenty of other help, or I wouldn't have been able to get away no matter how hard you made the worms squirm in my brain."

"Sorry, Les. It's just that with me leaving for Tirbat in two weeks, this is probably our last chance to share some fun."

Les punched Trevor's arm. "There's more to life than fun, y'know. Hey, your mom thinks you're in Essell buying clothes for Tirbat. Bus take a detour?"

Trevor hung his head. "Missed the bus to Essell," he said. Then he looked up and laughed. "Isn't this better than shopping?"

Uncle Matt cleared his throat. "Fellas, we'd best get home. Ellen'll have dinner waitin'."

"Les, you remember my Uncle Matt?"

"Couldn't forget him." Les stuck out his hand, and Uncle Matt grabbed it and pumped it.

"Great to see you again, son."

Trevor caught an undertone of anxiety beneath Uncle Matt's friendly greeting. He followed his uncle's quick glance toward the three or four other passengers who'd descended after Les. Two of them he didn't recognize, but he certainly knew Mistress Hanley, Maribeth's mother. A red and gray kerchief tied over her hair, she hurried into the general store when he turned to look at her. Through the window he saw her head for the crank telephone beside the counter. He remembered Maribeth speaking of relatives in Sharpness; her mother was probably calling to announce her arrival.

The fourth passenger was Jasper Ryles, who'd lived alone as long as Trevor had known him. He'd been married once, but his wife had died not long after the marriage, and he'd never wed again. Trevor had been told that the man had no relatives anywhere. What business could he have in Sharpness?

Uncle Matt cupped a hand around Trevor's elbow and steered him away from bus and store. Les followed.

"Keep walking," Uncle Matt whispered into Trevor's ear. "Don't look back. Guard your thoughts."

Trevor followed his uncle's instructions, though he found it hard to imagine that Jasper Ryles, curmudgeon though he was, could be bent on causing trouble.

Les caught up to him. "What's happening, Trev? Something wrong?"

"Uncle Matt thinks so." Trevor cast a backward glance at his uncle, walking behind them. "I guess he'll explain when we reach the house."

Relaxed, stuffed with good food, Les leaned back in his chair and grinned at Trevor, having forgiven his friend for using his mental powers to bring him here.

They sat around the large oak table on which Aunt Ellen had spread a feast: roast pork and gravy, turnips and carrots, peach dumplings and pear pie. A cool breeze drifted in through the open window, bringing the scent of fresh-mown hay to mingle with the lingering odors of the food. No one

E. ROSE SABIN

had said anything more about whatever had worried Trevor's uncle, and dinner was a joyous occasion.

Les shoved back his empty plate and patted his belly. "Best meal I've had in ages," he said. "You sure are a good cook, Mistress Blake."

"Call me Aunt Ellen, please, Les. After all, you and Trevor are closer than most brothers."

Delighted, Les jumped up from his chair, went to Aunt Ellen, and hugged her. "I'd be mighty proud to have you as my aunt."

She pulled his face to hers and kissed his cheek. "You and Trevor are very dear to us, Les. It's a pity his folks barred him from coming here for so many years. We were cheated out of the joy of watching the two of you grow up. We last saw you as children, and now you're young men ready to make your mark in life. All those years between——" She began to sob.

Les hugged her to him until the tears stopped. She raised her apron and used it to wipe her eyes. "It's been hard, not seeing you, not knowin' how you turned out. We'd hear reports now and then, of course. But we would've had you both here every summer if Trevor's folks hadn't been so opposed."

"I never did understand that," Les said. "Oh, I knew it had to do with Trevor's special powers, but I could never see why his folks were so bound and determined to keep 'em a secret. He said they thought other people would be jealous, but I knew about 'em and I never felt jealous. I wished I could do the things he could do, sure, but I accepted that I couldn't, because Trevor was special. And I was proud that he was, and proud to be his friend."

A curious look passed between Trevor and his uncle. Uncle Matt cleared his throat and waved Les back to his seat.

"There's more to it than jealousy, my boy," Uncle Matt said. "But right now I need to talk to you about something else. You say you aren't gifted, and Trevor thinks you can receive his mental sendings because the two of you have had such a long and close friendship. But that explanation doesn't satisfy me. Those who aren't gifted can't receive sendings. I think you're mistaken when you say you don't have the power."

Les shook his head violently, too startled to speak, his mind suddenly flooded with thoughts of all the times he'd tried in vain to duplicate Trevor's feats, of the nights when as a child he'd prayed for even a tiny portion of the power— prayed to his parents' gods and also prayed to the Power-Giver, as Trevor had confided his aunt and uncle had taught him to do on his memorable summer visit. But as he grew older Les resigned himself to being normal, though he didn't share Trevor's parents' belief that being normal was best.

Uncle Matt was regarding him with an expression both stern and anxious.

Les met Uncle Matt's gaze. "I don't have any gift, sir," he said.

"We think you do, Les," Aunt Ellen said in her soft voice. "Would you be willing to let us test you?"

"Test?" The word sent a chill laddering up his spine. "What kind of test? What will it do to me?"

"Nothing at all," Aunt Ellen assured him, rising from her place at the table. "It doesn't hurt, it won't take long, and it will settle the matter once and for all."

"Of course he'll have it," Trevor spoke up, his face eager.

"Let him answer for himself, son." Uncle Matt gave Trevor

a sharp glance before turning back to Les. "Being gifted can cause trouble. Trevor's gift has put a breach between him and his folks, as well you know. Your parents, now, they're good people, but they might be against what they don't understand. Reckon you wouldn't want them to turn against you."

Les sat up straight and directed his gaze at Uncle Matt. "I'm not a coward, Mr. Blake," he said. "Much as I love my parents, I wouldn't hide from the truth to spare their feelings. And I don't think they'd be opposed like Trevor's folks. So give me the test. I *want* to know."

Aunt Ellen left the dining room and returned in seconds with a candle and a small wooden box. She lit the candle, set it in the center of the table, and turned the stem that extinguished the flames in the gasolier above them. The dim light of the single candle sent shadows dancing over their faces, giving Trevor's familiar features a sinister look.

After returning to her seat, Aunt Ellen opened the wooden box, took out a pinch of gray powder, and sprinkled it into the candle flame. The flame flared, flickered, and returned to a steady glow. A sweet scent filled the room. Aunt Ellen spoke a word unknown to Les—perhaps from a strange language. After that, the room was quiet. No one spoke or moved; it seemed to Les they hardly breathed but sat like statues, hands resting on the table.

So gradually that Les thought at first it was only his imagination, the faces and hands of his three companions began to give off a pale blue light.

No, he was not imagining it. The ghostly aura shimmered around Trevor's head and played over his hands. It imparted an unearthly glow to Aunt Ellen's homey features. It transformed Uncle Matt's beard and sideburns into a silvery halo.

Les looked down at his own hands. Ripples of cold blue fire danced over them. He gasped.

"It's the gift light." Trevor's awed whisper broke the silence. "It's all around you."

"I've never seen it so bright." Uncle Matt sounded no less awed than Trevor. "You not only have the gift; you have it stronger than any of us."

"But I haven't . . . I can't . . ." Les's words failed. He stared at the blue radiance streaming from his hands.

"You have it," Aunt Ellen asserted. "You haven't discovered how to manifest it. You need training. We'll have to find a way—"

A loud banging on the front door interrupted her words. "Open up," a deep voice shouted. "We know you're inside."

A shriller voice screamed, "Come out, you godless sorcerers! Come out or be burned out!"

3

DOWNPOUR

Aunt Ellen jumped up, relit the gasolier, and extinguished the candle. The blue auras vanished with the snuffing of the candle flame.

Uncle Matt called out, "Hold on! I'm coming." He headed for the front door.

Trevor and Les started after him.

"Wait!" Aunt Ellen ordered, her voice sharp. "Let Matthew handle this."

Trevor wanted to disobey and take his place at his uncle's side. He headed for the door.

"No, Trevor. You'll only make it worse," Aunt Ellen said. "You and Les, come with me. We can watch and listen without being seen."

She led them upstairs to the bedroom at the front of the house, moving confidently through the dark rooms. The shouts and curses of the crowd at the front door carried clearly through the open window. But it was not, as Trevor at first assumed, the window that was to provide the view Aunt Ellen promised. She pointed to a grate in the floor, made visible by light from the room below. Through it they could see and hear what was happening without being seen.

The three of them knelt over the grate, their heads bent over it until they touched.

Trevor saw Jasper Ryles shaking a bony finger in Uncle Matt's face.

"You can't deny it, y'know. We seen you through the window."

"So you admit you were trespassing on my property," Uncle Matt thundered. "And what gives you the right to spy on people like a common Peeping Tom?"

"A man does what he has to do to protect his community, Mr. Blake. People got a right to know when their neighbors is conjurin' the Dark."

"Neighbors, you say? But you don't live in Sharpness."

"Aye, we're from Amesley, and so's those two young devils you're encouraging in evil ways. I can't turn my back on that. It's time I avenged my wife."

"That was an accident, and it was long ago." Uncle Matt's voice was soft, but Trevor could hear the sharp edge beneath the silk. "We aren't harming anyone now."

"That shameless nephew of yours has done plenty of harm." Mistress Hanley hopped up and down in her wrath. "You think we don't know the trial he's been to his folks? Oh, they tried to keep it hidden that he was cursed, and they forbade him to come here. I know that for a fact."

"And why should it be a crime for my nephew to pay his aunt and uncle a visit?" Uncle Matt asked.

"On account of the sorcery you're encouragin' him in," Mistress Hanley screeched. "Not that he needs encouragement. He'd never have won the scholarship that should have gone to my Maribeth 'less he used the dark arts."

"That's not true!" The words burst from Trevor.

Aunt Ellen clamped her hand over his mouth and drew him back, away from the grate.

He could no longer see him but he heard Uncle Matt say, "We've been doing no one any harm. We were just having a quiet family meal."

"No point o' you tryin' to hide what you are, mister," Ryles declared. "We seen you through the window, all o' you, a-shine with fox fire. We brung friends with us, and they all seen it. I've known what you are, and now all the folks hereabouts know, too."

Mistress Hanley said, "You can't deny you're callin' dark powers, not with what we saw through that window."

Trevor leaned close again, eager to see as well as hear what was happening in the room below.

"Doesn't make much sense that you're accusing us of using light to call the Dark, does it?" Uncle Matt asked reasonably.

Ryles sneered, and Mistress Hanley elbowed Jasper Ryles to one side and confronted Uncle Matt, her face contorted with hatred. "You needn't try to trap us with your conjure talk. We'll show you light. See those men outside with torches?" She waved her hand toward the door. "You bring out your nephew and his pal, or they'll torch the house."

Trevor jumped to his feet, his fists clenched. "They're crazy!" he said.

Les and his aunt pulled him back down. "Stay quiet," Aunt Ellen whispered. "Trust your uncle."

"We're going to haul 'em back to Amesley." Mistress Hanley glanced up at the grate and said loudly, "We'll take them before the council and show the council and everybody what Trevor Blake is. He won't be goin' to the university, not he.

A PERILOUS POWER

33

My Maribeth'll go, as she should have been chosen in the first place."

Trevor groaned. Mistress Hanley must have been watching him all the time, waiting and hoping for a chance to discredit him. And he'd given it to her by breaking the vow to his parents not to use his power.

"I'm going down," he said, standing again. "I'm the only one she really cares about. If I go out, maybe they'll leave the rest of you alone."

Les scrambled to his feet. "You're not going alone. I'll go with you."

Aunt Ellen rose and grabbed their arms. "Trevor, Mistress Hanley is here for you, but that Ryles fellow wants to get us all. He won't be satisfied until we're all dead."

"Well, we *have* to do something." Trevor pulled away from her and blundered through the dark room, hunting the door.

"Come back here!" his aunt said, her voice low but forceful. "We can stop them from up here if you keep your wits about you. They have us outnumbered, but they're afraid of our power. We can scare 'em off."

Trevor halted. "How?"

"We need water," Aunt Ellen's voice came through the darkness. "There's a full pitcher on the washstand against the wall to your right. Find it and bring it to me."

As Trevor groped for the pitcher, his aunt went on. "Les, you move quietly to the front window and unhook the screen. It pushes out, and you can crawl through onto the overhang above the front door."

"I should be the one to do that," Trevor objected. Pitcher in hand, he made his way toward the window.

"No!" Aunt Ellen's sharp rebuke halted him. "I need you

to help me in here. Do as I tell you. Now hold the pitcher steady."

Despite his impatience, Trevor held the pitcher as she instructed. Aunt Ellen spoke words over it, chanting in a strange language as she had done with the candle in the dining room. Finally, to Trevor's surprise, she leaned close and spat into the pitcher. In the meantime, Les had moved quietly to the window, eased open the screen, and climbed out onto the overhang, exactly as Aunt Ellen had directed.

"Pass the pitcher out to Les," she ordered Trevor. "Be careful. Don't spill it." She guided him to the window. As he handed the pitcher out through the open screen to Les, crouched on the narrow strip of roof, she whispered, "Les, when I tell you, empty the pitcher over the heads of the crowd."

Trevor leaned out and saw eight or ten people milling about, their lighted torches illuminating the area. Aunt Ellen grabbed his arm and pulled him back.

"Give me your hands," Aunt Ellen commanded, and intertwined her fingers with his. "Now," she said, "think rain!"

He hoped Aunt Ellen knew what she was doing. He had not seen her exercise her power before tonight. But as she ordered, he squeezed his eyes shut and thought of rain. Not a mere drizzle. He pictured a hard, pelting rain, a furious, driving rain. He remembered the worst rainstorm he'd ever seen, one that had come with slashing, blinding force, that peppered fields and livestock with hail, flattened the stalks of grain, filled the ditches and lanes, transformed cropland into marshland, and made houses into islands in a vast lake.

He heard a loud rumble. Was it thunder?

"Look! On the roof! One of 'em!" At the shout, Trevor

opened his eyes in time to see a flaming torch hurled onto the roof.

"Throw the water and come inside," Aunt Ellen shouted.

Les stood, kicked the torch from the roof, tossed the water after it, and scrambled through the window. He handed Aunt Ellen the empty pitcher.

Another torch landed on the roof. This one smoldered on the dry shingles. In seconds little tongues of flame sprang up and waggled like hungry nestlings screaming to be fed. Soon they would join and devour and grow and consume. Unless—

A bolt of brilliant lightning branched across the sky. Almost immediately a boom of thunder shook the house. With the thunder came rain, large drops that hissed into the flames. Then sheets, torrents, cascades poured from the skies, extinguishing the flames, drenching the torch throwers and their torches, plunging them into darkness, and squelching their cries.

Aunt Ellen lit her candle. "Good job, Trevor," she shouted to make herself heard over the pounding rain. "We can go downstairs now."

As they descended the stairs, Trevor saw that although the rain had driven away all their supporters, Jasper Ryles and Mistress Hanley remained inside, Ryles's face thrust near Uncle Matt's, Mistress Hanley's fists raised, ready to strike. But something was wrong. No one moved; no one spoke. The three could have been wax figures in a museum tableau.

Aunt Ellen hurried toward them and took her husband's arm. "You can release them, Matt. It's safe. The others have run away like scared rabbits."

"Very wet scared rabbits," Les put in, laughing.

Uncle Matt drew in a deep breath and stepped backward,

away from his two opponents. He looked toward the window as though noticing for the first time the rain that beat against the glass. With a smile he slipped his arm around his wife.

Jasper Ryles blinked. His rigid stance relaxed. He looked around in confusion.

Mistress Hanley's fists unclenched. Her arms fell to her sides. "Why, what time is it? I've got to be going. My sister Elsie will be worried sick about me. I've come to Sharpness to visit her, you know, and I only left her for a little while to pay my respects to you."

Jasper Ryles stared at her, his mouth agape.

"It's raining, dear." Aunt Ellen pointed toward the window. "You'll get soaked."

"Oh, I'm sure it's only a summer shower. It'll be over in a few minutes. A little rain won't hurt me."

Ryles gulped and seemed to find his voice. "That's a flood out there, woman. We can't go out in that."

However, Uncle Matt said, "Well, if you insist, I'm sure we have oilskins and rain boots in the hall closet. Ellen?"

Aunt Ellen hurried from the room and returned in a moment with rubber boots, yellow oilskins, and sou'westers. She held them out, and Mistress Hanley accepted a set and donned them with no hesitation.

Ryles balked. "I'm sure we ain't got what we came here for," he groused. "And even with rain gear, I don't like going out in that storm."

"Why, we've had a lovely visit," Mistress Hanley said. "And I've thanked Trevor for so graciously ceding to Maribeth the grant for the university." She bestowed a warm smile on Trevor.

Stunned, he tried to summon words of protest. Aunt Ellen

squeezed his arm in warning. He bit his tongue and kept silent.

Muttering under his breath, Jasper Ryles put on the boots and oilskins, jammed the sou'wester on his head, and followed Mistress Hanley to the door.

Like a gracious host, Uncle Matt hurried to pull the door open, and held it that way with some effort. Aunt Ellen waved a friendly farewell, and the two former conspirators struggled out into the storm.

Uncle Matt let the wind slam the door shut, and Les and Trevor hurried to the window to watch the two until they disappeared into the sodden darkness.

Trevor turned to Uncle Matt. "What did you do to them? And why did she say I ceded the grant to Maribeth? Do I have to do that?"

"One answer at a time, son." Uncle Matt said. "All I could do to Ryles was give him a mild amnesia. He's a normal, so his mind's closed to any thought adjustment. But Mistress Hanley, now, she's another matter. She's gifted."

"Mistress Hanley, gifted?" Trevor couldn't believe it.

"Not highly, I don't reckon, but there's no doubt she has a gift, though I suspect she keeps it hidden from everybody. But I made use of it. While I held 'em both in stasis, I went into her mind and adjusted her memories a tad. Did some readin', too. Sit down, boys. We need to talk seriously about this."

Uncle Matt sank wearily onto the couch, and Aunt Ellen sat beside him.

Trevor sank reluctantly into the wing chair, while Les perched on the edge of the seat of a rocker.

"Mistress Hanley's set on her Maribeth goin' to university," Uncle Matt continued. "Couldn't change that strong an ob-

session. No matter what I did, she'd o' remembered that and kept on makin' trouble. Matter o' fact, she's sworn to have you killed if that's what it takes. Don't know that she would really do it, but can you afford to take the chance? That's why I had to let her think you told her Maribeth could have the grant."

"She can't hurt me," Trevor scoffed. "I won't let her."

"She might not be able to hurt you, but *you* could hurt *her*—and maybe a lot of others, too."

"I wouldn't . . . What do you mean?"

"It's not a thing I wanted to have to tell," Uncle Matt murmured, looking down at his worn work shoes.

"He needs to know," Aunt Ellen said softly, patting Uncle Matt's hand. Trevor was shocked by how old and tired his uncle suddenly looked.

Uncle Matt nodded. "I was younger than you are now," he began slowly, as though the words were being pulled from him against his will. "Like you, I had power but wasn't trained in its use. My sister Oma was your father's twin; they were three years older than me."

Twin! Trevor hadn't known that.

"I was always full of mischief—loved to play tricks on people. Oma had gone to a quiltin' bee at Mary Elster's place. Lucinda Ryles was there, and so was Lorna Carroll, along with some other women."

Trevor recognized those names—the names carved on the base of the stone pillar in the cemetery. He leaned forward, not wanting to miss a word. Uncle Matt was talking very softly, as if to himself.

"My pa told me to take a lantern and go meet Oma and walk home with her. He didn't like the idea of her walkin' home by herself on a dark night. Marlon—your father—

A PERILOUS POWER

would have gone, but he was out in the barn with a colicky horse."

He paused, wiped his brow, and went on. "I thought it would be great fun to play a practical joke on Oma and the others. I'd just recently learned that my power let me use firelight to create illusions. The lantern fire was enough to make what I thought would be a marvelous illusion.

"I knocked on Mary Elster's door, and when it opened, I filled the doorway with the illusion of a huge bear, all aglow, its claws extended and its mouth open in a mean snarl.

"Oh, it was effective, all right. Oma'd been expecting me to come for her, so it was her that opened the door, with Mary Elster standing right behind her with a lighted lantern. Oma let out a horrific scream and jumped back, right into Mary. Mary dropped the lantern, and it broke, spilling oil and fire on her long skirt. Oma was too scared to realize what was happening and pushed against her, still trying to get away from the bear, and she caught fire, too, and Lucinda Ryles and Lorna Carroll, who'd been right behind Mary and Oma, they tried to put out the fire, but it caught them, too." Uncle Matt was speaking rapidly now, trying to get the story out and done with.

"By the time I dispelled the illusion and saw what was happening, it was too late. The whole place was on fire. The other women ran out the back way while the house burned, but Lucinda and Lorna and Mary and Oma, they all . . . they died. And it was my fault. I tried, but I couldn't save 'em. They died, and it was my fault."

His voice had subsided to a whisper; his head hung down so that his chin rested on his chest.

"It was an accident, Matt," Aunt Ellen said.

"Doesn't matter, Ellen," Uncle Matt muttered. "I was careless and cocky. I should've known not to use power that way."

"You hadn't had any training."

He shrugged. "Anyway," he went on, "a couple of the women that survived had seen the bear and knew it wasn't a normal animal, that it had a look of magic about it. They told my pa, and he figgered it was somethin' I'd done. When he confronted me, I confessed. Marlon wanted to kill me, and so did Jasper Ryles when the word got out. My pa decided to get me as far away as possible to keep me safe, and I suppose because he was furious with me, too, and didn't want me near him. He sent me to Port-of-Lords, where there was a very strong Community of the Gifted. They trained me in the proper use of power. I learned to use gifts I hadn't known I had, but I never again used the gift of creating illusions."

"How did Grandpa Blake know about the Community?" Trevor asked. "Was he gifted, too?"

"No," Uncle Matt said slowly. "His father had been, though. And the Community in Port-of-Lords was well known then all across the country for the good it did and the training it gave the gifted. It had been started by the Lady Kyla herself. Funny, you don't hear much about it these days."

"Maybe it's died out," Trevor said.

"No, it's still there. I have a friend I got to know back then, who's still in Port-of-Lords and belongs to the Community. I was homesick, so once I'd completed my training and knew I could use my power safely, I came back here. I wasn't welcome in Amesley, so I settled here in Sharpness, met and married Ellen, and here I've been ever since."

He raised his head, then, and gazed directly at Trevor.

"Now you understand why your father was so against you using power. He and I came to terms with each other, enough to let you come visit Ellen and me that time, but he never really forgave me. And now it's all stirred up again."

"Gosh, I'm sorry, Uncle Matt," Trevor said. "I didn't know."

"Course you didn't. Point is, you've gotta be careful how you use power. Your father thought he could keep you from usin' it at all, but it's too much a part of you to suppress all the time. You have to learn to use it responsibly."

Trevor sat up straight. "Say, maybe I could go to Port-of-Lords and get trained by the Community there like you did."

"But you can't give up the university!" Les protested. "It's your only chance to go!"

"I really did earn that scholarship," Trevor said. "I deserve it more than Maribeth Hanley."

"Well, it has to be your decision," Uncle Matt said. "But think about this. Some of the people outside with the torches were Sharpness people—neighbors, folks I've known all my life. I could tell they were embarrassed about being here. That's why they were content to stay outside and let Ryles and Mistress Hanley do the talking. But Ryles *did* get them stirred up, and they *would* have burned the house down if Ellen hadn't called the rain."

"Trevor helped," Aunt Ellen put in. "I couldn't have brought such a storm by myself."

Uncle Matt squeezed her hand. "Yes, well, my point is, don't y' see, that the rain put out their anger along with their torches. If nothin' stirs 'em up again, they'll let the matter drop. But Ryles won't. If he gets his memory back, he's likely to do anything, especially with Mistress Hanley egging him on, which she will if Trevor *doesn't* cede the grant to Maribeth."

"I guess you're right," Trevor said. "I hate not going to Tirbat. But if I could get trained in the use of power, it would be almost as good as going to the university. And going to Port-of-Lords would be exciting." He stopped, thought, and slumped back in the chair. "Except," he said, "that's way out on the west coast. I couldn't even afford the trip, much less find a way to live after I got there. I can only go to Tirbat because of the grant."

Uncle Matt stroked his sideburns. "You do need training, Trevor," he said thoughtfully. "There *is* a way you could go. Ellen and me, we've put a good bit away through the years. More than enough for our old age. We could give you enough to get there and live on for a while, till you get established."

"I couldn't take the savings you've worked so hard for," Trevor said, shaking his head.

"Of course you could," Aunt Ellen said. "We never had any children. We have no one to leave our money to. It'd make us real proud to give you some of what would have gone to our children. And you'd benefit so from the training. For you it would be better than any university degree."

"But go all that distance alone, with no assurance that it would work out?" Trevor couldn't help his skepticism.

"I could give you a letter of introduction to my old friend Doss Hamlyn," Uncle Matt said. "I understand he's done right well for himself in the shipping business. I'm sure he'd get you into the Community. Matter of fact, I know of another member of the Community who's supposed to be skilled at training young talents, a man by the name of Dr.

Berne Tenney. He wasn't there when I was, so I don't know him personally, but the skilled trainers that were there then would be too old now, if they're still alive. The information I have on Tenney isn't recent, but I think it's likely he's still active in the Community. I could give you a letter for him, too, asking him to undertake your training."

"Training," Les repeated slowly. "Training . . . I wonder. If I really am gifted, maybe they could find my gift and train me, too."

"I suppose they could, Les, but—"

"Oh, I'm not asking you to pay my way, Uncle Matt," Les interrupted. "I've saved some of what Dad's paid me these past three years for helping out on the farm. It was to set me up on my own, when I married, you know. But I haven't met a girl I want to marry, and I'm not ready to settle down. Dad can spare me—he's got plenty of hired help. If Trevor goes, I'd like to go with him. If you could include me in those letters you were talking about."

Trevor grinned. "That would be great, Les. What an adventure we'd have."

"Well, it's not for adventure you'd be going," Aunt Ellen said, frowning. "It's a big step, not one to be taken lightly."

"Oh, we'd take it seriously, I promise," Trevor said. "But are you sure you can spare the money? I don't have any set aside like Les."

"I wouldn't make the offer if we couldn't spare it," his uncle said. "We can help you both. And nothing could make us happier than seeing you both trained to use your gifts for good. You could change the way this area views the gifted— undo the impression left by what I did."

Trevor gazed at his aunt and uncle, recognized their sincerity, their deep desire for him to accept their offer. He turned to Les. "It won't be the university, but I never did like the idea of going off to Tirbat without you," he said. "So Port-of-Lords it is, then—for both of us."

4

A PORT-OF-LORDS WELCOME

The train clacked along, passing into territory new to them both. Les was excited, but Trevor seemed distracted and glum. Les figured that the disappointment of missing out on attending the national university was setting in. He decided a distraction was in order.

"Hey, Trev, you up for a game? Let's see who can spot the most new things—stuff we've never seen before. A point for every new thing; two or three if it's something really spectacular. What do you say?"

"I guess." Trevor shrugged, showing little enthusiasm. But then the train rumbled over a high trestle bridge crossing the Plains River, and Trevor, in the window seat, pointed and shouted, "Hah! I win the first points. See there! A paddlewheel riverboat and a tug pulling a line of coal barges. That should be worth three or four points."

"Two. Don't get greedy."

Trevor's mood lifted after that, and the game became a lively contest, to the amusement of the more seasoned travelers.

In the river port of Mercanton they both gained points rapidly as they saw their first buildings taller than six stories, their first fancy motorcars, bread and rolls being delivered by a truck instead of a horse-drawn wagon, electric street-lights, and a trolley with overhead wires.

Beyond Mercanton they passed through towns and villages like their own, but these gradually gave way to empty prairie, so featureless that the view grew monotonous and they slept.

When they awoke, they were lurching and swaying through mountains. Not gentle, mounded hills like those around Wickton but immense upthrust masses of stone terrifying in their grandeur. They resumed their game for the distraction it afforded from the threat of harrowing switchbacks and deep chasms and swift rivers with foam-wreathed rapids.

On a steep ascent the train squealed to a bone-jolting stop, everyone piled out, and the men were put to work clearing a rockslide off the tracks. Les and Trevor worked with the others, pushing and shoving to topple boulders over the embankment, hurling the smaller stones onto the tops of the trees below, and sweeping the tracks clear of dirt and pebbles so that the train could resume its journey.

Back on the train, Trevor again seemed lost in thought. He sat by the window but did not look out as the train completed its upward toil and began a slow but steady descent.

Les leaned across Trevor and nudged him with his elbow. "Look!" He pointed at a herd of wild horses that bolted and scattered at the train's approach. "They're worth five points at least."

Trevor shrugged. "Okay. I'm still ahead."

Determined to keep Trevor's mind on the game, Les said, "I haven't had the window seat for an hour. If I'd been there

as long as you have, I'd have you skunked. Those horses are spectacular, aren't they? I wish we could catch a couple and ship them back to the farm."

"I guess," Trevor responded, gazing out the window dispiritedly. Then something caught his eye, and he suddenly became more animated. "Hah! What's that?"

Les followed Trevor's pointing finger. Taking advantage of the herd's fright at the train, two large birds with huge wingspans swooped down on a foal that had gotten separated from its mother. The birds drove the terrified youngster farther from the main body of the herd. One landed on the foal's back, and Les saw blood spurt as the sharp talons sank into tender flesh.

"Not a pretty sight," he said. "It's hard seeing a foal destroyed like that."

"Too bad we don't have our shotguns," Trevor responded with a grin as the train carried them out of view of the carnage. "Those had to be condors. Thought they were mostly carrion eaters."

"They'll take live meat when they can get it," Les said. "I read about them. They prey on the weak, the sick, the newborn—any helpless creature they can find. It's a good thing they stay out here in the west and don't fly over our farm country."

"They're just doing what comes naturally," Trevor said. "You always were a sucker for sick and hurt animals. Remember when you brought home that baby bobcat?"

"Yeah." Les laughed. "I had scratches all over my arms. Dad made me turn it loose, but at least he didn't kill it—not where I could see, anyway."

Climbing away from the valley of horses, they were plunged into sudden darkness as the train entered a tunnel.

A PERILOUS POWER

Les held his breath, startled by the unexpected increase in the racket of the wheels and the ominous nearness of the tunnel walls.

With the abrupt restoration of light, the train plunged downward into another valley. This one held no horses.

"Look at those fields," Trevor said. "Those plants are worth a point. You'll never catch up."

Tall stalks of red flowers swayed in the wind like waves on a sea of blood.

Trevor peered out the window, the exhaustion of the five-day train trip falling away with the excitement of seeing Port-of-Lords. Les leaned over to gawk, too. The train slowed to a stately swagger for its passage into the city, allowing them time to stare at the broad boulevards with gardens of brilliant flowers stretched in narrow strips down the center. Too fascinated to continue their game, they passed statues and fountains, buildings so tall they could not see the tops through the small window, and more shiny new motorcars than Trevor had known existed. It was early evening, still light, but already the electric streetlights were winking on. Night was banished from this city; its citizens could work all day and play all night if they wished.

The train shuddered to a halt. Leaning his head out the open window and looking back, Trevor saw that the train had passed through a great arch to enter the station.

"We're here," Les breathed, and the unnecessary observation sounded like a prayer.

They stood, grabbed their carryalls, and pushed down the aisle past passengers gathering scattered belongings. When they were halted behind a fat woman juggling an armful of packages, Trevor chafed at the delay. But at last they stepped

E. ROSE SABIN

down from the train onto a marble platform. Trevor walked only a few steps before stopping, awed by the magnificence of their surroundings.

The train had carried them into a building more like a palace than a train station. High above their heads a ceiling of glass panels offered a view of the twilit sky. From the metal framing the panels hung immense chandeliers like nothing Trevor had ever seen, aglitter with dazzling tiers of electric bulbs and sparkling crystal reflectors. Passenger trains filled the center of the long building, and on the marble platforms between them and to either side, porters in natty green uniforms dashed among the passengers, helping with luggage, giving directions, checking tickets, and calling out to one another in an unintelligible jargon. None approached them. Trevor guessed it was obvious from their country clothes and shabby carryalls that they were poor prospects for tips.

They made their way through the crowd toward the shops and ticket offices beyond the platforms.

"Think we ought to get our coppers changed right away?" Les asked, pointing to a sign proclaiming MONEY EXCHANGE above a series of small windows. "We don't want to have to use the gold and silver for little things."

"I guess we should," Trevor shouted to be heard over the surrounding clatter and clamor. "And I wonder if we can find a place near here to stay overnight. I'd like to rest and get cleaned up. I feel too grubby and tired to meet Uncle Matt's friend."

"I agree," Les shouted back, adding to the cacophony. "Even with the letter of introduction, I don't think he'd want to take us in looking like this. We can ask the moneychanger about a boardinghouse."

They got in line at one of the windows, and when they

reached their goal, a young woman said, "May I help you?" in a bored voice.

His face burning, Trevor unbuttoned his shirt and unfastened one of two pouches strapped to his chest. Beside him Les did his best to block the view of curious strangers. Trevor was glad his uncle had advised him to keep the coppers separate from the gold dorins and silver triums. The dorins and triums were acceptable anywhere in the country, but each province minted its own coppers, and their values varied from province to province.

"I need to change these," Trevor said as Les prepared to extract his pouch. He shook the coppers onto the narrow ledge. Two or three rolled onto the floor and he had to scramble after them.

The clerk looked down her nose at the heap of copper coins. "You'll have to count them out and arrange them by value," she said with a sniff. "I can't take them like that."

Trevor began to sort through the pile and stack the coins by size. The woman stopped him with a look of disgust. "Not here," she said. "You can't hold up other people. You'll have to go somewhere else to do that and get in line again when you have them ready."

With Les's help Trevor scooped up the coins and stuffed them back into the pouch. He looked for an unoccupied bench where they could sit and separate the coins.

"Some welcome," Trevor grumbled. "Wonder if she eats sour apples all day."

"Guess they've got us pegged for a couple of ignorant hicks. Wonder how long it'll take us to learn city ways."

"If we were just treated to a sample of city ways, I never want to learn them, thanks. We can sit over there."

Trevor pointed to a bench near the arched entranceway,

but as they headed toward it, a mother installed her three young children on it and stood guard in front, her glare defying anyone to challenge the children's right to the bench.

"Excuse me, gentlemen, could I be of service to you?"

Startled, Trevor turned and saw a young man only a little older than he and Les, with wavy brown hair and a thin blond mustache.

"I hope I didn't startle you," he said. "Name's Carl Holdt." With a broad smile he thrust out his hand and held it out until Trevor grasped and shook it. He shook Les's hand, too, and in doing so steered them subtly toward the main doors. "I hope you won't think I'm being rude, but I happened to be standing near the currency exchange when that cashier was so discourteous to you. She should be reported. That's no way to introduce newcomers to our lovely city. This is your first time in Port-of-Lords, isn't it?"

Trevor nodded, all the answer Carl gave him time for before continuing, "Really, Port-of-Lords is a city known for its friendliness." He cupped his palm around Trevor's elbow and steered him toward the exit. "I got mad seeing you treated so rudely. So I decided to apologize for her and give you a bit of advice. The exchange here in the station pays at the official rate, but there are a lot of places where you can get a much better rate. If you'll permit me, I'll take you to a hotel not far from here where you can exchange your coppers and get a room and a good meal, all at reasonable prices. What d'you say?"

Trevor looked at Les, who, out of sight of Carl, gave a shake of his head. But Trevor saw no harm in saying, "We do need a place to stay for one night. We'll be meeting a friend tomorrow."

"I wonder. . . ." Les said slowly. "It might be better to stick

A PERILOUS POWER

with our plan to get our coppers changed here. We shouldn't impose."

"Naturally you aren't eager to trust me, a stranger," Carl put in quickly, dropping his hands from their arms. "I quite understand. You're being wise. There are a lot of people here who are more than ready to take advantage of strangers. I shouldn't have bothered you."

"You didn't bother us at all," Trevor protested, frowning at Les. He could not understand his friend's unaccustomed rudeness. "We don't know anything about the hotels here, and we sure could use a good hot meal. We've been traveling for five days and living on the cold snacks they sell at the stops."

Les put in grudgingly, "I guess we could look at the hotel."

"Then it's settled!" Carl exclaimed heartily. "I promise I'll give you no reason to regret this. You don't have any other baggage, do you?"

"Only these," Trevor said, indicating the carryalls with some embarrassment.

Carl clapped him on the shoulder. "That's smart, to travel light." They reached the exit, and he ushered them through the ornate glass doors. "It's hard to find your way around a new city, especially one the size of Port-of-Lords. And if there's anything I love to do, it's show off my city. I was born and reared here, and I love the place. I've done a lot of traveling, and I've never found any city that can compare to it. Of course, I suppose you gents think that about your hometown. Where did you say you were from?"

"Amesley," Trevor answered. "It's real small, no place you'd have heard of. It's in Plains Province."

"Ah, yes. The farm belt. Breadbasket of the nation." Carl's words and respectful tone invested their home with an importance that brought Trevor a rush of pride.

"Look across the street." Carl pointed to an oddly shaped building whose front resembled the prow of a ship. "That's the Maritime Museum. The shipping industry built Port-of-Lords, and the history is all laid out in there. You'll have to see it. Maybe I can take you tomorrow afternoon if you're not busy with your friend."

"It's good of you to offer," Les said, "but we *don't* want to trouble you." His emphasis on "don't" warned Trevor that Les didn't trust their new friend. But he was sure Les was being overcautious.

"Trouble!" Carl sounded hurt. "I wouldn't offer if it was going to be trouble. I like you fellows. I'm glad we've met, and I want the chance to know you better. Look across the street. That tall building with all the lights is the Telephone Exchange."

"Wow!" Trevor thought of the squat wooden building in Essell where two operators sat at a switchboard handling all the calls into, out of, and throughout the county.

"And here's the best restaurant in this part of town. It's expensive, but if you ever feel like splurging, I can promise you'll get the greatest meal you ever had."

Trevor was skeptical, thinking of the feast Aunt Ellen had prepared, but he kept silent. He had little choice, as Carl prattled nonstop, pointing out sights, giving bits of history— "At one time the famous shipping magnate Jeremy Carnaby had his offices on this very corner"—calling their attention to some passing phenomenon—"That car's a new Murphy, one of the first off the line. Must cost a hundred dorins."

Trevor couldn't imagine that much wealth. Uncle Matt had given him and Les each three dorins and fourteen triums, besides the coppers, and they had thought them-

A PERILOUS POWER

selves rich. He noticed Les rub his hand over the pouches hidden against his chest and guessed he had the same thought. Les was being uncharacteristically quiet, but then Carl wasn't really giving either of them much chance to speak.

"Now that street," he went on, pointing to a narrow side street, "that has nothing but shops selling exotic goods from across the ocean. Oh, and there's a small café that serves food in the style of the countries over there. My sister waits tables there. Too bad we can't pay her a visit and take a look at some of the shops, but we'll save that for another day, eh? I know you're tired now and probably can't wait for a meal and a hot bath."

Trevor was ready to agree, but Carl grabbed his arm as he started across a street. "Watch out! That car's coming way too fast."

Trevor stepped back to let the shiny black vehicle hurtle past.

Carl shook his head. "Some drivers are disgracefully care-less. They think pedestrians ought to watch out for *them*. There've been some nasty accidents because people buy these things and have no idea how to drive them.

"They say the horse-drawn carriages will all be gone in a couple more years," he went on, guiding them across the street. "Already they're getting scarce. Guess that'll put the street cleaners out of a job."

Carl's stream of comments, anecdotes, and information kept Trevor entertained until he noticed that they had en-tered an area where streetlights were farther apart, buildings older, plainer, and less well lit. He was on the verge of asking where they were, when Carl sang out, "Here we are!" and pointed to a lopsided sign illuminated by a spotlight above it. INN OF THE FIFTH LORD, the sign proclaimed.

Carl led them into a cramped lobby with nondescript dark sofas and chairs. "The desk clerk here can change your coppers, but first why don't we go into the pub and rest our feet? I'll buy you each a drink to celebrate your arrival."

Without giving them a chance to object, he led them through a curtain of glass beads into a narrow, dimly lit room with a row of dark wooden tables crowded along one side and a counter along the other. Trailing after Carl the length of the room, Trevor felt as if he were back on the train negotiating the narrow aisle between the rows of seats. They sat at the last table in the line, and Trevor wondered why, since they had passed several empty tables.

Carl went to the counter, and a man wearing a patch over one eye stepped out of the darkness behind it. Les poked Trevor and whispered, "I don't like the looks of this place, Trev—or that guy. I think he's a pirate."

"Shhh," Trevor cautioned. "They'll hear you."

But Carl ordered in his cheery voice, "I'll have my usual, Ned. And a Port-of-Lords welcome special for each of my friends."

The man nodded, disappeared, and reappeared in seconds with three tall glasses on a tray.

"We should get out of here," Les insisted.

"Don't be stupid," Trevor whispered. "Think of this as our first adventure."

Les rolled his eyes upward but said no more.

Carl carried the tray back to the table and handed around the drinks. Trevor noted that Carl's drink was a clear liquid while theirs was red and foamy.

Les gazed suspiciously at the tall glass. "What is this?" he asked.

"It's a treat for newcomers to our city, a house specialty. It's a blend of juices from fruit grown in the area, with just a taste of rum. I think you'll like it."

Sitting down, Carl raised his glass. "To your enjoyable and successful stay in Port-of-Lords," he proclaimed.

They clinked their glasses together, and Trevor took a sip. The strong fruit flavor was not familiar to him. Or perhaps the sharp tang of the liquor made the fruit unrecognizable. It seemed more than a "taste," and he would have preferred plain fruit juice, but the drink was cold, and he was thirsty.

Les raised his glass to his mouth, but Trevor suspected he only pretended to drink. To show Les how foolish his fears were, Trevor quickly downed half the drink. His ploy worked: Les took a few swallows of his.

Carl chatted on, allowing Trevor to relax, sip his drink slowly now, and listen or let his mind wander. His thoughts drifted dreamily over the long miles to Amesley.

He pictured his mother sitting in the old wooden rocker by the fire, remembered how as a small boy he used to crawl up into her lap and beg for a story. He'd grow sleepy as she talked. His head would droop against his mother's breast as her words drifted around him. As Carl's were doing. Words running together. Becoming like a lullaby. His eyes closed. He slumped forward, his arms spreading out on the table. His head rested on his arms.

No. All wrong. Shouldn't be sleeping. Got to wake up. But his head was too heavy and swollen to lift. And someone must have glued his eyelids shut and stuffed his mouth with cotton. He slept.

"Trevor. Trevor, wake up. You have to wake up." Someone shook his shoulders, sending waves of pain through his body. He groaned. A vile taste filled his mouth, and someone lifted him and held him while he vomited.

"Trevor, snap out of it. Come on." Les's voice. Good ol' Les.

"Trevor, listen. We were drugged. And robbed. That Carl. He took everything. Our money. Our papers. Our carryalls. Everything."

At that, Trevor got his eyes open and focused with effort on Les's face. It was pale, drawn, and he read panic in the blue eyes. The sight jolted him into awareness. He clutched at his chest where his coin pouches had been, felt nothing but his own flesh through his shirt.

"I came to a little while ago. I've been trying to rouse you ever since," Les was saying. "Can you stand up?"

Trevor got unsteadily to his feet and leaned against the building, breathing hard as the world spun.

"Take it slow," Les said. "You drank that whole drink he gave us. I only took about half of mine. I saw you pass out, but by then I was too far gone to yell for help. Next thing I knew, I woke up here—wherever here is."

Trevor discovered he'd been lying outside behind a stack of crates in a dusty alley. A shaft of light fell between the old brick buildings on either side. Sunlight. It was morning. From somewhere nearby came the sounds of traffic. He staggered toward the end of the alley.

"If anybody sees us," Les whispered behind him, "they'll take us for a couple of drunks. What are we going to do, Trevor? He even took your letters of introduction. If we find your uncle's friend, we've got no way of proving who we are. Do you remember his address?"

"No." Trevor groaned again. "The address and directions ˙

A PERILOUS POWER

59

were on the envelope. Guess I should have memorized 'em, but I didn't."

"Well, we do know his name. Maybe we can find him, and maybe he'll believe us when we tell him who we are and what happened. Right now we better get out of here. This doesn't look like a safe place." Les offered a supporting arm.

Leaning on Les's arm, Trevor took a few more steps. His head hurt, he was dizzy, and his stomach was churning. Les was right, though—they had to move, had to go somewhere.

But where?

5

A Clash of Powers

Although still shaky himself, Les supported Trevor as they turned from the alley onto the street. He looked up and down, searching for a recognizable landmark, hoping they'd been left behind the hotel Carl had taken them to last night. What was its name? His mind was fuzzy and his head ached.

Inn of the Fifth Lord, that was it.

They reached the corner and looked at the fronts of the buildings that abutted the alley. Old buildings, warehouses, mostly. No hotel.

"Maybe it's on the other side of the block," Les said. "Can you make it?"

Trevor nodded. "I'm feeling better. And sorry I didn't listen to you."

Les shrugged. "I'm just sorry we won't get that wonderful tour of the Maritime Museum."

"Okay, okay." Trevor gave a shaky laugh. "We'll miss out on that fancy restaurant, too. Hope Carl enjoys the meals he has there on our money."

"And all the exotic junk he buys in those fancy shops."

"Don't forget the meals in the café where his sister works,"

Trevor said. "If he even has a sister. I bet he doesn't."

They didn't find the Inn of the Fifth Lord on the other side of the block.

"They must have carried us away from the hotel to dump us," Trevor said.

"And get us thoroughly lost." Les glanced up and down the street. He had a feeling that they were far from the center of town, far from the train station, and in an unsavory area. The buildings were old and dilapidated, and an unfamiliar odor filled the air. There were no people nearby, and the vehicles passing in the street were mostly horse-drawn wagons. Maybe they could hail a driver and get a lift back to the train station, where they could hunt for Carl and try to recover their money and the all-important letters. Carl probably spent most of his time at the station, watching for victims, but if they couldn't find him, they could find their way to the hotel from the station and confront the sinister counterman. Carl had been no stranger to him; the two had worked together.

They could do little until Trevor regained his strength. They needed food. And for food they needed money.

They'd circled the block and headed along a street that seemed to have more traffic. As they walked, Trevor grabbed Les's arm and pointed across the street to an empty lot strewn with rubble from a building that had burned or been torn down. "Four points!" he said with an air of triumph.

At first Les thought Trevor had gone mad. Then he saw it. Not the lot. What lay beyond it. Water. Blue water.

They were only a block away from the ocean.

"Let's go!" Trevor said.

They picked their way through the trash, came out at last on a street that ran along a wide seawall, over which they could see, between the passing carriages and wagons, a sweeping expanse of ocean. They crossed the street, dodging traffic, and clambered up onto the seawall for a closer look.

The pungent smell was stronger here, and Les realized it was the salty, fishy smell of the water. Waves crashed against the seawall, dousing them with spray and sending foam scudding over the stone.

Several docks jutted out from the seawall, and at some of these large ships were anchored. His headache forgotten, Les stared in fascination at the activity on the quays. Men ran up and down, shouting and pointing and manipulating winches to load or unload crates, bales, sacks, and barrels. The dock nearest them was piled with lumber that was being loaded onto the deck of a battered freighter.

"Like a closer look, fellas?"

Les jumped, surprised by the stranger's silent approach. The man wore a blue uniform with gold braid on the shoulders and around the sleeves. His seamed face held a jovial smile. Les *did* want a closer look at both ships and ocean, but the man's manner reminded him a little of Carl.

"I'm first mate of that freighter." He pointed to the ship taking on the lumber. "Saw you two standing out here watching and thought mebbe you'd like to come aboard and look around. Matter o' fact, we could use a couple more hands with the loading if you've got two or three hours free and a will to work."

Les cast a glance at Trevor. "You feel up to it?" he asked, uneasy enough about the offer that he hoped Trevor would say no.

"I'll do what I have to," Trevor said with a shrug. "How much do you pay?"

"Five mid-coppers an hour."

A PERILOUS POWER

The answer conveyed little information, since they had not had a chance to learn the value of Port Province coppers, but they were in no position to bargain. At the least, they'd earn enough for a meal and a bus ride back to the station.

They followed their new employer onto the quay and over a none-too-sturdy gangplank onto the ship.

The freighter was larger than it had appeared from shore, but no cleaner. The first mate put them to work helping to guide the bundles of lumber onto the stacks, secure them into place, and, when a stack reached maximum height, tie tarpaulins over it. The work was hard and dangerous. The bundles of lumber, lowered from the hoists, came down swinging and had to be caught and steadied. Les's hands grew raw and studded with splinters; his muscles ached despite his farm conditioning. He cast frequent glances at Trevor, but his friend seemed to be holding up well and had probably sweated out the residue of the drug. Les was lightheaded from not having eaten, and Trevor must have felt no better, but they persevered until the work was done and the first mate beckoned them away from their fellow workers.

"Time to settle up," he said and led them through an open hatch down a ladder to a narrow passageway belowdecks. He took them into a tiny cabin. The door closed behind them, and Les started at the sudden sound of the ship's motors.

"Warmin' up to leave," the first mate explained. "We're behind schedule. That's why I needed your help." He stepped to a locker and opened it. "I made a good choice when I went after you two. This crew needs strong, healthy men."

He turned, a long-barreled pistol in his hand. "Sorry,

E. Rose Sabin

boys. You *will* get paid for your work, but not till the end of the run. You just signed on for a two-month cruise."

The mate's hand was steady on the pistol and his gaze was hard. To Les's horror, Trevor closed his eyes and sagged against the wall.

You can't pass out on me, Trevor! We've gotta get away.

But Trevor didn't fall, and when Les looked again at the pistol he saw the barrel bend slowly back toward its owner. The mate swore and dropped the gun.

"Nice use of power, Trev!" Les leaped forward and slammed his fist into the man's face.

"Nice use of those farm-boy muscles, Les!" Trevor yanked open the cabin door and raced for the ladder, Les at his heels. They clambered up onto the deck, shoved startled crewmen aside, and sprinted to the gangplank.

It was gone. A width of dark water the height of a man stretched between ship and dock.

"I always did want to see the world," Les quipped.

"Yeah, but not just yet." Trevor gripped Les's arm. "Jump on three," he said, crouching, poised to spring. "One! Two! *Three!*"

They launched themselves into the air, Trevor clutching Les's arm. A blur of water passed beneath them, and they fell sprawling on the quay. Les didn't need to hear the amazed shouts of the ship's crew to know that their leap had been spectacular. Trevor's power had saved them again.

Les struggled to his feet and glanced back at the freighter, expecting to see it return for them. But it moved steadily out to sea, gray smoke puffing from its stacks. He gave the staring crewmen a jaunty wave.

Looking down, he saw that Trevor hadn't moved. "Trev, you okay? Trevor?" He shook his shoulder, and Trevor

A PERILOUS POWER

groaned and rolled over to look up at him, his dark eyes dull and deeply shadowed.

"No strength left," he said. "Used too much power . . ."

"You got us off the ship. I'll find a way to get us out of here."

He walked off the quay and watched the traffic rumbling past. Could he trust anyone in this city? If he made a mistake and picked the wrong person, with Trevor too exhausted to use the power again, they might not escape a third time.

A horse-drawn wagon clattered toward him. He scrutinized the driver's face as the wagon neared, but gave up trying to decide whether the man looked friendly. Carl and the first mate had both looked friendly enough. He'd have to take a chance.

"Ho!" he shouted, running alongside the wagon. "Can you help me? My friend is sick, all our money's been stolen, and we need a ride to the train station."

The driver, an old man with a thick gray beard, halted the horse and squinted down at Les. "What makes y' think I might be headin' toward the station?"

"Nothing. I was only hoping."

"Where's your friend?"

"Back there on the quay." Les pointed to Trevor, who'd managed to sit up but was resting his head in his hands.

"Can you get him here and into the wagon?"

"You bet I can!"

"Okay, make it fast. Ain't got all day. I'm not goin' all the way to the train station, and I won't go out of m' way for you, but I'll take y' far as Carnaby Park. That's not but five blocks from the station."

The man's brusque, no-nonsense manner made Les inclined to trust him. He ran to Trevor. "I've got us a ride." He helped him to his feet and practically carried him to the wagon.

The wagon ride jolted Trevor and brought back the pounding in his head. He was relieved when the surly driver halted his horse and announced, "This here's Carnaby Park. You'll have to walk to the station from here or hitch another ride. Go alongside the park and straight on for five or six blocks more, and you'll see it."

They thanked him, jumped down, and watched as he shook the reins and drove away.

Trevor sniffed the air. A strong odor of frying meat reminded him of his hunger. If only they had money . . .

Les pulled him in the direction the driver had indicated. "Come on, let's get going. I smell it, too, but why torture ourselves?"

But Trevor broke away and entered the park, not stopping until he found the source of the scent. In a kiosk set among trees, a woman was frying meat cakes on a griddle. The sight made his mouth water.

He spied an empty bench near the kiosk and dropped onto it.

Les joined him. "What good's this going to do?"

Trevor leaned his head against the back of the bench, closed his eyes, and breathed in the aroma, trying to imagine he was eating. His stomach refused to be fooled. It needed the real thing. If he hadn't already used so much power today . . .

He opened his eyes and watched the woman in the kiosk. With a spatula she scooped a meat patty off the griddle, flipped it onto a bun, covered it with peppers and onions from a simmering pan, wrapped it in waxed paper, and

A PERILOUS POWER

handed it to a customer. Several more people waited in line.

When the cook was busy making change, he focused his mind on the buns stacked on a tray beside the griddle. Tired and weak as he was, he had to strain to find the power, draw it out, and send the lines of force, wavering, uncertain, snaking toward the stack of buns. He concentrated on the usually effortless process of snagging his quarry, lifting it, reeling it back along the lines of force.

Two buns flew through the air and landed in Trevor's outstretched hands. Resisting the urge to pop one into his mouth, he opened them and watched the cook. She tossed more meat cakes onto the griddle and turned to speak to a customer. Two of the frying patties sailed through the air and landed on the open buns.

"Good job!" Les exclaimed, a wide grin splitting his face. He reached for a bun.

"Wait," Trevor said, and sent his mind reaching for the peppers and onions.

That trick proved his undoing. The cook turned in time to see a mess of onions and peppers lift out of the pan, dripping hot oil, and slither through the air like eels. With a scream she swatted at the phenomenon with her spatula. The clump exploded and greasy strands of onions and peppers showered cook and customers. Only three or four strands reached their destination.

Amid the confusion, one small boy retained the presence of mind to follow the flight of the garnishes. "*They* did it!" he shouted, pointing straight at Les and Trevor. "Look! Thieves!"

In the act of taking the first bite of his meat-filled bun, Trevor found himself the focus of a crowd of hostile stares. He ate faster.

E. Rose Sabin

The child kept shouting. "They did it. Get 'em! They stole the patty cakes!"

"I think we better run for it, Les." Trevor got the words out through a mouthful of sandwich.

Les nodded, crammed more of his patty cake into his mouth, and jumped to his feet.

"They're running away! Stop them!" screeched the obnoxious boy.

Jamming the rest of their food into their mouths, Les and Trevor raced toward the street. They leaped over a hedge, pounded through a flower bed, and veered around a fountain and several startled strollers. Trevor could hear their pursuers swarming behind them.

A shrill whistle blasted his ear. He looked up to see ranged in front of him three police officers, billy clubs raised.

Trevor skidded to a halt, and Les pulled up beside him. The crowd encircled them and the policemen, screaming accusations.

"Hold it!" an officer bellowed. "One at a time. What's going on?"

The cook pushed forward, wiping sweaty hands on her grease-stained apron. "They're thieves and sorcerers, that's what," she said in a voice shaking with anger. "They stole meat cakes from my stall—lifted them right into the air and made them fly. This lad saw it; he can tell you."

The police looked skeptical, but the boy jumped up and down. "I seen it, yes, I seen the whole thing. It was magic! They used magic to steal patty cakes."

One policeman pulled a notebook out of an inner pocket of his jacket and began writing down the testimony of the cook and the boy. The other two—big, burly fellows—grabbed hold of Les and Trevor.

"Wonderworkers, eh?" one said. "And thieves to boot. We've got good, secure jail cells for the likes of you. Come along. No tricks." He slapped his truncheon against the palm of his hand. "We don't put up with your kind in Port-of-Lords."

6

A COSTLY RESCUE

Les sat on the ledge that served as a sleeping platform in the tiny, windowless cell. Resting against the brick wall, he watched Trevor pace back and forth, back and forth in the small space. He ought to be dizzy; Les felt dizzy from watching.

Since being locked into the cell, they'd been fed a watery but edible stew and both had slept for several hours, taking turns stretching out on the narrow, bare ledge. Trevor had slept first, then Les napped as well as he could on the hard stone. He'd awakened to find Trevor pacing like a caged cat.

"Trev, stop wearing a hole in the cement and sit down," he begged.

Trevor continued pacing as though he hadn't heard.

Maybe he could distract Trevor with conversation. He asked a question that had been bothering him. "Trev, if there is such a big Community of the Gifted here in Port-of-Lords, why does any display of power surprise people, and why are they so antagonistic?"

"Guess we'll find out when we find the Community," Trevor said, not slowing his pacing.

"Your uncle said he hadn't had any contact with his friend

here in years. You don't suppose the Community's dispersed or been wiped out and he never heard, do you?"

Trevor merely grunted.

Les reconciled himself to waiting until Trevor worked through whatever was driving him.

Abruptly Trevor broke from the pattern and threw himself down beside Les. "I'm going to risk sending a call for help. When I called you to come to Sharpness, Uncle Matt said every gifted in the county could hear. I'll cast out in every direction, and we'll see what happens."

"Is that wise? You know what happened in Sharpness."

"I don't know what else to do," he said. "I can't open the door. I tried to use my power on the lock, but it doesn't work."

Les glanced at the heavy iron door. "Maybe you just haven't gotten enough strength back yet. Why don't you relax and give yourself more time?"

Trevor shook his head. "We didn't come to Port-of-Lords to spend our time in jail. I thought you wanted to see the Maritime Museum."

"If our jailers find out what you're trying, it'll add to the case against us."

"They won't find out unless they're gifted, and if they are, they may be willing to help us." Trevor leaned back, eyes closed, a frown of concentration puckering his forehead.

A moment later all Les's thoughts were blocked by a cry that screamed through his mind, sending his hands crashing against his temples, squeezing in a futile effort to stop the explosion within.

Help us. Strangers here. Robbed. Jailed. Need rescue. Help.

Over and over the message shrieked through his brain. He slid from the bench to crouch on the ground with his arms over his head. But the relentless blast continued, nauseating him, forcing him to crawl to the rank hole in the corner of the cell and heave up his recent meal. After that, he huddled against the wall as far from Trevor as the tiny cell permitted, clutched his head, and felt himself slipping into unconsciousness.

As from a great distance he seemed to hear a new voice cut across the racket in his head. *Hush,* it said. *I hear. I come.*

Trevor lifted Les onto the ledge. He'd been so absorbed in his call he hadn't noticed his friend's distress. He should have known how the sending would affect Les at such close range.

Les was unconscious, his breathing shallow, his pulse rapid. Trevor wished that healing were one of his talents. But it seemed he was only able to cause hurt, not cure it.

Help *was* on the way. He only hoped he hadn't bought that help at the price of Les's life.

He gave Les's shoulders a gentle shake. "Les," he said. "Les, I'm sorry. Come out of it, please."

Les gave a low moan but did not wake. Driven by anxiety and guilt, Trevor sent a soft mental call into Les's mind. Careful to keep the sending tightly focused, he pictured Les waking, feeling well and strong.

Les did not move, did not respond, did not wake.

Trevor pounded on the door of the cell. "My friend is sick," he shouted. "He needs help. A doctor."

A face appeared at the tiny barred window in the otherwise solid door. "Shut up in there," a gruff voice shouted.

"My friend. He's sick. Please, get a doctor. I'm afraid he's dying."

"Well, ain't that too bad! You was both healthy enough when they brought you in here. I don't fall for that old trick,

A PERILOUS POWER

and I ain't opening the door. You try anything else and you'll get no supper tonight."

"It's not a trick. Look at him. He—"

But the face had vanished. Trevor turned back to Les. He had to get help, but the only thing he could think of might kill Les before help arrived.

Hurry! he sent at full strength. *Help! Friend hurt.* He sent the image of Les lying unconscious, scarcely breathing.

He could do no more. He sat beside Les to wait.

He checked Les's breathing. Was it really weaker, or was it only fear that made him think so? If he'd killed Les . . .

He rose and paced.

He sat again, checked Les's pulse and breathing. Weaker. No question about it.

He walked to the door, peered out the tiny grate, saw only a gray wall.

He paced. He sat. He paced. He wanted to scream for the promised help to hurry, but he dared not weaken Les more. What was keeping the person?

Suppose he never came? Maybe he should try again to rouse the jailer. Maybe a different one would come, one who could be persuaded.

He rose and walked to the door. It swung open. A guard, one of those who had put him into the cell, said, "Somebody to see you." The guard stood aside to let in a short, dumpy woman with scraggly red hair.

Trevor barely restrained a shout of disgust. The visitor wore mismatched and wrinkled clothes that might have been fished out of a trash bin and a ridiculous straw hat topped by a pink bow out of which stuck a fuchsia feather. A stuffed bluebird perched on the bow in front of the feather.

E. ROSE SABIN

"Yes, these are my nephews," she said, glancing back at the burly jailer. "Foolish, naughty lads. Had a mite too much to drink, I'd suppose. It's not the first time, I'm ashamed to say. No doubt they think they've pulled off a wonderful joke, convincing you their sleight-of-hand tricks were real sorcery. They can't believe they can get into serious trouble with their parlor tricks. The folly of youth, you know."

"Yeah, well you'd better convince 'em," the jailer growled. "If it happens again, they won't get off with a fine."

"I'll see they work hard to repay the money," she announced with a grim smile. "That'll impress 'em where words won't."

She marched to the ledge where Les lay. "This scapegrace is still sleeping it off, is he? Well, he'd better come around and get up onto his feet if he doesn't want to be left here." She caught hold of Les's earlobe and gave it a cruel twist.

A sharp voice in his mind prevented Trevor's angry outcry. *Don't say a word. Follow my lead if you want help.*

He bit his tongue and glared at the ridiculous creature. This was not the help he'd expected.

"Come, lad, up with you," she was saying to Les.

"He's sick," Trevor said, rebelling against the mental command to silence.

"I don't doubt it." She glared at Trevor. "That's what comes of carousing." *Call me Aunt Veronica.*

She gave Les's ear another tweak. His eyes popped open. He gazed up at her with a bewildered look.

"Come, lad, up with you if you want to get home today. I've better things to do than waste my time on ne'er-do-wells."

"Yes, Aunt Veronica," Les said in a meek voice.

Trevor could scarcely conceal his relief at seeing Les awake and able to speak. He formed a mental *thank you* and tried to send it to her.

A blast of pain blocked the sending. *No more of that!* spoke the voice in his head. *You'll send nothing more until you've learned control.*

Aloud, she said, "Come, both of you. I've paid your fine, and an outrageous one it was. You'll have months of work paying it off."

She herded them to the cell door, and the jailer stood aside and let them pass.

Trevor waited until they were outside the oppressive stone prison and striding along unfamiliar streets before he dared to say, "Thank the Power-Giver, you heard my call for help. You must be from the Community of the Gifted we came out here to find."

"Community!" She turned her head and spat on the ground. "I have nothing to do with that bunch of fools."

"Why?" Les asked. "What's the matter with them?"

"They've lost sight of why the Community was established and turned it into a social club," she said. "Instead of sharing the power gift, they want to keep it all to themselves. You'd have rotted in that cell before any of *them* came to help you. Not that they wouldn't have heard your friend's call. There's probably not a gifted within ten miles doesn't have a headache from it. It's no surprise it nearly killed you."

"I didn't know." Her characterization of the Community shocked Trevor; she had to be wrong about it. But she wasn't wrong about what he'd done to Les. He turned to him. "It's not enough to say 'I'm sorry,' but I don't know what else to say. All I could think about was getting out. I didn't realize—"

E. ROSE SABIN

Les waved a hand. "Forget it, Trev. I'm fine now."

Trevor looked at their rescuer. "You're a healer?"

"Sometimes," was her vague reply. "How'd you know about the Community?"

He suspected she had asked in order to change the subject, but Trevor told her about Uncle Matt's plan for them, about the money they'd had stolen, about the abduction attempt, the escapade in the park, and their arrest.

"Hmmph! Good I came for you. You want looking after, that's clear. Matter of fact, I remember your uncle. The Community was still on track then, and I helped train him."

Trevor was surprised at that, and not sure he believed it. If what she said was true, why hadn't Uncle Matt spoken of her? If Uncle Matt had trusted her and thought her able to train him and Les, he would have written a letter of introduction to her. Trevor decided not to trust her or her description of the Community.

He cleared his throat. "We really appreciate all you've done. Healing Les, getting us out. We'll never be able to repay you. But we should find the Community and carry out the plan my aunt and uncle intended for us. To do that, we'll have to recover the letters they gave us."

"Aunt Veronica" put her hands on her hips and fixed Trevor with a firm gaze. "Young man, I just finished telling you that the Community isn't what your uncle thinks. It's changed. Though Doss Hamlyn's not so bad. He *might* help you. He could certainly train you if he cared to. But Berne Tenney's the worst of the lot. You'd do well to stay clear of him."

"What's he a doctor of?" Les asked. "Medicine?"

"Not him. If he's a doctor of anything, it's mischief. I suspect he just likes the title."

A PERILOUS POWER

77

"Well, even if we don't go to him, we should go and talk to Doss Hamlyn," Trevor insisted.

"Now you listen to me," Veronica said, stomping around a corner into a narrow lane. "I was putting on an act for the police, but one part was true enough. I had to pay a substantial fine to get you boys out of that jail, and I work hard for my money. Now you tell me you don't have so much as a single copper between you. Well, sirs, you'll be staying with me and working until your debt is paid. Until it is, you'll go nowhere."

"But we *will* repay you. We'll get our money back along with the letters. And our carryalls. We don't even have a change of clothes. With my power I can find Carl and force him to give back all he stole."

Hands still on her hips, the little woman whirled in front of him, halting him in midstride. "You're more of a fool than I thought if you expect to see your things again. Your friend Carl is a skilled thief, and possibly gifted himself. You're not clever enough to trap him. You'll not go chasing after a chimera. You'll work off your debt to me before you go anywhere."

"What kind of work?" Trevor asked. "What do you do?"

"I'm a cleaning lady," she said. "I hire out to people who don't need a permanent maid, just somebody to come in on a temporary basis."

Trevor couldn't believe it. "You're gifted, and you work as a *maid*?"

"Why not? It's good, honest work. And I can pick and choose the jobs I want and those I don't want."

Trevor's opinion of this woman dropped lower. "But for someone gifted . . ."

"My gifts aren't for hire," she snapped.

Trevor bristled. "But you used your gifts to help us, and now you want us to pay you."

"I want you to repay me for the money I used to pay your fine. That has nothing to do with my gifts—or yours. I can find plenty of work for you that won't require any use of power."

Les said, "Of course we'll work to pay our debt to you."

"What we need to do is to find Carl," Trevor insisted. "Or find Doss Hamlyn and see whether he'll help us."

"But, Trev," Les said, "it's not just money we owe. I owe Veronica my life, and I'll never be able to repay her for that. We can pay a visit to Doss Hamlyn later."

"*You're* a good lad, that's clear. And a sensible one." She glared at Trevor as if to be sure he hadn't missed the implication.

Again Les spoke before Trevor could find a way to revoke his friend's ready acceptance. "Maybe you can tell if I really am gifted."

Veronica looked startled. Her sharp gaze probed Les. "Gifted? Of course you are. The way you were affected by this one's sending shows that." She gave a contemptuous nod toward Trevor. "A normal would have felt nothing. That you felt it so strongly proves a high talent."

"But I can't do any of the things Trevor does."

"That merely means your talent is different from his," she said. "How old are you?"

"I'm eighteen."

"You ought to have discovered your gifts by that age. Hmmm." She took Les's chin in her hand and turned his head to one side and then the other before releasing it with a frown. "Well, if anyone can help you, I can. Yes, indeed, I've developed many a young talent in my time. My guess is

A PERILOUS POWER

you've been so overshadowed by this flashy friend of yours that you didn't recognize the signs of your talent. But I can remedy that, indeed I can."

So she was blaming him for Les's failure to find his gift. And now more than ever Les would be determined to serve this woman.

Trevor knew he would have to yield, for a short time, at least. He found the prospect deeply disturbing.

7

BEYOND THE DOOR

Les had long since lost any notion of where they were in relation to the few landmarks he knew. After walking for many blocks, turning down numerous side streets, and passing through several twisting alleys, Veronica stopped before an odd, dome-shaped hovel set back from the street and hidden in the shadows of the taller buildings on either side of it. Those buildings were rundown tenements with sagging window screens, cracked windows, and weathered siding. Half-naked children with runny noses and faces streaked with dirt played on the sidewalk and in the street in front of the apartments. Les noticed that they avoided the area in front of Veronica's small home as though barred by an invisible fence.

Veronica paid no attention to the ragged urchins, but led the way along a gravel path to her front door. She pushed the door open. "Watch your step," she said.

Les was surprised to see a stairway leading down into an interior considerably below ground level. Veronica stopped at the foot of the stairs and lit an oil lamp resting on a small table. As the lamp flared, the door above them swung shut.

Apparently the house consisted only of this single, circular, windowless room. The air was surprisingly cool and fresh with a pleasant, spicy scent. As his eyes grew accustomed to the dim light, Les stared at the peculiar and fascinating place.

The entire floor was covered with animal pelts, though from what animals he could not imagine. The furs were of unusual colors and patterns unlike those of any animal he knew of. One was configured with concentric circles in shades of gray and brown. That animal would have made an easy target for a hunter.

Small tables, some round, some square, some triangular, but all the same height, were scattered about the room. Each stood as high as Veronica's waist and held a single object. A crystal ball rested on one, another held a mortar and pestle; an empty birdcage stood on a third. A knife lay on a triangular table, an hourglass stood on a round one, while a square one held a thick, leather-bound book.

The only furniture in the room other than the tables was a flat-topped wood-burning stove with a metal stovepipe that curved in an inverted **L** and exited through the wall. An empty woodbin sat beside the stove, an ax leaning against it.

From the ceiling a weird assortment of items both strange and familiar dangled from strings and ropes or hung in nets. Les noted bunches of onions and garlic, chili peppers, sprigs of herbs, pots, kettles, ladles, and cork-stoppered bottles. Those things he understood, but he wondered what use she had for the skulls of small animals, a thick hank of what looked like human hair, a string of shells, and a dried fish. He marveled at the weird combination of articles like a delicate porcelain doll, a black wand, and a snakeskin. There were several oddly shaped items that he could not identify.

E. ROSE SABIN

He glanced at Trevor, curious to see his friend's reaction, and was surprised to see an expression of revulsion.

"Hex materials," Trevor said in a tone of contempt. "A true talent has no need of such things."

Les was appalled by Trevor's rudeness, but Veronica ignored it. She removed her ludicrous hat, revealing a tangle of faded red hair mingled through with strands of white that gave it a pinkish cast. Combing the fingers of one hand through the tangle with no noticeable effect, she set the hat carefully on an empty table. Then she pulled off her shawl and tied it onto the end of a dangling cord, crossed the room, and lit another lamp.

"Now," she announced, "I'll fix us a pot of tea, and we'll talk."

"Tea!" Trevor snorted in disgust.

"Tea is calming," she said. "It settles the nerves."

"My nerves don't need settling," Trevor snapped.

Les understood, probably better than Trevor himself, what lay behind his friend's irritability. Trevor's pride had suffered a succession of blows since their arrival in Port-of-Lords, culminating in their rescue by this dowdy little woman. To Les it was clear that she was far more than what she seemed, and he thought it should be equally clear to Trevor, but he was refusing to see it. Les guessed that Trevor couldn't stand being obligated to Veronica when he wanted to find Carl, punish him, and recover what he could of their money. Les wanted that, too, but he owed Veronica too much to walk out on her just to satisfy a thirst for vengeance.

Ignoring Trevor's rudeness, Veronica puttered around, lighting a fire with a bit of wood that was in the stove, filling a kettle and setting it to heat, finding cups and spoons among the hanging objects, all the while keeping her back to her guests. Only when the kettle began to whistle did Veronica turn and look at Trevor.

"Young man," she said, "since you don't care for tea, and your nerves need no calming, you take the ax and go fetch more wood for the stove. Your friend and I will have tea, and he will listen to what I have to say. Until you are ready to learn, I can teach *you* nothing."

Trevor glared at her and Les expected him to refuse. But he stalked to the woodbin and picked up the ax. "How do you expect me to find wood to cut here in the city?" he asked, his voice taut with anger. Les didn't like the way he was gripping the ax.

"From the forest."

"Forest! What forest?"

"The one beyond the door." She stooped where she was standing and, beginning at the floor and moving upward, then over and down again, traced a door-sized rectangle in the air with her index finger. The finger left a visible line, and when Veronica finished her drawing, a wooden door appeared within the lines. Veronica pushed it open, and Les caught a glimpse of green beyond it.

"Go through and gather the wood quickly. Don't try to chop down a whole tree; just cut dead branches off trees within sight of the door. Don't get lost. And be on your guard. Wild beasts prowl that wood. Go, hurry."

Trevor stared at the door. The flush of anger faded from his face, leaving it pale. He inhaled deeply, marched through the open door, and vanished from Les's view.

Veronica shut the door. It looked odd standing upright in the middle of the room, a plain wooden door attached to nothing. Les stared at it. "Is that a real place—where you sent him?"

E. ROSE SABIN

84

"Quite real," Veronica said.

"Then he's really in danger?" Les headed for the door.

Veronica stretched out her arm and stopped him. "Danger is everywhere. He must learn caution. Where I've sent him he'll have the opportunity to learn it without endangering anyone else while he does so."

She hadn't eased his concern for Trevor. Les tried to move around her to reach the door. She clasped his wrist in a steely grip and pulled him back as easily as if he had been a child.

"That door is not for you. You may not pass through it. Come, let us have tea."

She scooped tea leaves into a ceramic teapot, filled the pot with boiling water, and set it on one of the small tables along with two cups. Les noted with mild amusement that the teapot was old, its lid cracked and glued together. The cups didn't match, and one had a chipped rim. He saw no chairs in the room. Probably she did not often have guests.

"While the tea steeps, you can tell me more about yourself," she said. "I especially want to know why you are so willing to follow your reckless friend. You should be the leader. Why do you let him lead you—into trouble, it seems."

"He's not always reckless," Les defended Trevor. "Not usually—well, not often."

"Mmm. So you say. I'll wager you don't believe that yourself."

He had to grin then. She had both him and Trevor neatly pegged. "We've been friends for a long time—all our lives, in fact."

"So you're both eighteen?"

"I'm a few months older; he's still seventeen."

She scowled. "You're older, yet you seem content to let Trevor lead. Why?"

"I guess," he said slowly, "it always seemed natural to let him take the lead because of his special powers. When we were younger, I was in awe of them. Then, well, he didn't use them much as we got older, but I always knew . . . I mean, he could do so many things I couldn't do . . ."

He let his voice trail off as he realized how lame his explanation sounded.

"Hmmph. Well, let's have our tea." She lifted the teapot, poured the tea into the cups, and handed him one. A few leaves floated in the amber liquid, and he wondered absurdly whether she read them.

"Do you take sugar, cream, or lemon?" she asked.

Seeing none of those items anywhere about, he shook his head and sipped the tea. It was surprisingly good, with a mellow taste that made him think of a rain-drenched forest. He did find it soothing, and drinking it while standing encouraged him to finish it quickly. He set the empty cup back on the table.

She drained her cup and set it beside his. "Now," she said, "let's discover your gifts." Taking his arm, she led him to the table that held the crystal ball.

"Put your hands around it, like so." She demonstrated, placing her hands on either side of the crystal. He followed suit, his larger hands encircling the sphere so that only its top was visible. Cold at first, the crystal warmed beneath his touch.

Veronica stared at the portion visible between his hands. "Soon," she muttered softly as if to herself, "soon we shall know."

*   *   *

E. ROSE SABIN

86

Trevor stumbled dazedly through the door and found himself in a grassy meadow sprinkled with wildflowers. Golden butterflies darted from flower to flower. In the nearby woods, a bird sang. No gift or power that he had heard of could create a door into another place. This must be an illusion. But if so, it was an incredibly good one. Breathing deeply the fresh, sweet air, he strode toward the trees.

It was impossible for that eccentric old woman to have created such an elaborate illusion. Or to have sent him here, if it was real. Something or someone else had to be behind this feat. He resolved to ferret out the answer.

He recalled how easily she had healed Les. But healing was not an unusual gift. This was something new, something beyond his understanding.

Passing into the woods, he looked back to be sure he could see the door. How odd it looked, the plain wooden door standing in the middle of a grassy field. He peered beyond it, where the grassland gave way to rolling hills. Nowhere did he see evidence of human habitation.

Hefting the ax, he searched for dead branches or fallen limbs. A partially uprooted tree leaned against its healthier neighbors. He recalled Veronica's warning not to chop whole trees, but this tree was nearly dead, and by itself it would provide all the wood he needed. It was large for his ax, but its dry wood would burn well. He could use power to increase the force of the ax.

A jade green snake with eyes like opals glided across the path, slithered among the uplifted roots of his chosen tree, and vanished.

"Hope that's not your home, fella. If it is, you're about to be evicted."

He raised the ax, brought it down against the trunk of the

tree. Chips flew, the tree shook, a gash sliced into its side. He lifted the ax and brought it down again. The gash widened.

A third blow split the tree. Its top fell away and crashed onto the leaf-carpeted ground.

Green tentacles sprouted from the hollow trunk and resolved themselves into snakes—hundreds of them. Hissing, ruby tongues darting, opal eyes glittering, they poured from the tree and streamed toward him.

He turned and ran. The rustling of leaves behind him told him they followed. He dodged around trees and leaped over stumps and low shrubs. The snakes surged over the obstacles and pressed close behind him.

A stream crossed his path. He saw it too late to check his speed. He leaped across, slid on the other bank, sprawled full-length in the mud.

The sound of splashes told him the snakes were crossing the stream.

He hauled himself to his feet and ran forward. A furious splashing and thrashing made him slow and risk a glance back at the stream.

He stared transfixed. An eely creature with a long snout had stuck its sinuous neck above the surface and was gobbling down the snakes, some of which hung from its jaws like strands of seaweed.

The snakes that escaped that toothy maw slithered up onto the muddy bank and glided about aimlessly, their crusade forgotten.

Trevor shouldered his ax and walked away from the stream. He'd gone only a few steps when he realized that his wild dash had taken him far from his point of entry, and he no longer had any idea where the door was.

E. Rose Sabin

And he hadn't gathered any firewood.

One thing he knew: He had to get back across the stream. But he had no desire to encounter either the snakes or their fearsome nemesis. He struck out on a course that took him parallel to the stream so that he could cross it well beyond the place of danger.

A fallen limb blocked his path. He raised his ax and considered. Would this one, too, contain snakes?

But he had come for firewood and would be ashamed to return empty-handed. He swung the ax. It split the limb.

A swarm of bees flew up at him. Surrounded by their angry buzzing, pierced in arms, neck, and face with dozens of fiery stingers, he swung the ax to fend off the enraged insects and leaped into the stream.

It was deeper than he'd thought. He plunged beneath the water until the clinging bees floated off. The icy water eased the agony of the stings.

He stayed beneath the water until his lungs ached and he had to breathe. He surfaced and drew in another breath. A wild buzzing and sharp stabs on his scalp and forehead sent him back beneath the water. He swam upstream to get away from his tormentors.

Powerful jaws closed over his leg; pain stabbed through his ankle. He twisted around. The snake killer had grabbed him, was tearing at his leg, pulling him beneath the water.

He aimed the ax and used his power to drive its blade through the creature's long neck.

The water turned red, the jaws loosed their hold. He called the ax to him. It flew toward his hand, green snakes clinging to its handle and pouring into the water from the creature's severed neck.

A PERILOUS POWER

With a cry he let the ax fall into the water, and he clambered up onto the bank.

Which bank? He didn't know, and with the snakes behind him he couldn't worry about it.

Weaponless, dragging one foot, he looked for a way of escape.

He stumbled forward a few steps, heard a loud buzzing, saw the cloud of bees descending on him, and tried to run faster. A low growl in front of him stopped him as the bees descended.

A creature the size of a large bear ambled toward him on two legs. Its front paws bore long, curving claws. A long, hoselike snout seemed to sniff the air.

Trevor groaned and tried to turn aside and run in another direction. His injured foot gave way. He sprawled forward, and a blanket of bees spread over him. Snakes slithered over his legs. He fainted.

He awakened to pain in every part of his body. Something hot and moist was moving back and forth across his legs. The snakes? He lay still, not daring to move, not sure he *could* move. But he heard no more buzzing of bees, and gradually he became convinced that what he felt moving across his back was not the snakes. He remembered the beast he'd seen. He turned his head, got one swollen eye open enough to make out a blurry image.

The creature was bending over him, swinging its nose across Trevor's skin and clothing. As he watched, the nose stopped, a long slender tongue snapped out, snared a bee, and retracted with its prize. Trevor let his head fall back to the ground. The probing and the licks continued. Trevor fainted again, or perhaps he merely slept. When he woke, the creature had left.

E. ROSE SABIN

He managed to roll over and sit up despite his swollen flesh. A few dead snakes lay scattered around him; the rest were gone. He leaned forward and looked at his injured leg. It was soaked in blood. He tore his trousers away from the wound and examined the deep gashes left by the water monster's teeth. One of those gashes went all the way to the bone, and although the bleeding had slowed to a trickle, if he tried to walk it would start again. He had lost a lot of blood. To keep from losing more, he fashioned a strip torn from his trousers into a tourniquet.

He tried to stand. A wave of dizziness slammed him back to the ground. Black swirls enfolded him; he struggled to stay conscious.

If he could find the strength to send, who would hear? This place, wherever it was, was far from Port-of-Lords. Only the door linked it with Veronica's strange house, and he wasn't sure a sending would be heard beyond that door.

He had to try. But in his weakness he could manage only a plea so feeble he sensed that it did not pass the nearest tree.

It seemed that he was doomed to die here in this terrible, nameless place.

8

Lost

Les stared at the portion of globe visible between his encircling hands. Veronica's gaze had been fixed unblinkingly on that circlet of crystal for some time. Her lips moved occasionally in the way of one reading to herself. To him she said nothing, and her expression of intense concentration warned him not to distract her with questions. He leaned closer, hoping to see what she saw, but viewed only the reflection of his own face, its features distorted by the curved surface.

He grew weary standing and wondered that Veronica did not. The room held no chairs or furniture other than the profusion of tables.

He itched to examine the odd assortment of articles hung about the room. Hex materials, Trevor had called them in derision, but the door that stood mysteriously in the center of the room and opened onto another place, perhaps another world, offered proof that Veronica was no mere hex witch.

His gaze swung to the door. Such an ordinary-looking object, had it been in a normal place. So alien, so obtrusive where it was. He kept his gaze fixed on it for a time, willing it to open and Trevor to stride through with an armload of firewood.

The door remained closed. He returned his gaze to Veronica.

"Most peculiar," she muttered, shaking her head. She removed her hands from the crystal, and he dropped his own away. He tried again to peer into the globe, but it was clouded; nothing could be seen within and its surface no longer reflected an image.

"What did you learn?" he dared to ask.

"That the problem is more complex than I'd thought," she answered.

"The crystal didn't tell you anything?"

"The crystal told me much. It confirmed what I'd suspected: You are a great conduit of power."

"Conduit of power? What does that mean?"

"We say the gifted *have* power, but that isn't accurate. We receive power from the Power-Giver. The power is one, but as it flows through different people, it produces different gifts and manifests itself in various ways."

She plucked a small packet from a dangling net, slipped a flask from a looped cord, and untied the knotted thread that held a slender glass wand. She carried these items to a triangular table holding a silver goblet.

"In some the power falls like a slow and gentle rain, soaking a wide area but with a diffuse force." Opening the packet, she sprinkled a white powder into the goblet. "Such people have many talents, and often impress and even frighten others by the range of their abilities, but they cannot sustain or focus the power to achieve important and long-lasting results. They are often called witches or illusionists, because their gifts, while genuine, have the quality of parlor tricks.

"Into others the power pours like a fountain." She uncorked the flask and poured a red liquid into the goblet.

"These are gifted with no more than two or three talents, but those are strong and deep. It is they whom normals fear for the harm they can do. Some can bind demons to their bidding. Others can coerce weaker subjects to do their will. Some can shapechange and roam as an animal, often inflicting harm. Others create havoc by mimicking the appearance of another person. But in this group also are those who use their talents for great good. Some are healers, some are truth readers, some are finders of the lost.

"Into a very few the power strikes deep and sure like an arrow." She thrust the glass wand into the goblet. "Those rare souls have but a single talent. It may be of such nature that it can be used but once. But it is of immense strength; none can overcome it.

"Finally, there are those, drawn primarily from the second group, on rare occasions from the first, who through rigorous self-discipline, meditation, and sacrifice are able to open themselves fully to the flow of power, allowing it to so permeate them that they become nothing more than channels of power. They are the Adepts." With the glass wand she stirred vigorously until the powder dissolved fully.

"You are an Adept, aren't you?" he asked as the insight burst on him.

She smiled and held the frothy mixture out to him. "Drink this."

"What is it?"

"It will place you in a dream state that I can enter to explore the paths of power within your mind."

"You mean it will let you read my mind?"

With a pained look she drew back the proffered goblet. "I read no one's thoughts without express permission. Had I intended such a thing, I would have told you. You must trust me. Your thoughts and memories will remain inviolate."

Shamed, he reached for the goblet. It was less than half filled with the foamy red liquid.

"The effect lasts only a short time," she told him as he gazed into the cup. "Less than an hour, I'd say."

Without a word he drank it down. The taste was not unpleasant—fruity and a little sweet. Only that.

"Good," she said when he handed back the empty goblet. Taking him by the wrist, she led him across the room. He looked closely at the door as they passed it, standing solid and substantial in the room's center. Shouldn't Trevor have returned? He opened his mouth to ask but yawned instead. No point in voicing his concern. Veronica knew what she was about. He would trust her as she'd asked.

She released his wrist and piled together several of the pelts that covered the floor. "Lie down," she said.

He was glad to do so. His limbs were growing numb, and he wanted to relax.

The pelts were soft and inviting. Smiling, he stretched out on them. "Feels good," he murmured, overwhelmed by a marvelous sense of well-being. A wonderful place, this was, and Veronica was kind and wise and generous. Too bad Trevor wasn't here. Good old Trev. Best buddy a guy could have. He yawned again, a yawn that stretched the muscles of his face. He curled up, burrowed down into the soft fur, eyes closed, drifting in happiness.

Trevor would enjoy this. *Where is Trev? Have to find him.* So much fog. Trev. Lost in fog. *Trev. Trev, where are you?* No answer. *Can't find him. Nothing here but fog and shadows.* Shifting, twisting shadows. Swirling shapes. Gray. Black.

And white. One white form. Tall, graceful. Moving

through the shadows. *Here. I'm here.* But the form moves past, drifts away. Gone. Alone.

No, not alone. Other shapes form, dissolve before he reaches them. *Trevor.* He's sure one is Trevor, but it turns away, drifts out of reach, disappears. He's alone again. Alone.

He tossed, moaned. Opened his eyes.

Veronica bent over him, frowning. "There, now, had a bad reaction, didn't you? I didn't expect that. Shouldn't have happened."

She helped him sit up. "You should have felt content, happy—nothing more."

"I did feel that way." Les shook his head to clear it. "Until I started seeing shapes. I thought I saw Trevor. Why isn't he back?"

Her scowl deepened. "Trevor, always Trevor. He'll be the death of you, lad."

"But *shouldn't* he be back with the firewood by now? How long was I out?"

"About half an hour. And, yes, he should. I suppose I'll have to go see what trouble he's got himself into. He wants looking after, he does, but you shouldn't have to be the one who always has to do it."

"I won't be this time. Not if you go," Les pointed out reasonably. "And you haven't told me what you read in my mind. Did you discover my talents?"

She pursed her lips, looked toward the freestanding door, and didn't answer.

"Well?" he prodded.

She walked to the door. "Some things you're better off not knowing."

He pushed himself to his feet and headed after her. Still woozy, he stumbled, regained his balance, but failed to reach

A PERILOUS POWER

the door before she stepped through it and closed it behind her.

He twisted the knob. It refused to turn. He pulled, afraid he'd pull down the whole door. It stayed firmly in place, and it stayed firmly shut. He walked around it and tried to open the other side, wondering whether, if he did so, he'd go through to the place Trevor had gone or to somewhere else. He would never know. The door resisted all attempts to open it.

Frustrated, he walked back to the pile of pelts, sat down, knees drawn up, and watched the door. Time passed. Veronica did not return. What could he do? He had never felt so helpless.

As time dragged on, he began to feel that Trevor had been right after all. They should not have come here. He shouldn't have refused to listen, shouldn't have dismissed his friend's distaste as mere reluctance. He could not undo what was done, but it galled him to do nothing but wait. Could he break through the door? Use a table as a battering ram? That probably would not work on a magical door, but if Veronica did not get back soon, he'd have to try.

Trevor woke with a start. He hadn't meant to doze off. With all the dangers in the woods, he had to stay on guard. The loss of the ax left him weaponless, and in his weakened state he couldn't use his power. Helpless to defend himself, he didn't want anything sneaking up on him.

What had awakened him? He heard a twitter of birds, a background chorus of chirring insects. Those sounds had been present all along. He sat up, cocked his head, and listened.

Was that a footstep, that soft crunch of leaves? Yes, someone—or something—was walking toward him. He tensed, looked for a place to hide.

Too late. He should have crawled earlier to a more sheltered spot. With his injured leg, he'd never make it now. The footsteps grew louder, closer.

A woman stepped out from among the trees. A young woman, unusually tall, wearing a long, loose-fitting white garment of soft cambric, a dressing gown, unsuited for tramping about through the woods. Her hair fell in two long braids that hung over her shoulders and curved over her breasts.

She saw Trevor and stopped short, her hand flying to her mouth as if to stifle a scream. She whirled, ran back the way she'd come.

"Wait!" Trevor called after her. "Help me! Please!"

She'd already passed from sight in the gathering dusk. He held his breath, waiting, hoping.

He heard her footsteps approach, slow and cautious. She came into sight but stopped several feet distant. "What—who—are you?" she asked in a quavering voice.

"I'm Trevor Blake. I came here to gather firewood. I was chased by snakes, stung by bees, and a water monster took a bite out of my leg." He used both hands to lift his injured leg so that she could see the bloody wound.

"Oh!" She came a step nearer. "But how did you get here? There shouldn't be anyone else here."

He didn't think he should tell her of Veronica and the door. Instead, he said, "Are these your private woods?"

"No, I guess not." She took another step toward him. "But I've never seen anybody here before." She looked wary, frightened. "Though I've never come this far. I was following a ghost."

"A ghost!" Just his luck. The only other person anywhere near, and she was insane.

"Well, I don't know what else to call it. It was like a white mist drifting down the trail in front of me. It was shaped a little like a man. I could see through it. It vanished just before I saw you."

Trevor despaired. This woman was not going to be of any help to him.

She walked to his side, stared down. She was younger than he'd thought, maybe sixteen or seventeen. A nasty bruise discolored the left side of her face.

His own face must look much worse, he thought, puffy as it was from the bee stings. Maybe his appearance was what was frightening her so.

She knelt beside him, touched him lightly on the cheek. He winced from the pain of even that soft pressure on his swollen flesh. She jerked her hand away, but slowly extended it again and placed her palm on his cheek. He cried out in pain, lifted his hand to push hers away.

Her other hand caught his. "Be still," she said. "I'll heal you."

As she spoke, he felt the swelling go down. The pain lessened.

In a moment she moved her hand. "That takes care of the bee stings," she said. "Now I'll look to your leg." She shifted her position to sit beside the mauled leg. This time she placed both hands over the wound, and again the pressure of her touch made him yell. She grimaced but did not pull her hands away. The process took longer than with the bee stings, but he felt his leg warm and tingle and itch like a healing scab so that it was all he could do not to push her hands away and scratch. He gritted his teeth and waited, and

E. ROSE SABIN

minutes later the itching stopped, and a few minutes after that she moved her hands, and he leaned over to look and saw only healthy skin with not a trace of a scar.

She stood, and he rose to stand beside her. She was taller than he by several inches.

"Thanks," he said, embarrassed by the inadequacy of the word. "I don't know your name."

"It's Miryam," she said shyly.

He lifted his hand to her face, brushed the bruise with a finger. "You're hurt, too," he said. "Why don't you heal yourself?"

"It—it isn't that bad." She dropped her gaze, backed away. "I have to go."

"But you can't leave me. I don't know how to find my way out." He heard the plaintive whine in his voice and, angered with himself, said gruffly, "Finish what you started, girl. What good will your healing do if you refuse to guide me out of here? You seem to know the way, and this place is dangerous."

"Yes," she said slowly, "I guess it is for someone who doesn't belong here."

"Well, I *don't* belong here. I have no protection against wild animals, and night's coming."

"You're gifted, aren't you? You couldn't be here if you weren't."

He couldn't deny it. Now that he was healed, he could use his power. But even with power he had no desire to stay in these woods, weaponless, after dark. "A woman named Veronica sent me here," he said. "Do you know her?"

"No. I've heard the name." Her frightened look returned, and she turned and headed down the path.

A PERILOUS POWER

He caught up with her and grabbed her arm. "I'm coming with you," he insisted.

"Can't this Veronica get you out?"

"I don't trust her," he said. "She may never come back for me. You have to lead me out."

She awarded him a long, measured look. "Danger is not only in the woods." She touched her bruised face. "But come on, then. I've stayed here far too long."

She set off at a brisk pace. He had to step quickly to match her long strides. Concentrating on keeping up with her, he paid scant attention to his surroundings. In the growing darkness he could see little beyond the path. The trees became banks of shadow, distinguished only when they thrust out their roots to trip him, or stretched their limbs across the path, forcing him to duck.

They encountered a jumble of roots, intertwined in such a way that they had to ascend them like steps.

Very like steps.

Trevor looked at the tree from which they protruded. His gaze followed the massive trunk upward to a mat of branches high overhead, solid as a ceiling.

Eyes off the path, he stumbled, put out a hand to catch himself, rubbed his palm along the trunk of the tree.

No tree was that smooth. And surely these *were* steps he climbed. They were too evenly spaced, too carefully shaped to be anything else.

Wooden steps ascending along a frame wall. At the top of the steps a sharp turn. In front of them a heavy gray curtain. From beyond it a man's voice shouting, "Miryam. Miryam, where are you hiding, you lazy slug? Get in here."

His guide's shoulders slumped; she seemed to shrink.

Her white-sleeved arm swept aside the curtain, and she

stepped through the passage. Trevor followed into a narrow hallway lit by a single bright overhead light. She'd led him out of that strange world into which Veronica had sent him and back to his own world, without using Veronica's mysterious door.

"Miryam," the voice bellowed again. "If I have to come find you—" The angry voice sounded vaguely familiar.

"I'm coming," Miryam called out. But her steps dragged as she trudged toward a door.

Trevor caught her arm. "What's happening? Where are we? Who is that?"

She yanked her arm from his grasp. "I warned you not to come," she whispered and opened the door.

Trevor glanced behind him to find an escape route. The gray curtain was gone, replaced by a solid wall. However, the wall beside him held a second door, so this was not a dead end. Reassured, he followed Miryam.

She stood before a man lounging in an overstuffed easy chair. "Damn you," he harangued her, "you know what time I expect supper. Where is it? Get it up here! I—"

He broke off, craned his neck to peer past her at Trevor.

Sitting up, he pushed Miryam aside, giving Trevor a clear view. No wonder the voice had seemed familiar. The man who glared at him, face suffused with anger, was Carl.

9

DECOY

Trevor! What a surprise." Carl leaped out of his chair.

The shock of recognition paralyzed Trevor for a single fateful moment. By the time he lunged for Carl, the con man had lowered his head and slammed into Trevor's chest, knocking him backward through the open doorway.

He recovered his balance barely in time to fend off a second blow and get in a punch and knee jab of his own. Carl staggered back, and Trevor threw himself on top of him. The two thrashed about on the hall floor, slamming into the walls, battering each other, neither able to gain the advantage.

Belatedly Trevor thought to use his power. He hurled a blast of force that at such close range should have knocked Carl unconscious.

The force bounced harmlessly off Carl and boomeranged. Trevor hadn't thought to shield. The rebound slammed into his brain, bringing pain and blackness.

Consciousness crept back in a haze of hurt. His head throbbed, his ears buzzed, and his muscles ached. When he tried to move, he discovered that he was in a straight-backed wooden chair, his arms pulled behind the chair's back and his wrists bound so tightly that his hands were numb. His ankles were also tied, and rope was wound around his legs and the legs of the chair, making it impossible for him to shift position.

He lifted his head and willed his eyes to focus. His gaze fell on Carl, straddling a second wooden chair and leaning forward against its back. Carl broke into a broad smile and rocked his chair exuberantly.

"Welcome, my friend. I can't tell you how delighted I am that you decided to drop in. You're exactly who I needed to see. You couldn't have come at a more propitious time." The thin blond mustache bobbed up and down as Carl delivered his hearty greeting.

"You lousy thief! You stole everything I had. What more do you want?"

Carl rubbed his hands together in glee. "Ah, what more do I want? That *is* the question." He scooted his chair with a loud screech across the bare wooden floor and thrust his face so close to Trevor's that Trevor could smell his garlic-and-wine-laden breath. "What I want is entry into the Community of the Gifted. I've been intrigued by the letters of introduction I found in the packet along with the gold and silver you so generously provided for me. I decided to impersonate you, present the letters, and see what opportunities they open up for me. Unfortunately, the letters speak of your friend Les and his problem of not being able to find his gift. I thought I was going to have to recruit a friend to play Les's part, which would have been tricky. It isn't easy to impersonate someone who tests high in talent but doesn't exhibit any evidence of gifts. With you as a lure to acquire Les's cooperation, I'll have the original article."

He threw back his head and laughed.

E. ROSE SABIN

Trevor spoke through teeth clenched in anger. "If you think I'll help you find Les—"

"Oh, I know you will," Carl said through his laughter. "You won't have any choice." He jumped to his feet and swung the chair behind him. "Miryam!" he shouted. "Come here!"

The girl who'd led him into this trap entered the room. She'd changed out of the dressing gown she'd had on before; she was wearing a brown twill skirt, a long-sleeved white blouse, and over them a white muslin apron. She looked frightened; her eyes were red as though she'd been crying, and she avoided Trevor's gaze.

Carl grabbed her arm, jerked her toward him, and with his other hand grasped her chin and forced her face upward. "Trevor," he said, "this is my sister, Miryam. She's a bit foolish, but she has enough sense to do what I tell her. Don't you, Miryam?"

His fingers dug into her flesh. She couldn't have answered if she'd wanted to, not with his grip on her jaw. He shook her head, released his hold, leaving ugly red marks on her face. "Don't you?" he repeated.

She nodded.

"Miryam has some useful talents," Carl said. "She'll stay here with you. You'll tell her where Les is, and she'll go and fetch him for me."

Trevor strained uselessly against his ropes. "You're crazy! You won't drag Les into this. I won't tell her or you anything."

"You will, though. Sooner or later you will. I'll leave you two to chat while I eat the supper Miryam so lovingly fixed for me." Smiling, he brushed past Miryam and left the room.

Miryam collapsed onto the chair Carl had vacated and sat

hunched over, her hands between her legs, rocking back and forth, moaning. Her hair fell across her face, hiding it from him, but her misery was obvious.

As furious as he was with Carl, Trevor could not be angry with the unhappy girl. She clearly did not approve of Carl's actions, but for some reason she was terrified of him. If Trevor could persuade her to help him . . .

"You don't want to help Carl, do you?" Trevor asked gently. "Is he really your brother? You're Miryam *Holdt*?"

"Miryam Vedreaux," she said in a barely audible voice, still rocking. "He's my half brother."

"Why do you let him treat you that way?"

She didn't answer, didn't raise her head.

Trevor tried again. "Miryam, you must have a lot of power. If you don't like what your brother is doing, you can fight him. You don't have to suffer like this."

She spoke in a soft whisper without raising her head. He had to strain to hear her. "You don't understand. He controls me. I can't break free."

"That's nonsense. Look, I'll help you. With my power added to yours, we can defeat him. Untie me."

She shook her head.

"You can't let him get away with this," Trevor said urgently. "You don't have to. Help me. Let me help you."

"You can't help me. No one can," the sad voice murmured.

"Don't be such a weakling! Of course you can be helped." The words burst from Trevor. "Let's get out of here, and I'll show you what I can do."

She looked up, meeting his gaze at last. "We can't get out, and you can't help me. You can't do anything except what Carl wants you to do."

Trevor's anger flared. "You're just being stubborn!" He

struggled uselessly against the tight ropes. "How can you let him treat me like this?"

"I don't have any choice. The only way . . . Look, tell me about your friend. About Les."

The request calmed Trevor. Maybe if he talked quietly to her, he'd win her confidence. She was terrified of her brother; he'd have to overcome that. He had to think, to block out his physical discomfort: the chafing ropes, the cramping muscles. *Take it slow*, he told himself. *She's got a soft heart. Play on that. Take her mind off herself—make her think of Les.*

"Les and I grew up together," he told her. "Our families lived on adjoining farms. All through school we got in mischief together, helped each other out, shared dreams." As he spoke, his mind reviewed all its pictures of Les and him together as children, as schoolboys, as teenagers helping their fathers with the plowing and harvesting, caring for the animals. "My parents didn't want anyone to know I was gifted. They forbade me to use my power. But Les knew. I guess he envied me a little, but he never let it hurt our friendship. He's a great friend—the best. Your brother's crazy if he thinks I'd put Les in danger."

"My brother probably *is* crazy," she said quietly. "But he's clever. He always knows how to get exactly what he wants."

"Well, this time he won't. I couldn't lead him to Les if I wanted to. I don't know how to find him from wherever it is I am."

"But you can mindsend. You could call him to you."

"How would he know how to get here? Anyway, I won't do that. He's in a safe place, and he'll stay there." Trevor thought of Veronica. Much as he mistrusted the little woman, she had power, plenty of it. She'd heard his sending,

A PERILOUS POWER

healed Les, and gotten them out of jail. As long as Les was in that crazy-looking house of hers, he was safe from Carl.

His mind played over their rescue, the walk from the jail with Veronica haranguing and lecturing him the whole way. He saw again the odd, domed house, so incongruous in the block of ugly tenements, so seemingly impervious to the degradation of the neighborhood. That round house was a magical fortress; unless Les was lured outside, Carl would never be able to get to him.

Miryam jumped up. "Be careful," she shouted, and with that despairing cry, she ran from the room. Puzzled, Trevor stared after her.

He was still trying to make sense of Miryam's unexpected flight when Carl strode into the room. "Good boy!" he boomed, walking over to slap Trevor on the shoulder. "I knew I could count on you. You gave Miryam the information she needed to find your friend."

What was he talking about? He'd given nothing—His mind! She'd read his mind! He should have known. He knew she had extraordinary talent. But no more than Veronica.

He had to warn Veronica. He launched a strong mental sending: *Veronica! Guard Les! Carl has me. He wants Les. He—*

Trevor's head spun. "No more messages," Carl said.

Trevor tried to speak, but his head was heavy, his tongue thick. Carl's face blurred; his vicious laughter swept him into oblivion.

Les explored the room, examining the odd objects hanging everywhere. The avid curiosity he'd felt earlier was gone; he was only trying to divert his mind from worry over Trevor. He found himself wondering about each object, whether it would aid in helping Trevor, dismissing most things as useless for that purpose.

He wished he knew how much time had passed since Trevor's disappearance. How long had it been since Veronica went after him? The windowless room offered no clue to the time of day—or night. He climbed to the outer door and tried to open it to look outside, but it was locked, and the lock refused to yield to his efforts.

The place was acquiring the feel of a prison. What could he do if neither Trevor nor Veronica returned? He cursed his powerlessness. A gifted person could find or make a way of escape; he was trapped.

He returned to the magical door and glared at it, angry that its secrets were hidden to him. Veronica should have returned.

On another tour of the room, he selected a sturdy metal table with a round top on which rested an astrolabe. He removed the instrument, set it on the floor, and carried the table back to the door. Holding it by its wrought-iron legs, he swung the dinner-plate-size top against the door.

It thudded against the wood with a force that jarred his bones and sent a wave of pain smashing through his arms and shoulders. He put the table down and, rubbing his upper arms, examined the door. The wood was undented, the lock undamaged.

He picked up the table, braced himself, and swung again. Again the agonizing jolt, again no visible damage to the door.

"Once more," he said grimly, hefting the table and throwing all his strength into the swing.

The iron table passed into and through the wooden door, and both table and door vanished in a flash of light. Unbalanced by the absence of the expected resistance, Les sprawled forward. His hands hit the floor, and he yelped with pain. When he picked himself up and examined his palms, he saw red and blistered flesh where the iron table legs had burned as they dissolved into nothingness.

He had succeeded only in destroying the door. He sank back on his haunches and stared at the place where the door had been, unable to think of anything more he could do.

A moth dipped down and fluttered in front of his face. He grabbed for it, only to see it dart beyond his reach. Driven by the need to vent his frustration, he jumped to his feet and lunged for the moth. His fingers brushed its wing.

It spiraled down and landed on the floor near his feet. He lifted a foot to stomp on it.

It shimmered, expanded, and as he blinked his eyes, Veronica took shape before him.

Caught by surprise, he fell backward and sat heavily on thick fur. "Y-you were the moth?" he asked, so stunned he found it hard to form the words.

"In a manner of speaking," she said, gazing sharply around the room. "My consciousness was riding in it." Her dark eyes fastened their gaze on him. "And you, don't you know better than to touch things you don't understand?"

"I'm s-sorry," he stammered. "I—I was worried about Trevor. When you didn't come back, I—"

"You panicked," she finished for him, too accurately.

He bowed his head and nodded, jerked it up again as his wits returned. "Where's Trevor?"

Her frown cut deep furrows into her round face. "Not where he should have been. I found tracks. As I might have guessed, he didn't follow my instructions. He wandered far out of sight of the door. Got himself into a good bit of trouble from the signs I saw, but he managed to stay alive. He managed something else, too, and I'm not sure how, but I'd bet he had help."

"What? What did he do and where is he?" Les struggled to his feet and stared down at her.

"He got himself out of the place I sent him. Or someone else got him out. That's more likely, but I don't know who'd have the power." Her face wrinkled even more, its folds almost hiding her eyes. She fell silent, lost in thought, as though she'd forgotten Les's presence.

"Well, but can you find him?" Les asked. "There must be something you can do."

She sighed and walked to the astrolabe Les had left on the floor. "Careless," she muttered, stooping to pick up the instrument. "Where am I going to put this? I'll have to replace the table you demolished."

He strode to confront her. "I'm sorry about the table, but it's not as important as finding Trevor."

"I've half a mind to let the young scapegrace find himself," she sniffed. "He'd likely learn more that way."

Les wanted to shake her. "He's in danger. Isn't that what you said? You've got to help him."

She ignored him and wandered from table to table until she found one with enough space for the astrolabe. Only then did she turn back to him. Her face had smoothed out as though settling the astrolabe into its new location had brought her peace.

"Trevor isn't helpless, you know. He has considerable talent, but he must learn to use it wisely. He'll learn nothing if someone bails him out of every trouble he gets into. Relax. I imagine you're hungry. We'll have supper."

"I'm *not* hungry. I can't eat while Trevor's lost somewhere."

"Well, you won't be much use to him if you're weak from lack of food." She bustled about, unhooking a kettle from a cord, untying a bunch of herbs from another string.

Regardless of Veronica's advice, Les could not set aside his concern for his friend. He started through the maze of tables, halted abruptly when Trevor's voice shouted in his mind: *Veronica! Guard Les! Carl has me. He wants Les. He—*

The shout cut off. Les ran toward Veronica, heedless of the tables, knocking one over in his rush. "Did you get that?" he demanded. "Carl has him. He *does* need our help!"

Veronica stood on tiptoe and slammed her palm against Les's cheek. "Calm yourself!" she ordered. "Of course I heard. Settle down. Go pick up that table you pushed over. Hope you didn't break anything."

"But Carl! Carl is the guy who drugged and robbed us. *Do* something."

"Silence!" Her voice crashed over him, freezing him in place.

"I'll keep you like that until you get hold of yourself," she said. "I *am* doing something. I'm fixing supper."

She went back to gathering items from tables and cords while he stood helpless. Her activity carried her behind him where, unable to turn, he could no longer see her, though he heard the clatter of pots and the clang of a spoon stirring something. After a time she came and stepped in front of him.

"Listen to me. We're going to have company in a short while. Someone looking for you. Remember, Trevor said Carl wants *you*. He was warning of danger to you, so be careful when you talk to this person. Understand?"

Suddenly he could move. He nodded. "But you'll be here, won't you?"

"I'll be nearby, but I think it best that you talk to the visitor alone. You might want to invite her to supper." She motioned toward the side of the room.

Following her gaze, he saw a larger table, which certainly had not been in the room earlier, set with steaming bowls of vegetables and a platter of sliced meat. Two places were set, and two chairs had materialized along with the table.

"You use power to get your food?" he asked, amazed.

"No, of course not. I have meat and vegetables delivered by the market boy, and I cook it myself the normal way. I did use power just now to arrange the table because time is short. I don't waste power on everyday tasks, unlike some in the Community. Now get ready to receive your guest."

Still staring at the mouthwatering spread, he asked, "But where did the table and chairs come from?"

When he heard no answer, he turned. Veronica was gone. A moth fluttered among the dangling cords.

Someone knocked on the outside door. He hurried to it before remembering that it was locked and he could not open it. Still, he put his hand on the latch and lifted. The door swung open.

He was not prepared for the sight of the frightened girl standing on the doorstep; he must have stared at her for several minutes before she said in a shy voice, "Are you Les? Trevor's friend?"

"Yes," he said, suddenly aware of the dirty clothes he was wearing, the only things he had to wear since Carl had stolen the carryalls.

"I've come to take you to Trevor," she said.

A moth swooped past his face. He raised his hand to brush

A PERILOUS POWER

it away, remembered Veronica's warning of danger. But when Les saw the ugly bruise on one side of Miryam's face, he felt an impulse to protect her.

"Won't you come in?" he said, stepping back so that she could descend. "I was about to have supper. Perhaps you'll join me?"

"Oh, I couldn't." Her hand fluttered to her throat, its motion reminding him of the moth.

"Please," he urged, smiling encouragement. "I haven't eaten all day, and I'd be glad for your company."

Slowly she stepped inside and let him lead her down the stairs.

10

Friend or Foe?

Les escorted the girl to the table, helped her into a chair, and sat opposite her. She looked around the room in bewilderment, her gaze lingering on some of the more mysterious items. Perhaps she understood their purpose.

"You live here?" she asked with evident awe.

"No," he said. "I'm a guest of the owner."

"Where is the owner?" With anxious eyes the girl scanned the room.

"She went out for a while." Les didn't like to lie. He cast a guilty glance at the moth flitting overhead. Hurriedly he picked up the platter of meat. "May I serve you, uh—I'm sorry. I don't know your name."

"It's Miryam. I'm not hungry. Give me only a small portion, please."

"Miryam. That's a lovely name." He placed a slice of meat on her plate, went on to serve her vegetables and bread before filling his plate.

It had been a long time since he'd had a decent meal, his stomach demanded filling, but his appetite deserted him. His attention fixed on Miryam, he scarcely knew what he was eating.

Veronica had said he was in danger, and Trevor had implied the same, but he found it hard to believe that Miryam would lead him into a trap. He watched her as she picked at her food, her eyes downcast.

He gathered courage to say, "Miryam, I know Trevor's in some trouble. What about you—what kind of trouble are you in?"

She sighed, set down her fork, and met his gaze. Her eyes held a desperation that reminded him of the foal when the condor had swooped down on it. "I know Trevor mindcalled to you and told you he's with Carl. Carl is my half brother. He sent me to find you. I—I was able to locate this house from images I read in Trevor's mind. He didn't realize. He doesn't want you to come back with me, but I think you should. Carl wants to use you, but he's more likely to hurt Trevor than you. He'll keep Trevor tied to a chair until you come, and I can't promise he won't do worse to him if I don't bring you back with me. The only way to protect Trevor is to do what Carl wants."

"What does he want?"

"He wants to use the letters of introduction he stole from Trevor to gain entrance to the Gifted Community," she said. "He intends to impersonate Trevor, but because the letters give detailed information about you, he feels he can't succeed without your cooperation."

"He must be crazy if he thinks I could help him convince the gifted that he's Trevor. They'd never be fooled. Their talents would spot the deception immediately."

She shook her head. "They might. But Carl believes he can use power to convince them. My power," she added bitterly. "Don't underestimate what he can do."

Les pushed his plate away and dragged his chair around the table to sit beside her. Unsure what to do, he wished Veronica would rematerialize and give him advice. After an awkward silence he asked, "Why should a rogue like Carl want to get into the Community, anyway?"

"I don't know." She dropped her hands into her lap, stared at her interlocked fingers. "He hasn't told me what he intends. I'm sure it's a plan for getting more power or wealth or both. Those are the things he cares most about, though he also enjoys getting away with things like cheating and swindling people. He even makes me work in a café where I can spot marks for him." Her voice was low and bitter.

"Why do you help him? What hold does he have over you?"

"He . . . It's a long story."

"I'm willing to listen." He kept his gaze fixed on her, waiting for her to look up.

Instead, she pushed her chair away from the table and rose as if in sudden panic. "I can't. I've already delayed too long. Carl will be furious. He may take his anger out on Trevor."

Les kept his seat, though he wanted to jump up and comfort her. "What will he do if I don't go with you?"

"Oh, please!" She knelt beside his chair, placed her hands on his arm. "He'll torture Trevor. Maybe kill him. And he'll force me to help. Please, I can't bear that!"

Tears spilled from her eyes, washed over her cheeks. Awkwardly he tried to wipe them away. Her skin was soft, and he let his hand linger on her cheek. Their eyes met. "I'll go with you," he said.

He stood, lifting her to her feet at the same time. Although

A PERILOUS POWER

she was taller than he, she seemed frail and defenseless. He was torn between the desire to take her in his arms and the need to hurry to Trevor's side.

She has power, he reminded himself. *She read Trevor's mind. Who knows what she's picking out of mine?* The thought made him step away from her. He looked for the moth, couldn't spot it anywhere.

Yet surely Veronica would stop him if he'd made the wrong decision. After all, she'd set up this meeting, had practically forced him to invite Miryam to have dinner with him. Miryam would not have been able to enter if Veronica had not willed it. Likewise, if Veronica did not will it, they would not be able to leave. With that assurance he accompanied Miryam up the stairs that led to the door.

He grasped the latch, was surprised when it swung open. As he hesitated, peering into the darkness, Miryam pushed past him. How late was it? He'd lost all track of time. Deciding it didn't matter, he shrugged and followed Miryam out into the night.

She led him confidently through dark and deserted streets. Light, music, and a strong odor of liquor spilled out of occasional doorways, and twice they overtook small groups of men weaving along, shouting and laughing in drunken glee. Les tensed, fearing trouble, but Miryam glided past the revelers without so much as a glance. No one took note of their presence.

Every patch of light they passed through Les scanned in vain for the moth, hoping that Veronica had not abandoned him.

They reached an apartment building only marginally nicer than those surrounding Veronica's home. Miryam took a key from her skirt pocket and unlocked the door, led him into a corridor and up a creaking stairway to the second floor. Two doors opened onto the stair landing; she knocked at one of these. "Carl," she called softly, "I'm back."

Trevor! Wake up, boy. Hear me. The insistent voice buzzed in his ear, dragging him out of fogged sleep. He tried to sit up, but his head swam, and he let it fall back onto the bed.

Bed. He was stretched out on a bed, not tied to a chair. Not tied at all. That discovery took precedence over the voice. He needed to sit up and see where he was.

Trevor, listen to me. I haven't much time.

He shook his head, trying to banish the annoying voice. The movement flooded him with waves of dizziness. While he waited for them to subside, the voice persisted. *Trevor, Miryam will be here with Les any minute. You must hear me.*

It was Veronica's voice, he realized. And as the import of the message penetrated his drugged mind, he struggled again to sit up. Les was coming! He had to think straight, had to get ready. Couldn't let Carl get Les in his clutches.

By the Power-Giver, you are the most stupid, stubborn, aggravating young man I've ever had to deal with. You don't deserve your talents. I've half a mind to strip them from you, and don't think I can't. If you don't lie still and listen to me, I may do that.

The angry outburst seared his mind. He sank back on the bed, helpless to do anything but listen to the infuriating woman who'd invaded his brain.

Hmmph! Now, then. You must agree to go along with Carl's plans. He'll do Les no harm so long as you and he both cooperate with him.

That's ridiculous! He couldn't speak the words, but he

A PERILOUS POWER

thought them with all the force his mind could muster.

Shut up! Don't you dare send. You have absolutely no sense of focus. Carl and everybody else will hear you.

Get out of my mind, he sent, heedless of her warning.

I'd cheerfully let you get yourself killed, but I've taken a liking to Les. With that comment, the voice ceased. He felt its absence in his head and breathed a sigh of relief. Now, to get his wits together and get ready to defend Les against Carl.

A moth fluttered toward him, growing larger as it descended in slow spirals. He thought he was hallucinating when he saw it change shape, grow still larger, until Veronica stood by his bed.

She placed her hands on her ample hips. "It's dangerous for me to be here, you young fool. Don't know why you can't listen to reason."

He tried to open his mouth to protest and discovered that he could neither move nor speak. He could only glare at her.

"Your power's no match for Carl's," she went on. "You act rashly, and Carl can destroy both you and Les. I could get you both safely away from here, but doing so wouldn't stop Carl or solve Miryam's problem."

How did she know about Carl and Miryam? Why did she think he'd care about their problems? Unless she was in league with them!

Her scowl made him think she'd read his thoughts and knew his suspicions. "Far more is at stake here than the money and letters you lost to Carl," she continued. "The man is a leech. The only real talent he possesses is the ability to steal power from others. He's got his suckers so firmly into his sister that the girl can't break away. She has tremendous talent, and he'll use it all even though it drains her. He can do that to you, too. He could do it to me if he catches me here, but he won't be able to use Les that way. Les is the key to stopping him.

"He wants to use Les to help him impersonate you and gain entry into the Community of the Gifted. He's had little contact with other gifted. Getting into the Community will give him access to unlimited power—or so he thinks. In reality, it will let us trap him and put a stop to his power thievery. And—" She rubbed her hands together. A smug smile spread over her face. "It will provide an opportunity for the Community to function in the way it was intended."

So. She had her own agenda. He should have known. If he went along with her scheme, she'd use him and Les for her own purposes. Thinking more clearly now, he had to admit that much of what she said made sense. But he didn't, couldn't trust her. In his present condition he was in no shape to rescue himself or Les. That would change; he was sure of it. And when it did, he'd act on his own. Veronica, whatever her real purpose was, seemed to have no interest in helping him and Les recover their stolen money and letters. He'd use her help to protect Les, but he'd watch for a way to defeat Carl and get back what belonged to him, no matter what Veronica said or did.

"They're coming," she whispered. "I have to leave. Be sensible for once. Do as I've told you."

She vanished. A moth flew up to the ceiling. When the door opened, it flitted from the room.

Trevor found himself able to move. He raised himself on one elbow and watched as Carl escorted Les into the small room. *Oh, yes*, he thought. *I'll be sensible. I'm a lot smarter than you think, lady.*

11

COOPERATION

Les was uneasy. He would have been even more so, had he not seen the moth fly from the room in which Carl had imprisoned Trevor. His relief at seeing it (he never doubted that it was *the* moth) had doubled when he assured himself that Trevor had no serious injuries, only bruises. The worst Carl had done was to drug him, and he'd promised not to repeat that so long as Trevor cooperated.

Thankfully, Trevor had been disposed to cooperate, though Les knew him well enough to recognize signs of a coming explosion. Les could only hope that with Veronica's help they'd get this mess cleared up before Trevor attempted some reckless act that endangered them all.

That concern was only one reason for his nervousness as he waited with Carl at the door of the imposing brick home that bore the address on Trevor's first letter of introduction. To find the house, they had turned down an elm-shaded street not far beyond the Maritime Museum, with its distinctive ship's-prow front. At the end of the street they passed through high gates of wrought iron and up a curving driveway to the largest private home Les had ever seen.

The size and opulence of the house clearly delighted Carl.

Looking disgustingly pleased with himself, he lifted and dropped the heavy bronze knocker.

A maid in a neat black uniform with a starched white apron opened the door. "Sirs?" she inquired with the merest hint of deference.

"Trevor Blake and Lesley Simonton with a letter of introduction for Mr. Doss Hamlyn," Carl said, displaying the envelope, expertly resealed. Knowing that Carl had opened it and read the letter, Les could nevertheless see no clue that the seal had ever been broken.

"One moment, sirs." The maid retreated into the house, reappeared in seconds with a gold plate. "Please step inside and wait in the foyer," she said. When they entered the spacious foyer, she extended the plate. "I will be happy to carry the letter to Mr. Hamlyn."

Carl placed the envelope on the plate, and the maid carried it off. "It seems 'my' Uncle Matt has important friends," he said, grinning at Les. "This is getting better and better."

Les turned his back on Carl and gazed at the two oil paintings in heavy gold frames, the silken wallpaper, the highly polished parquet floor. Two antique chairs on opposite sides of the ample area looked too fragile for actual use, but the gleaming brass umbrella stand and beautifully carved coatrack were utilitarian as well as ornamental.

Carl hummed annoyingly throughout Les's survey, breaking off when the maid returned. "Mr. Hamlyn will see you," she reported with a bob of her neatly coifed head.

She led them through rooms and corridors so quickly that Les had to be content with brief glances at damasked walls, plush carpets, and elegant furnishings. He had never seen anything like the wealth of paintings and sculptures that graced the walls and niches.

E. Rose Sabin

The maid directed them into a paneled study. A mahogany desk stood in front of bookshelves filled with leather-bound volumes. The chair behind the desk was empty; their host rose from one of four thickly cushioned reception chairs. With the letter of introduction in his hand, he stepped forward to greet them, a broad smile on his mustached face.

With dark, wavy hair and clear, blue eyes, he looked much too young to be a contemporary of Uncle Matt. "Welcome," he said in a hearty voice. "What a delightful surprise. It's been years since I've heard from Matthew. Please sit down. You must tell me all about Matthew and his charming wife." He indicated two of the chairs.

Carl sat in one, crossed his legs, brushed imaginary lint from his trousers. "It is good of you to see us, Mr. Hamlyn. My uncle has spoken so highly of you. He and Aunt Ellen are well and send you their warmest regards."

Les sank into his chair and watched Hamlyn's face for some sign of incredulity, some evidence that he detected the deception. If Uncle Matt had told Trevor what the man's talent was, Les had not heard it. Could he truth read? Was he testing Carl?

Carl seemed fully at ease. He responded to Hamlyn's request for details in his smooth way. "They have not prospered as you so clearly have, sir, but they are content. Their farm provides a comfortable income and they enjoy the respect of their town."

Les recalled how close the people of that town had come to burning down their home with them inside it. Trevor probably hadn't told Carl about that.

"Excellent!" Hamlyn enthused. "But their gifts, man. How do they make use of their gifts?"

A PERILOUS POWER

"They use them seldom," Carl answered without hesitation. "In our rural county, people mistrust the gifted. They have had to conceal their talents. But they did help me to develop my power. As I believe my uncle mentioned in his letter, my parents opposed such training. I was allowed few visits with my uncle and aunt, but they took full advantage of those rare occasions to teach me as much as they could. With no children of their own, they looked on me as a son. Because they realized that my opportunities would always be limited in Amesley, they arranged for me to come here, and for my friend Les to accompany me."

"Ah, yes, Mr. Simonton." Hamlyn turned to Les. "Matthew's letter refers to your undiscovered talent. I would like a fuller explanation of that peculiar phenomenon, please."

Les was sure he had not imagined the note of hostility that had crept into Hamlyn's voice. It added to his nervousness as he described the process Uncle Matt and Aunt Ellen had used to determine his potential.

"Interesting," was Hamlyn's comment when Les finished. "I'm familiar with that test. I wouldn't call it foolproof. But it is significant that you can receive Trevor's sendings. That suggests to me a passive rather than a latent talent. Not, I'm afraid, a basis for admission into our Community."

"You mean I'm *not* gifted?" Les experienced more relief than disappointment, having seen the trouble power could cause.

"Being able to receive a mental sending *is* a gift, but one of little significance. I'm sure it has been a convenience for you and Trevor on many occasions, but it offers nothing of value to the Community."

"I see." Les nodded solemnly. The man's attitude confirmed Veronica's dismissal of the Community as arrogant and exclusive. No, he was definitely *not* disappointed. But he had to pretend to be.

"The Blakes—Trevor's aunt and uncle—were so sure of my power, sir. Couldn't you at least arrange for another test?"

"Yes," Carl broke in. "Les has come so far. We had hoped not to be separated. Surely you won't send him on the long trip back to Amesley without giving him a chance."

Clever. Carl's speech conveyed regret, but it also made clear that he *would* enter the Community even if they rejected Les, that he would not pass up his own opportunity for Les's sake.

What would the real Trevor have done? The thought crept unbidden into Les's mind. He dismissed as unworthy the suspicion that his friend might have done the same.

"I have another letter from my uncle," Carl continued before Hamlyn could answer. "I believe it specifically concerns the matter of developing Les's gifts. It is intended for a Dr. Berne Tenney." He reached into his vest pocket and pulled out the second letter, but he did not hand it to Hamlyn.

Hamlyn frowned. "Dr. Tenney, eh? That's odd." His mouth clamped shut. If he had intended to say more, he apparently thought better of it.

Trevor must not have told Carl what Veronica had said about Tenney.

"My uncle did not have Dr. Tenney's address," Carl continued. "He said you could direct me to him."

Hamlyn's carefully manicured fingers tapped the arm of his chair. He gazed distastefully at the letter in Carl's hand.

Clearly alarmed by Hamlyn's change in demeanor, Carl shoved the letter hastily back into his pocket and leaned forward. "I believe my uncle was not personally acquainted with Dr. Tenney but knew him only by reputation. If he has made a mistake . . ."

The smile that returned to Hamlyn's lips was tight and lacking in sincerity. "Quite so," he said. "Your uncle is not aware of the politics of our Community." He ran a thumbnail caressingly over his mustache. "I think . . . I'm not sure it would be wise for you to see Dr. Tenney." His smile acquired a sardonic twist as he met Les's gaze. "Yes, I think you should not deliver that letter."

"Sir, I shall gladly defer to your judgment," Carl said. Les wanted to laugh at the trickster's struggle to repair the damage.

"I wonder," Hamlyn said slowly, "I wonder whether your uncle made a mistake in sending you here. The Community has changed since he was a part of it. It is not as welcoming as it once was. We do little training of new talent these days."

Carl leaned forward, his hands open in a plea. "But, Mr. Hamlyn, we've come so far. My uncle was certain that we would at least be given the chance to prove ourselves."

"Hmm. Yes." He gave Carl a long, appraising look. "Perhaps you *should* see Dr. Tenney."

Good! Hamlyn had grown suspicious, though Les had no idea what had aroused his suspicion.

Hamlyn rose and walked to his desk. He slipped into his desk chair and took pen and paper from a drawer. "I'll write instructions for finding Dr. Tenney's residence. After you've seen him, return here if you are still interested in entering the Community, and we will then discuss your admittance, though I advise you not to count on a favorable reception."

"But, sir, I don't understand this at all."

Ignoring Carl's protest, Hamlyn scrawled lines on the paper, folded it in half, and left his desk to hand the paper to Carl and pull a bell rope hanging by the door. The maid appeared promptly, ushered them from the office, and escorted them to the front door.

Carl fumed all the way home, railing at Les as if he were personally to blame for Doss Hamlyn's change of mood. Les let him rant, resolved not to speak of Veronica and her assessment of the Community in general and of Tenney in particular. He did ask Carl why he didn't go directly to the address on the paper Hamlyn had given him.

"I want a talk with Trevor first," he explained in a surly tone. "I'll bet he knows more about this than he's told me."

Les feared for Trevor. He had little doubt what methods Carl might use to extract information. He could possibly spare Trevor that by passing on what Veronica had said about Tenney, but he decided to leave it up to Trevor to share that information, if he chose.

Trevor paced the narrow confines of the room. He had attempted several times to use his power to open the locked door, but the lock resisted his talent. Carl must have warded it in some way.

He already regretted his decision to cooperate with Carl. He had no reason to do so except to keep Les safe, and no reason to trust Carl to do that. He was sorely tempted to send to Veronica, demanding that she free them both. But she was right—he couldn't direct his mental power, and if Carl received the sending, he would almost certainly harm Les.

If Hamlyn discovered Carl's trickery, that discovery could have an adverse effect on his chance of being received into the Community of the Gifted. And he was certain that the

A PERILOUS POWER

plot would be discovered before long. Without Miryam, Carl's gifts were limited. He would never be able to convince the Community.

Would he be able to convince Doss Hamlyn? The suspense was maddening. He could not endure this waiting. If Miryam would come to the room, he'd try again to persuade her to help him. Persuade her or force her. Despite her power, she was frail and easily frightened. He was certain he could bend her to his will if he could get to her.

With his talent, he ought to be able to focus enough to transmit a single message. Miryam was somewhere in the house, so he didn't have to reach far. He could do a controlled sending; he was sure he could.

He sat on the edge of the narrow bed and built a picture of Miryam in his mind. Not pretty. Taller than a girl should be. (Carl was tall, but not overly so for a man. Strange that his sister would have such height, but she was only a half sister, he recalled.) Nothing remarkable about the pale skin, the shadowed brown eyes. With her long brunette braids and her simple, unstylish clothes, she could have been a farm girl, except she wouldn't have the physical strength.

When he'd last seen her she was wearing a dark skirt, brown, he thought, like her eyes, with the tips of plain black shoes showing beneath it. Her white blouse with its long sleeves and high neck was also plain, with only a bit of lace around the collar and cuffs. He wondered whether she wore such austere dress by her own choice or whether Carl forced her to do so.

Not important. He had the image built in his mind. Concentrating on it, he attempted a mere whisper of a sending. Nothing more than *Miryam, come here.*

He waited impatiently. Several minutes passed. He tried

again, re-creating the image, injecting more force into the sending: *Miryam, come here. I must talk to you.*

Maybe she didn't know the sending came from him. *It's Trevor*, he sent again. *Please come.*

A sharp blast beat into his brain: *Danger!* Terror. Grief. *Quiet. Can't come.* Outrage. Menace.

A mingling of pain and fury twisted his mind. He doubled over, head between his knees, the heels of his hands pressing his temples, trying to drive out the storm.

It stopped abruptly. Dazed, he lifted his head. The door burst open and Carl strode into the room. He caught Trevor by the shirt, hauled him to his feet, and slammed a fist into his jaw.

Trevor sprawled back onto the bed. Carl loomed over him, fists clenched. "Keep out of my sister's mind!" he shouted. "Don't ever try that again!"

Trevor didn't move, resisting the urge to rub his aching jaw. He hadn't expected Carl to return so soon. He didn't dare ask what had happened. He kept his gaze fixed on Carl's angry eyes.

Gradually the mad rage subsided. In a calmer voice, Carl said, "I want to know more both about Doss Hamlyn and about this Dr. Tenney. Especially Dr. Tenney. I want you to tell me everything your uncle and aunt said about him."

The demand confirmed Trevor's suspicion: Something had gone wrong. He wasn't sorry; in fact, he was delighted, though he was careful to keep his face expressionless. He waited a moment before answering, needing to be sure he could also control his voice.

"I've already told you everything," he said. "My uncle talked mostly about Mr. Hamlyn, said they'd been friends as young men. Uncle Matt and he both worked as stevedores.

Hamlyn stayed on after Uncle Matt left and worked his way up in the shipping company. For several years Uncle Matt and Doss Hamlyn corresponded, but—"

"You told me all this before," Carl broke in. "What did Hamlyn say in his letters to your uncle? About the Community, that sort of thing? And what about Dr. Tenney?"

"He didn't tell me much," Trevor said. "Nothing that I haven't already told you. He only said about Dr. Tenney that he knew him by reputation, and that if anyone could uncover Les's gifts, he could. He didn't tell me anything more about the Community except that it had been established long ago, and Hamlyn and some others were a part of it and felt it provided protection from hostile normals."

"He didn't tell you how rich Hamlyn is? That he owns the company now? That he lives in a mansion? That he doesn't like Dr. Tenney?"

"No, no, and no!" Trevor said.

"You must know more." The madness flashed back into Carl's eyes. "Guess I'll have to refresh your memory."

He yanked Trevor up and hit him again. This time Trevor tried to fight back. He got in a single hard punch to Carl's chest, gasped, and fought for breath as he felt his throat close. Carl's power made invisible fingers tighten around his neck, choking off his breath.

Les and Carl had entered Carl's apartment through the back door. Carl had ordered Les to wait in the kitchen and had stalked off to confront Trevor. Les would have followed him despite the order, but loud sobs called him instead to Miryam's side.

He found her huddled on the floor of the small living room, clutching her head. Her breath came in ragged sobs.

He knelt beside her and gathered her into his arms.

"What is it?" he asked.

She couldn't answer. Her hair, unbraided, hung loose over her shoulders. He stroked her head. "What's wrong, Miryam? Try to tell me."

"It's Carl," she gasped. "In my mind. Twisting it. Ohh!" Her face contorted and she clutched her head. "So much pain."

Her agonized cry tore at his heart. "I'll stop him. I'll find a way."

"No." She grabbed for him, pulled him against her. "He'll hurt you."

"He can't do any more to me than he's doing to you."

She clung to him. "He can kill you. Stay here."

"He won't kill me. I won't let him." Les gave her a reassuring hug and rose to his feet. Muffled shouts led him to Carl.

He burst into the room to find Trevor rolling on the bed and tearing at his throat while Carl stood over him, laughing. He hurled himself at Carl, grabbed him, pinned his arms to his sides.

"Stop it! Stop hurting them," Les yelled in Carl's ear. "I swear I'll kill you if you don't."

Carl made no attempt to break Les's grip or to fight back. He stood still and said quietly, "You can't kill me without killing Miryam as well."

Behind him he heard Miryam's voice. "It's true, Les. Leave him alone."

Trevor sat up, rubbing his neck and glaring at Carl. "You're crazy," he said in a hoarse voice. Then his eyes met Les's. "He's killing her himself," he said. "He's absorbing all her power."

A PERILOUS POWER

Les released Carl and stepped back, poised to attack him again. "You'd do that to your own sister?" he said.

"Oh, come on. Don't be so melodramatic." Carl was smiling again. "It's not that bad. Yes, I borrow a little power from her. She has plenty to spare. But if you're so worried about her, the best thing you can do is help me get into the Community. There I'll have plenty of people to borrow power from; I won't have to use any more of hers."

"I've been helping you," Les retorted. "You were the one who wanted to come back here instead of going to find Dr. Tenney."

Carl adjusted his vest and smoothed his trousers. "Yes. Well, I'm ready now," he said with another of his mercurial mood swings. "It seems we can't rely on Doss Hamlyn's help, so let's go find this mysterious doctor."

12

$\int$MOKE

For the second time that day, Les descended from a hired carriage and walked with Carl to the front door of a large house. This house, however, was no mansion. It reminded Les of the haunted houses in the ghost stories told around campfires on school hayrides. It was a rambling structure of two stories plus an attic beneath a high, sloping roof. Loose shingles on the roof flapped in the wind; some had been torn off, leaving ugly bald spots. The windows were dirty and cracked, and some were missing panes of glass. Whatever paint had once graced the structure had long since worn away, and the boards had weathered to a dull gray speckled with leprous patches that looked more like mold than remnants of old pigment.

The house hadn't been easy to find; it sat at the end of a dirt road on the outskirts of town, with no other houses nearby. The carriage driver had grumbled at having to travel to such a desolate area where he'd have no hope of a return fare, but Carl had mollified him with a generous tip. Carl could afford to be generous; the money he lavished he'd stolen from Les and Trevor. But this time Les didn't object, because the driver agreed to wait for them. Les did not want to be stranded out here with no way of escape from whatever lurked in such a house.

Trevor had told Carl the truth about what he knew of Dr. Tenney from Uncle Matt, but Les was all but certain he had not told Carl what he had learned from Veronica. Trevor might not believe Veronica, but Les did and felt apprehensive about meeting the "Doctor of Mischief," as Veronica had labeled him.

The steps leading up to the sprawling front porch were splintered and treacherous. Carl paused and regarded them thoughtfully. "I don't like this," he muttered, more to himself than to Les. "This place looks deserted. I'll bet Hamlyn is playing some kind of trick on us."

Les said nothing, merely watched with mild amusement as Carl struggled to decide whether to venture up the rickety steps and across the sagging porch.

"I'll make Hamlyn pay, if this is a joke," Carl said and set his foot on the first step.

Les waited until he reached the porch before starting up himself, carefully stepping where Carl had trod, expecting the rotted wood to give way beneath his weight.

It did not. He trailed Carl across the porch to the battered front door. While Carl knocked loudly, Les turned to be sure the carriage was waiting. Only an hour or two remained before sundown, and he did not want to find himself stranded here at night. He was reassured to meet the driver's gaze and know the man was following their progress and could come to their rescue if they slipped through the rotting floorboards.

Or if whatever he heard approaching the door should be something other than human.

E. Rose Sabin

138

The heavy tread sounded ominous. Les stepped back as the door creaked open. The pungent odor of pipe tobacco flooded the porch. Les craned his neck to peer around Carl. The being in the doorway was obscured by a cloud of smoke. Les could see a bald head about level with Carl's chin. Onyx eyes glittered through the heavy smoke. A pipe's crimson glow pointed to the mouth.

"Dr. Tenney?" Carl sounded doubtful.

"Of course. I've been expecting you. What took you so long?" Without waiting for an answer, he leaned out to wave at the driver. "It's all right, my good man," his deep voice boomed. "You may go."

"No, wait!" Carl shouted.

Too late. The man was already driving off, eager, no doubt, to be away from this place, and Carl's shout was lost in the clopping of the horse's hooves.

"He was to wait for us," Carl said angrily. "How will we get back into town?"

"That won't be a problem," the man said with a smile. "I believe you have a letter for me?"

Carl placed into his hand the letter from Uncle Matt. Dr. Tenney puffed on his pipe as he opened the envelope and read, but Les, standing beside Carl, could see more now through the smoky veil. The man had a short, blunt nose and a pointy chin graced by a neat triangle of beard. A curly fringe of gray hair swept around the back of his head and up and around each ear. He was nattily dressed in a tan waistcoat and dark gray cravat. A gold watch chain hung from his trousers pocket. His appearance in no way fit that of the dilapidated house; he seemed, in fact, so out of place that Les also suspected that some trick was being played

A PERILOUS POWER

on them. He'd been expecting them, he said. Les wondered whether he was really Dr. Tenney or someone Hamlyn had sent to this deserted house to deceive them.

Whoever he was, he finished the letter, refolded it, and returned it to the envelope. "Hmmm. Well, come in." He motioned them inside.

Les followed Carl through the doorway and down a dark and dusty hallway. They ascended a creaky stairway, Les with his hand on the wall, feeling his way despite the cobwebs snagging on his fingers. Hearing something scuttle past him down the stairs, he resisted the urge to bolt. If Carl was going to go through with this, he must. For the sake of Miryam and Trevor he had to follow Carl's lead.

They reached the top of the steps and proceeded some distance down a corridor past several closed doors, until at the last one their host stopped, took a key from his waistcoat pocket, and unlocked the door.

A sickly yellow light filled the room into which they were taken. Small tables cluttered the room, putting Les in mind of Veronica's strange abode. But peculiar as that place had been, he had felt at home there.

The objects on the tables here were mostly made of metal twisted into odd shapes and sprouting wires and coils in all directions. As Les passed by a table, he brushed a protruding wire and it sparked, sending a jolt through his arm and into his shoulder. He jumped back, more surprised than hurt, and when he moved forward again, a coil off another device snagged his sweater, unraveling threads to leave a long tear. Dr. Tenney tut-tutted but offered no apology.

Les had to stop, remove his sweater, and ease it off the offending coil. As he worked to free the sweater, a sharp-ended wire jabbed his wrist, drawing a bead of blood. It seemed to him that the wire had extended itself for the purpose, though he told himself that he'd imagined its movement.

Les held the sweater and kept his arms close in front of him as he moved on into the center of the room.

Here three cushioned armchairs were arranged in a circle. "Be seated, gentlemen," Dr. Tenney said, plumping himself into the nearest chair.

Carl sat opposite their host, and Les lowered himself gingerly into the remaining chair. It squeaked despite his caution, and, as though in concert with it, an apparatus on a nearby table emitted a loud squeal. Dr. Tenney chuckled at Les's startled jerk.

The strangeness of the place had no apparent effect on Carl. "I gather," he said, leaning forward, "that Mr. Hamlyn informed you of our coming and our purpose."

Les guessed that he was attempting to grasp the initiative, but the ploy failed. Dr. Tenney merely puffed on his pipe, and studied the rising smoke as he said to Les, "So, Mr. Simonton, you hope to uncover your gifts. How old are you?"

"Eighteen, sir," Les answered, disliking having to impart even that innocent piece of information.

"When a gift remains hidden for so many years, there's always a good reason. Sure you want to stir things up?"

"I—I'm not certain," Les said, and dared to ask, "Are you a medical doctor, sir?"

"Not sure I'm qualified to help you, eh? I assure you that I am, though I am not a doctor of medicine but of engineering." He puffed thoughtfully and added with a sly smile, "Yes, indeed, of engineering."

"Mr. Hamlyn said he couldn't enter the Community unless his gift was known," Carl said, clearly uninterested in Tenney's credentials.

"Ah, and *you* wish to enter the Community." Dr. Tenney directed that statement at Carl with a hint of suppressed laughter.

"I do, sir, very much. And so does Les. But he will defer to the Community's judgment."

"But will the Community defer to my judgment, that is your question, is it not?" The man jumped to his feet. "No doubt it will, but only if I've tested you both."

"But my power is evident," Carl protested. "My gifts aren't in question."

"Maybe not. But things are not always what they seem. Your uncle expressed confidence in my abilities. You surely can have no fear that I will do you harm."

"Sir, my uncle had not the privilege of a personal acquaintance with you as he had with Doss Hamlyn. He knew you only by reputation, and that based on information garnered many years ago. I must know more about you and your place in the Community before I allow you to test me."

"You are willing for me to test your friend, but not to undergo the same test yourself?"

Carl tugged nervously at his collar. Les enjoyed watching him squirm.

"I'm only willing for Les to be tested because he's come so far to enter the Community, and I don't want to see him disappointed."

"You've come equally far, have you not?" Laughter lurked behind the doctor's words.

"Of course. But Mr. Hamlyn assured me I would be welcomed by the Community."

Hamlyn had said no such thing.

While Carl assumed the attitude of righteous injury, Dr. Tenney circled Carl's chair, puffing furiously on his pipe. Smoke gathered around Carl, concealing him within a blue haze. The acrid smell made Les cough.

Coughs came from within the cloud as well, followed by a sudden, ominous silence. Dr. Tenney laughed aloud.

"What are you doing?" Les demanded.

"Reading," came the puzzling answer, followed by a triumphant "Aha!"

Dr. Tenney bounded across the room and snatched from its table a tall, slender metal cylinder with wires poking from its top and squiggling all about it. He set it on the floor in the middle of the three chairs. The cylinder sat on a base that was a shorter, wider cylinder of opaque glass. Lights sparked within the glass.

Les regarded it with apprehension. "What is that thing?" he asked.

"You'll see, my boy. You'll see."

A black void formed above the device, a horrid gaping emptiness. It grew to sufficient size to swallow a man.

Dr. Tenney clapped his hands together. At the sharp sound the smoke swirled away from Carl and was sucked up into the void. Carl sat with eyes open, staring after the smoke. He seemed dazed.

Dr. Tenney wandered over to a nearby table and knocked the bowl of his pipe against a ceramic dish, emptying the ashes into the dish. Ignoring Les and Carl, he picked up a pipe cleaner and slowly and methodically cleaned his pipe. When he finished, he laid his pipe carefully on the edge of the dish and wandered back to stand before the void.

"You know your friend's uncle well, boy?" he asked in an offhanded manner, not looking at Les but peering into the

A PERILOUS POWER

void as though something in that inky blackness was visible to him.

"Not really," Les said, unsure how much to tell him. "I spent a short time in his home when I was a child and didn't see him again until Trevor and I visited his aunt and uncle before making this trip to Port-of-Lords."

"Haven't been here long, have you?"

"Only a few days." Les spoke the words with some amazement. So much had happened since their arrival that it seemed they'd spent years in Port-of-Lords.

Dr. Tenney turned and bent toward Les. His hands clasped behind his back, he thrust his face near Les and sniffed, his stubby nose twitching like a rabbit's.

"Hmmm," he said, drawing out the sound like a dying note on an organ. "I wouldn't think—no, I'm sure that's been too long. Wouldn't last that many days; not so strong, anyway." He frowned and his gaze probed Les's face. "You've got a strong smell of magic about you, boy. Not your own. Your gift, whatever it may be, is too deeply hidden to give off a smell. And it's not your friend's." He nodded contemptuously at Carl, who hadn't moved. "Want to tell me who else you've spent time with recently?"

This man could *smell* power? Les thought quickly. Instinct warned him not to mention Veronica. Or Miryam. "We visited Mr. Hamlyn this morning, sir."

The doctor's eyebrows dipped and rose. "Hmmm," he murmured again. "Maybe. But I think not. Well, we'll know soon, won't we?"

Dr. Tenney turned back to the void and again peered into it. "Come, come," he called, the words muffled as though the hole was drawing them deep within.

Suddenly Dr. Tenney smiled. "Ah, here we are at last."

E. ROSE SABIN

He reached into the blackness, his hands disappearing as they entered the void. When he pulled them out, they clasped two other hands. Arms followed, then a white-gowned body, a terrified face.

Dr. Tenney swung Miryam down and over the device below the void, helped her to stand uncertainly on the wooden floor.

"Miryam!" Les leaped to his feet.

She stumbled forward and fell into Les's arms. He eased her into the chair he'd vacated and turned to confront Dr. Tenney.

But Carl, released from whatever spell he'd been under, was also on his feet and facing down the smaller man. "Why'd you bring her here? What's this about?"

Carl could be extremely dangerous with Miryam available to draw power from. Les stood protectively in front of her. She grasped his hand, her fingers icy.

"Is that Dr. Tenney?" she whispered.

He nodded and massaged her hands to warm them. In his concern about Miryam, he'd missed what Dr. Tenney had said to Carl. Whatever it had been, it had caused Carl to back down, though he looked ready to explode at any moment.

Dr. Tenney gazed back into the void. "Ah, I believe my seeker has found something else," he announced. "Let's see what it's sending me this time."

Trevor glowered at the faded wallpaper on the four walls of his prison and plotted how he might defeat Carl. He would first have to separate Carl from Miryam.

He didn't understand how Carl drew power from his sister, nor did he care. If Miryam was too weak-willed and frightened to break the link between her and her brother, that was her problem, not his. What he had to do was to keep her away from Carl for a while. Les seemed drawn to her; maybe he could use that—persuade Les to lure her away. When Les and Carl got back from their visit to Dr. Tenney, he'd find a way to talk to Les alone. He'd need no more than a couple of minutes. He lay back on the bed, eyes shut, planning a ruse that would get him those minutes.

An odor of pipe smoke filtered dimly into his consciousness. His eyes popped open; he saw no one else in the room. Someone must be smoking a pipe outside his door. Carl must have returned. He'd never seen the con man with a pipe, but he hadn't really known him long. If it wasn't Carl, someone else besides Miryam was in the house.

He got up, crossed to the door, and sniffed. The smoke odor was no stronger. He pressed his ear against the door, heard nothing.

A curl of smoke drifted past his face. Another. The building could be on fire. He beat on the door.

More smoke swirled around him. He coughed and pounded harder. The smoke spun around him like a cyclone. He waved his arms, trying to beat it away, and shouted hoarsely for help. He could no longer see the door. His eyes smarted; his throat ached. Waves of dizziness swept over him.

Suddenly someone caught hold of his arms, yanked him forward, and swung him outward. He landed with a jolt.

He didn't recognize the stout, bald man who helped him out of the darkness, but he spotted Carl standing near him, and then saw Les standing not far from Carl. In a chair behind Les sat Miryam.

"Well, now, the gathering is complete. I'll close down the

seeker, and we'll have a chat." The man bent down and did something to the contraption at his feet. The blackness above it vanished. He lifted an assembly of glass, metal, and wire, carried it to a table, set it down, took a pipe from another table, and returned to the group. It dawned on Trevor that he was no longer in Carl's apartment but had been transported somewhere else. The presence of Les and Carl convinced him that this was Dr. Tenney's house, and the doctor himself had brought him here.

"We'll need two more chairs. I suppose I could fetch them myself, but that's what servants are for, eh?" He went to another table and fussed with a horn-shaped apparatus mounted on a square box. He turned a handle on its side and cocked his head as though listening.

A shrouded figure approached, though Trevor didn't see where it came from.

"I require two chairs for my additional guests," the man said to it.

It bowed its head and glided silently from the room, returned a moment later carrying two heavy chairs as though they were feathers. It set them down near the others and faced its master, who remained by the device he'd used to summon it.

"That will be all," he said.

The figure bowed and vanished. The doctor turned to his guests. "Please make yourselves comfortable," he invited. "Allow me to introduce myself to the lady and gentleman who just arrived. I am Dr. Berne Tenney. Come, come, take your seats, please. We have much to talk about."

Trevor was quick to follow Dr. Tenney's suggestion.

Carl dropped sullenly into another chair. Seeing his discomfiture made Trevor want to laugh.

A PERILOUS POWER

Les pulled a chair close to Miryam's and sat holding her hand and regarding his host with a look filled with suspicion. That look puzzled Trevor. Dr. Tenney had rescued them.

Dr. Tenney leaned back, crossed his knees, and extracted a pouch of tobacco from his waistcoat pocket. As he occupied himself with filling and tamping his pipe, he said conversationally, "It seems we have mysteries to unravel. Kind of you to brighten an old man's life with challenges."

No one responded. Dr. Tenney examined the bowl of his pipe, appeared satisfied with the result of his labor, and snapped his fingers. A flame flickered at his fingertips. He kindled the tobacco and waved the flame out of existence. He placed the pipe stem into his mouth, drew deeply on the pipe, blew out a cloud of smoke, and chuckled.

"Quiet bunch you are. Not going to offer any help, eh? All right, guess I'll have to sort things out for myself."

His wrinkled forehead didn't fool Trevor; the doctor had already grasped the whole situation, he was sure. He should speak up, accuse Carl of imprisoning and impersonating him. It could be that Dr. Tenney was waiting, giving him that chance. Trevor cleared his throat. But when he tried to talk, no sound came out.

He glared at Carl, but Carl's gaze was fastened on Dr. Tenney.

Dr. Tenney removed the pipe from his mouth and pointed its stem at Carl. "You're a clever lad and a daring one, that's clear. You almost had Hamlyn fooled, you know, and he's not easily deceived. You might have gained entrance to the Community if it hadn't been for the second letter, the one to me. My guess is that Matthew Blake wanted to be certain that his nephew, Trevor, did not accept entrance into the Community without his friend Lesley Simonton. I'd reckon that Blake feared an unfavorable reaction to admitting someone with only a hidden, undeveloped talent. And maybe he couldn't depend on his nephew to stick by that friend and refuse to be admitted without him. That right?"

"No!" Trevor found his voice and the word exploded from him. "No, I wouldn't have done that."

A broad smile spread across Dr. Tenney's face. "So, you *are* Trevor Blake." The smile vanished. A sharp gaze scrutinized Trevor; he felt he was being looked *into* as well as looked over. His face burned, though he couldn't explain the flush.

"I wonder why you let this fellow borrow your identity," Dr. Tenney mused, as though he expected to have to puzzle out the matter himself.

"He forced me to," Trevor said. "He stole the letters and held me prisoner. He threatened to kill me if Les and I didn't cooperate."

"It wasn't like that," Carl interrupted. His blue eyes were wide, his gaze earnest. "I was afraid my meager talents would never be enough to get me into the Community, so I persuaded Trevor to let me borrow the letters in return for lodging and board. I'd get Les in as well as myself, and then help Trevor get in as well. His gifts are great enough that he could be admitted on his own merits."

Carl did not flinch at Dr. Tenney's hard stare. He exuded sincerity and innocence.

"I see," said Dr. Tenney. "But you fail to explain the presence of this young lady." The pipe stem pointed to Miryam, who cringed and did not meet the doctor's gaze.

"She's my sister," Carl said, retaining his innocent demeanor. "We're linked by a strong psychic bond. Maybe that's why your magic brought her here."

A PERILOUS POWER

Trevor's gaze fastened on Dr. Tenney's face, watching every twitch, every nuance of expression, trying to judge the doctor's reaction. He wouldn't believe Carl; Trevor was sure of that. But the doctor's mild response to the accusation against Carl was disturbing.

Trevor knew better than to hope that Miryam would speak up and add her grievances to his. The girl was an utter coward, totally dominated by her brother. Even with Les patting her hand, encouraging her, she huddled in her chair like a whipped puppy.

"I find that bond extremely interesting," Dr. Tenney was saying to Carl. "Useful, I should imagine." He watched his pipe smoke spiral toward the ceiling.

"It gives us a closeness most brothers and sisters would envy," Carl said in a voice that oozed affection.

Trevor couldn't understand Les's continued silence. Carl must be preventing him from speaking as he had prevented Trevor.

As for Miryam, she slumped against Les's shoulder, her eyes closed.

"Your sister, for whom you show such tender regard, seems to be near fainting," Dr. Tenney observed. "Her transport here may have been too much for her. Perhaps we should take her to a room where she can lie down."

Les jumped up and lifted Miryam in his arms. "I'll carry her," he said. "Tell me where to take her."

"No, no, my boy," Dr. Tenney said. "Her brother will carry her. You stay here."

Carl sprang to his feet and reached for Miryam, who seemed to be in a swoon. Les at first refused to relinquish his hold on her, then released her with a suddenness that would have sent her crashing to the floor if Carl had not caught her. It was clear to Trevor, and surely Dr. Tenney could also see, that Les's attempt to resist had been countered with power. The doctor offered no objection.

"Wait here," he told Les and Trevor. Puffing on his pipe, he led Carl from the room, the gangly Miryam limp in her brother's arms.

As soon as they passed through the door, Les grabbed Trevor's arm. "Hurry!" he whispered. "This is our chance. We'll go find Veronica and get her to rescue Miryam."

"Are you crazy?" Trevor stared at his friend. "We've *been* rescued. Dr. Tenney's going to expose Carl."

"That man's worse than Carl. Remember what Veronica said." Les tugged at Trevor. "Hurry! Before it's too late."

Trevor shoved him away. "Veronica! Always Veronica. Did she find your gift?"

"If she did, she didn't tell me what it was."

"So why do you trust *her*? I think she lied about the Community. I'm going to take my chances with Dr. Tenney."

"Trev, don't be a fool. We need to get out of here."

"You sound like Veronica. I'm not going anywhere. Run if you want to. I'm staying to see the fun when the doctor gives Carl his comeuppance."

Les glanced toward the door. "Don't trust him," he pleaded. "Come with me."

"Afraid to go by yourself?" Trevor taunted.

Les shot his friend a hurt look and bounded from the room.

Trevor hadn't believed he would really go. If Les involved that busybody Veronica, he could mess up everything. Veronica didn't like the Community; she could ruin their chance for admittance.

He got to his feet to go after Les, but at that moment Carl

A PERILOUS POWER

and Dr. Tenney returned. Dr. Tenney looked around. "Where's your friend?" His surprise seemed unfeigned.

"He was afraid," Trevor said, and in his embarrassment he embellished that truthful statement. "He thought you'd blame him for helping Carl try to trick you. I told him to wait, but he wouldn't listen."

"Well, well. That's a pity." Rapid bursts of smoke spurted from the doctor's pipe. "Don't concern yourself, though. He won't get far." He took the pipe from his mouth and winked. "Let's sit down, shall we, and await his return."

13

TURNINGS

Les reached the top of the stairs but did not descend; he could not bring himself to abandon Miryam. Carl and Dr. Tenney had taken her into an upstairs room, but he did not know which one. He risked discovery by lingering. The light was dim here in the hall, but he tried the door nearest the stairway, found it unlocked, and opened it. It gave access to a storage closet. He crowded in and pulled the door almost closed, leaving only a crack through which to see out.

He had concealed himself just in time; he heard a door open nearby. Peering through the narrow opening, he held his breath, not daring to move.

Dr. Tenney and Carl came out of a room a short distance down the hall. Sure he'd be caught when the doctor paused and sniffed, Les stifled a sigh of relief when the doctor moved on toward the room where Trevor waited. Carl shuffled along behind, as though walking in his sleep.

Les edged quietly to the door of the room they'd left; it had to be where they'd put Miryam. He eased the door open and slipped inside the dark room, groped his way forward, bumped into a bed. "Miryam?" he whispered.

No answer. He bent, touched the bed, found the still form

lying on it. It had to be Miryam, but he couldn't rouse her; this was no mere faint.

He shook her gently. "Miryam, wake up," he pleaded.

She didn't wake. He lifted her and held her in his arms. He could carry her a short distance, but the way back to town was long and he had no transportation.

Reluctantly he lowered her onto the bed. "Miryam," he whispered, though she wouldn't hear him, "I have to leave you and get to Veronica. She'll help me rescue you. I'll hurry, I promise." He brushed her hair back from her forehead and kissed her.

He found his way to the door and stepped into the hall, muscles tensed, ready to fight his way free.

The hall was empty. He headed toward the stairs, not believing his luck. Hands on the wall, feeling his way in the darkness, he descended the creaky staircase. It was impossible to move silently. Anyone looking for him would know exactly where he was. His toe caught on the upraised edge of a loose board and he stumbled and slammed against the wall to keep from falling. He might as well have yelled out, "Here I am!" But he heard no sound of pursuit.

He reached the bottom of the stairs and peered into blackness. The front door, he remembered, was straight ahead at the end of the hall, which had been empty of obstacles. He walked forward.

The walk took too long. He quickened his pace. His foot smashed into something and he pitched forward, hands outstretched to catch himself.

His hand slid over a rough board and slivers of wood dug painfully into his palm. He'd stumbled against the stairs and caught his hand on the same upraised board that had nearly tripped him as he'd descended.

He'd passed through no doorways, had never taken his hand off the wall. Yet somehow he'd wound up back at the bottom of the steps.

This time he'd try the opposite wall. He groped his way to it and set off again, moving slowly this time, making certain he came to no corners or turns. He proceeded straight ahead; he could have sworn he did. Yet again he stumbled into a barrier that his exploring fingers determined to be the stairway.

"Looks like I have to go back up," he muttered to himself. "I'm trapped."

The house itself couldn't have changed; that was impossible. And he knew he hadn't simply gotten lost. Dr. Tenney had used his power to confuse him, turn him around. No wonder there'd been no pursuit!

He could stay down here and try again, but he'd only waste time and wear himself out. Better to go up and confront Dr. Tenney. Not, he thought bitterly, that he could do much with no power to counter the doctor's.

He trudged up the stairs. When he reached the door to the room where he'd left Miryam, he entered to check on her.

A frightened gasp told him she was awake. "Shhh," he cautioned. "It's me, Les."

He reached the bed and found her hand in the darkness. "Are you all right? What did he do to you?"

He sat on the edge of the bed, and she sat up and leaned against him. "It was Carl," she whispered. "Dr. Tenney put Carl into some kind of trance. And Carl shared it with me as he does everything."

"Carl has to be stopped. So does Tenney. We have to get away. But Tenney's done something to me so I can't reach the front door." In a whisper he described his fruitless attempts to find the way out.

"Tenney's an Adept," Miryam said. "I'm not sure we *can* escape. Carl knows you're with me—the link between us lets him know everything I do. Except . . ." Her voice trailed off and she straightened. Her fingers dug into his arm.

"Except?" he prompted.

"Wait," she said. "We might have a chance. If I can . . ."

Again she left the sentence unfinished, but rose to her feet and pulled him up beside her. He felt her tension, sensed a series of small movements, but in the darkness he could not see what she was doing.

Abruptly she touched his arm, slid her hand to his wrist, and clamped her fingers tightly around it. "Follow me," she breathed.

She moved forward, pulling him after her. The door to the room burst open and light flooded in. Dr. Tenney rushed toward them, face suffused with anger.

Miryam moved calmly onward. The doctor, the room, the light all vanished. Les thought at first that Dr. Tenney must have done something to them, but Miryam's steady forward motion reassured him.

She stopped so suddenly that he bumped into her. She released her hold on his wrist.

"What is it?" he asked, reaching out and placing a hand on her shoulder. "Where are we?"

"Shhh!" She stood stiff, unmoving.

Seconds lengthened into minutes while they stood like a pair of statues. The darkness and silence were so complete that only his grip on her shoulder told him he had not lost her.

Suddenly he lost even his sense of touch; his own body

did not signal its existence. He was nowhere, nothing.

He was not—and then he was. He felt ground beneath his feet, smelled Miryam's clean sweet scent, felt her shoulder beneath his hand. Heard her voice.

"Tenney almost had me," she was saying. "He's so strong. I don't *think* he can find us here, but I can't be sure. It's the one place I can go to get away from Carl, and if Carl can't track me here, I hope *he* can't either."

They were no longer in utter darkness; a dim light allowed him to see her and to see that they stood among trees. A cool wind ruffled his hair and clothing. Clicks and chirps of night insects surrounded them.

He glanced up; patches of sky grew and shrank between waving branches. His efforts to connect the star patterns failed; these were not the constellations he'd grown familiar with as a boy on the farm. They were not in the world he knew, the world of Amesley and Port-of-Lords and the vast stretches between.

"We've crossed to another plane," Miryam said, answering his unasked question. "It's the only power I have that Carl has never been able to share. I don't know why. He *can* call me back from it, though. Not easily. It takes him an hour or more, so we have a little time. Unless Dr. Tenney boosts his power."

"How does it work? Can you get to another place from here?" In his confusion he wasn't making himself clear. "Could you get to the place where you first found me? We'd be safe there, I know."

"Mmmm. I'm not sure. I can try. It would be easier to find the way to my apartment, but that's where my brother will expect me to go."

"If we can get to Veronica's house, we'll have help. She's

A PERILOUS POWER

an Adept, but she's not evil like Dr. Tenney."

Miryam pressed her fingers over his mouth and said quickly, "Better not mention his name here again. Don't mention any name. They may be able to find us that way."

He nodded, and she lowered her hand. "Come on," she said, and led him along a scarcely visible path.

At a wide place in the path Miryam stopped. "This is where I found your friend," she said. "From here I may be able to find the place you want to go. It will take some time and require all my concentration. Keep guard. Wild animals prowl these woods—Trevor was attacked. It's usually safe enough by day, but at night, well, that's another matter."

"I'll watch," he said, wondering what he'd do if a beast charged them. Without a weapon, he had no way of defending himself and Miryam.

She stood in the center of the clearing, her eyes closed, her lips parted, arms raised to about waist level and stretched out to either side, her cupped hands palms upward. Whatever it was she was doing produced no outward sign; nothing at all happened.

She hadn't told him not to move, so he prowled around the clearing, looking and listening for any sign of the beasts she'd warned against. Something rustled through a nearby bush, but he caught no glimpse of anything threatening.

Miryam sighed, and he turned toward her to see her hands drop to her sides. "It's no use," she said. "I'm blocked."

"Tenney?"

"Maybe. I can't tell. This Veronica—it might help if I knew more about her. Describe her."

Les told her how Veronica had come to their rescue when he and Trevor had been jailed and Trevor had nearly killed him with his sending. He described her frumpy appearance and how, without changing clothes, she'd acquired a strong air of authority as they reached her home.

While he spoke, Miryam gazed into his eyes. He could not tear away his own gaze; he felt drawn through those brown irises into the mind behind them.

She blinked, releasing him. "I thought for a moment I saw her," she said slowly, as if awakening from a dream. "She slipped away."

Her shoulders drooped with fatigue. He stepped forward, drew her into his arms. She sagged against him, resting her head on his shoulder. "I'm sorry," she breathed.

"Please, Veronica," he pleaded aloud, "help us."

A moth darted in front of his face.

"Come on," he said.

The insect was winging its way out of the clearing. Leading Miryam, he followed it.

"What is it?" Miryam asked.

"A chance. Maybe." He kept his eyes on the moth.

It wasn't easy to spot when it darted through the trees. Its light color made it visible, but only as a ghostly fleck that winked out among the leaves of a low branch, reappeared beyond it, and vanished again.

He searched where he had last seen it, caught a fleeting glimpse of something fluttering over a patch of ground shrub, and forged on.

Miryam stayed with him. They splashed across a narrow and fortunately shallow stream. He squished along in wet shoes over rocks, through brambles, under low-hanging branches, on an erratic course that led them from the trees into a broad meadow. Only a short distance into it he realized he'd lost the moth. Or maybe it had never been there. He had wished for help so desperately that perhaps his mind had created the moth out of nothing more than a speck of starlight reflected on glossy leaves.

Miryam regarded him with bewilderment. He had no idea what to tell her.

"You both give up too easily."

Les whirled around.

Veronica, hands on her hips, regarded them with a stern look. "You've got to be made of stronger stuff if you hope to defeat Berne Tenney," she said. Glaring at Miryam, she continued, "Make no mistake, he *must* be defeated now that you've shown him how much power you have. He has Carl, and Carl controls that power. You've been thrust into a war, and you'll need to employ every weapon at your command if you're to survive."

Miryam threw herself at Veronica's feet.

"Please," she said, embracing Veronica's ankles, "we'll do whatever you say if you'll only help us."

"Will you, now?" Veronica asked, gazing down at Miryam's bowed head. "You won't like what I tell you to do. You have to stop letting your brother use you."

"Do you think I don't want that?" Miryam was sobbing. "I don't have any choice."

"Stand up," Veronica commanded. "I can give you a choice. But it won't be easy."

Miryam continued to cling to Veronica's feet. "Tell me what to do," she begged. "He's pulling at me."

"Stand up," Veronica repeated.

Les bent to lift Miryam to her feet, but a sharp gesture from Veronica made him retreat. He watched helplessly as Miryam struggled slowly to her feet and stood with bowed head and sagging shoulders.

"Straighten up!" Veronica snapped.

"I have to go," Miryam wailed. "He's drawing me. I can't help myself."

"You can," Veronica said, "if you can endure the pain."

"Let me help her," Les said, reaching toward her.

"No!" Veronica's order checked his movement.

Miryam straightened her shoulders. She gave Les a quick glance, then looked directly at Veronica. "I won't go," she said in a low but firm voice.

"Good," Veronica said. "Keep saying that, and mean it."

Miryam's face spasmed; her eyes rolled back. But she did not fall. "I won't go," she repeated. "I won't."

Veronica motioned to Les, signaling him to stand behind Miryam. When he did, the Adept reached forward and caught his hands, so that Miryam stood within the circle of their arms.

Miryam's whole body trembled. Les was sure she would fall. But she stayed on her feet and opened her eyes. "He stopped," she said. "Not for long, I don't think, but—"

"We don't need long," Veronica said.

She dropped Les's hands, raised her arms, and outlined a rectangle. A door appeared within the lines, she opened it, and they passed through into her table-filled room. After pulling the door firmly shut, Veronica waved her hand, and the door vanished.

"Come on," she ordered, leading Miryam across the room. She pushed her down onto a thick, glossy black pelt. "We have to work fast. We have no time to waste. Get over here, Les. I'll need your help."

He hurried around the tables, knocking his elbow against one while dodging the cords and ropes that swung clusters of herbs, small pots, and artist's brushes into his face. When he reached Veronica's side, she ordered him to sit next to Miryam on the pelt.

"We're going to disentangle the strands of power that bind her to her brother," Veronica explained. "It will take a long time and cause her great pain. I can't promise it won't kill her."

She stopped and looked down at Miryam. "Are you willing to risk your life?"

"If I truly have a chance of being free from Carl, yes," Miryam said decisively. "I'll take any chance for that."

"Good," Veronica said. "Let's begin."

14

Entanglement

While Veronica gathered materials from tables and untied objects from strings, Les sat beside Miryam on the fur. He wanted to encourage her but could think of nothing to say; he could only pat her hand.

Veronica came up beside him and put her collection of items on the pelt. They looked harmless enough: a candle, a needle, a mass of black and white yarn tangled together, a pair of sewing scissors, a china cup, a sprig of some sweet-smelling herb, a pot filled with water, a hand mirror, and a smooth, oval stone that might have come from a river.

"It is essential that you both trust me," Veronica said. She sat opposite them on a pelt with broad gray- and -yellow stripes. "This is an extremely delicate procedure. If you resist at a critical moment, it can be fatal."

"What are you going to do?" Les asked.

"I'm going to separate the strands of Carl's power that are entangled with Miryam's."

"Carl always told me that could never happen," Miryam said in a timid voice. "He said we were bound for life."

"He certainly intended for that to be so," Veronica said. "Yet I think separation is possible. The fact that your power allows you to enter another plane and he cannot follow you into it shows that a point of uniqueness remains to you. That is our starting point. We can work from that area to disentangle the mingled strands."

"He'll know what you're doing," Miryam said. "He'll fight it."

"Yes, of course he will," Veronica said. "That is where Les comes in. Because he has power but his talent is inactive, he provides the perfect buffer. I'm going to follow a complicated procedure. I can't explain it all, but briefly, Miryam, it involves channeling Carl's power into Les as I separate it. It will be unpleasant for you, Les, but it won't do permanent harm. The risk is to Miryam, not to you. It will put the power where Carl can't draw on it. As he grows more helpless, you, Miryam, will be able to take over more of the work from me and direct your own freeing. You will see clearly what to do.

"The process is extremely painful, and once begun, it cannot be stopped. If you attempt to halt it, you will not survive. You must understand that."

Les looked at Miryam. Always pale, her face was bleached of all color. Her hands shook. But she said, "I do understand. Go ahead. I'm ready."

"You, Les?" Veronica turned her gaze on him. "Are you willing to let me use your mind as a trap for Carl's power?"

"You're sure *he* won't be able to use *me*?" Les asked.

"I'm sure," Veronica stated firmly.

"His power won't stay in my mind, will it?"

"I don't know." Veronica frowned. "It won't be of any use to you if it does stay. It won't combine with or change your gift. And the discomfort will last only while the procedure is under way. Afterward you won't be aware of it at all."

"All right," he said with a sharp intake of breath. "I'm ready to do anything that will save Miryam."

Veronica crumbled the sprig of dried herb into the pot of water and held the pot in her cupped hands. After a few seconds, steam rose from the pot, carrying with it a pleasant, lemony scent. Veronica poured the hot liquid into the cup and handed the cup to Miryam.

"Drink this," she said. "It will only relax you, not put you to sleep. I need you awake to help with the separation."

Miryam raised the cup to her lips, breathed deeply the scented steam, and drank. She handed the empty cup back to Veronica, and the Adept nodded her approval.

"You I must put into a trance," she said to Les. "It will be light; you will be able to see and hear me."

She placed her fingertips on his temples and gazed into his eyes. His heartbeat slowed, his breathing deepened, and his limbs grew heavy. Veronica, seated in front of him, was bathed in an aura of light. The rest of the room receded into darkness.

Miryam lay back, her head resting on Les's thigh. The corona of light enveloped her. She smiled up at Les. "Give me your hand," she whispered drowsily.

He couldn't move. He seemed to be in a waking dream. Miryam found his hand and clasped it against her breast. Veronica picked up the small stone and set it on Miryam's forehead. Slowly it became transparent and acquired a golden glow as though a flame burned inside it.

Les stared at the glowing stone. Reflected in it he saw Veronica, distorted by the curve of the stone, so that her body was tiny and distant but her hands, holding the mess of yarn, were large, filling the reflective surface of what was

A PERILOUS POWER

no longer a stone but a gleaming orange gem.

And he was seeing *into* and *through* that gem, as though it were a window into Miryam's head. Within, Veronica's fingers plucked delicately at the yarn.

"Miryam, I want you to think about the world you visit to get away from Carl," Veronica instructed, her voice seeming to come from a great distance. "Think about it as though you were going there, though you will not do so."

As she spoke, her fingers slipped deeply into the tangle of yarn. Les watched them draw out a frayed white end piece.

"Good, Miryam. Draw back slowly from that point, and follow the line of your power to where it joins with Carl's."

The Adept's hands tugged on the end of yarn; her fingers followed the white strand until it slipped into a knot of black yarn. Patiently her fingers worked at the white end, poked it through a black loop, and drew it out, followed it to another, larger knotted mass, worked at the snarls and loops, pushing and pulling, weaving her white thread in and out.

Miryam gave a sudden moan and shook her head. The orange gem slid. Veronica caught and steadied it. "Don't move," she said. "I have to cut the knot."

Les saw the reflected hands take up the scissors, insert the points into the knot, pry apart and snip a piece of black yarn, and pull the white strand loose. When she cut, Miryam gave a sharp cry and arched her back.

"Easy," Veronica muttered, her fingers continuing to unravel the yarn. She held a black end as well as the white one and was untwisting the two and rolling them into separate balls in the palms of her hands.

A stab of pain shot through Les's head, passing through a spot at the top of his nose, between his eyes, and exiting through the back of his head. Something like a burning rope stretched between those points, sawing back and forth, bringing blinding agony. He couldn't cry out, could hardly breathe, fought against being sick. His eyes remained open, but the gem window that had reflected Veronica's movements became only an orange blur in which white and black threads twisted and writhed like snakes. The black snake grew larger. It slithered, hissing, up onto the burning rope and along it into Les's head, where it struck, sinking its fangs into his brain, tightening its coils around his consciousness, squeezing, squeezing. Its black poison filled his body.

"Hang on, Les," came a voice from far away. "Hang on, or you'll kill Miryam."

The snake wrapped around him, crushing him, melting his bones.

"Miryam," the voice, or perhaps an echo, repeated.

"Miryam." The word came from his own strangled throat, and with it a draft of icy air that drove the fiery serpent back, coiling in on itself, tearing its searing way through his brain to come to rest in a tight, hot ball in the back of Les's head.

Dazed, dizzy, breathing heavily, leaning his weight on his hands, he kept himself from collapsing. He heard the snick of scissors and Veronica's voice saying, "It's over."

Miryam's head lifted from his thigh. Hands pushed him back to lie flat on the fur. The weight in the back of his head tugged at him, pulling him down into the softness, down into darkness.

"I'm free!" a sweet voice said. "But what's happened to Les? You said it wouldn't hurt him."

"It shouldn't," said a voice that was not sweet but tart like vinegar. "It's something they're doing—Dr. Tenney's doing— at the other end. Hush, girl, while I try to figure out what it is."

A PERILOUS POWER

Les tried to stay awake, but his eyes refused to open, and the weight in his brain pulled him into oblivion.

Dr. Tenney chatted amiably about inconsequential matters, and Trevor let his mind wander, hearing only snatches of the conversation. He understood that the doctor was waiting for Les's return before moving on to important topics, and Trevor grew increasingly uneasy about Les's continued absence. But the doctor showed no sign of concern.

Trevor thought of many things he wanted to ask the doctor. That the man was highly gifted was obvious, and the prospect of learning from him excited Trevor. Yet, voluble as the doctor was, Trevor found it impossible to fit his questions into the doctor's rambling dissertation. Each time he opened his mouth to frame a query, Tenney launched into an involved and seemingly pointless tale.

Carl also listened without interjecting comments. His eyes were open but appeared unfocused, and he sat as though bespelled.

Carl was one of the things he wanted to ask about: how he used Miryam's power, how he had so easily overcome Trevor, and whether the Community would punish him for his misdeeds. Trevor wanted to be certain that he and Les got all their money back, as well as their other belongings.

Carl stirred and blinked; he was coming out of his trance. Before he was fully alert, Trevor *must* get his answers. He waited for a pause in the doctor's prattle, determined to change the subject and launch his interrogation.

He didn't get the chance. Carl jerked upright. "He's with her," he said, cutting off the doctor in midword.

The doctor cocked his head as though listening, though

Trevor heard nothing. "So he is," he said. "He seems quite attracted to the young lady. What will they do? I wonder. She cannot exert her power without your consent, can she?"

"No, not when I'm this close to her." Carl's worried frown belied his assertion.

"I sense something you are not telling me." A hint of menace lurked behind Dr. Tenney's mild tone.

Carl's eyes narrowed. He hesitated, then said slowly, "She can . . . disappear. Only for an hour or so. I can always bring her back from wherever it is she goes. But I've never been able to follow her."

"Fool!" Dr. Tenney leaped to his feet. "You should have told me that before. Come with me."

He trotted toward the door, and Carl followed. Trevor got up and strode after them, not sure whether the doctor's order had been directed to him as well as to Carl but unwilling to let Carl out of his sight. They dashed through the dark hallway to a room nearer the stairs. Trevor passed through the doorway and collided with Carl, who had halted abruptly just inside the room. Dr. Tenney stood only a couple of steps in front of him, cursing.

Trevor glimpsed two ghostly figures vanishing into a distance too great to be contained within the walls of the room.

He recalled how Miryam had found him in the place to which Veronica had sent him through her mysterious door. Miryam had created no doorway, but somehow, Trevor was sure, she'd forged a path back to that place and had taken Les with her.

Dr. Tenney whirled on Carl. "You said you could draw her back. Do it."

"I—it takes a while. It's hard to reach her."

A PERILOUS POWER

"Get busy. Don't waste time." He snapped his fingers and created a flame, with which he lit the wick of a glass hand lamp on a bedside table.

Carl walked past the doctor and stood by the bed. He shut his eyes; a look of intense concentration furrowed his face. The doctor, wheezing from his rush, plopped into the room's only chair, a plain wooden rocker that creaked beneath his weight.

Trevor felt awkward, uncertain what he should do or whether he dared speak and perhaps disturb Carl's concentration. He didn't understand the doctor's alarm. Surely Dr. Tenney could either follow them or bring them back himself. His power must exceed both Miryam's and Veronica's. But he sat rocking and watching Carl and seemed to have forgotten Trevor entirely.

A long time passed. Tired of standing, Trevor lowered himself to the floor and sat cross-legged, waiting. Dr. Tenney continued to ignore him; his attention remained focused on Carl.

Abruptly Carl straightened. His look of concentration changed to one of triumph. His arms made pulling motions as though hauling on a rope. Dr. Tenney stopped rocking and his hands gripped the arms of the rocker. His tongue licked his lips.

Carl's shoulders strained as though he tugged at a great weight. Sweat broke out on his face; the look of triumph faded.

His arms fell to his sides. He shook his head. "I lost her. She's never resisted me like that before."

"Keep trying," Dr. Tenney snapped.

"No use. She's gone." Carl sank wearily onto the bed.

Dr. Tenney pushed himself to his feet. "Wait here—both

of you." With that tardy recognition of Trevor's presence, he hurried from the room.

Carl's fists clenched and unclenched. He didn't speak, but Trevor could see the rage building in him and hoped Dr. Tenney got back before Carl decided to vent his fury. Although with Miryam gone, he ought to be a match for Carl. He scrambled to his feet and marshaled his power.

Dr. Tenney returned, followed by the ghoulish figure he'd called on earlier to bring chairs. Trevor shrank away from it without knowing why.

"The path your sister took is unfortunately closed to me," the doctor said. "I can't go after her, but I can send my servant to track her down. He will not tire and cannot be distracted from his search."

The shrouded figure glided silently to the center of the room. Its cowled head swayed back and forth, reminding Trevor of a hunting hound. It moved slowly forward, toward the wall, seemed to shimmer for a moment, and vanished as if it had passed through the wall.

"He will not return without his prey," the doctor said, rubbing his hands together. "Come, let's return to my workroom where we can wait more comfortably." He clasped Carl's arm and led him along, again ignoring Trevor.

He trailed unhappily after them, worried about what that thing would do to Les and Miryam when it found them. For the first time it occurred to him that Les might have been right about Dr. Tenney. But possibly the doctor did not yet understand what kind of person Carl was.

Trevor vowed to make him understand. He'd ask his questions, make his accusations, and demand his answers. No more sitting idly while Dr. Tenney spun meaningless tales to fill the time.

A PERILOUS POWER

171

They entered the workroom and Dr. Tenney gestured toward the chairs. "Sit down, gentlemen. I'll join you shortly." He went to a table at the room's far end and fussed with the device that sat on it.

Carl sat as instructed. Trevor's resolve wavered, but his concern for Les would not let him join Carl. He navigated the maze of tables and came up beside Dr. Tenney. The doctor did not seem to notice him, being absorbed with adjusting the angle of a brass hemisphere balanced on a slender, stiff spring and wrapped erratically with thin strands of copper wire that looped around the missing half of the sphere as well.

Trevor cleared his throat. "Sir, you do understand that Carl forced Les to come here with him, don't you?"

The doctor looked up from his tinkering. "Forced? That's an interesting word. It has so many different shades of meaning."

"The point, sir, is that Les came here unwillingly and left of his own volition. I'd like to ask why you are so determined to bring him back. What do you intend?"

"Would you and he not have come to me willingly, bringing the letter from your uncle, if your plans had proceeded without interference?"

"Yes, we would. But in that case Les would have had no reason to be distrustful. We've had bad experiences, sir. Instead of pulling Les back here against his will, it would be better to let him go. He'll come back on his own, if you give him time. And if he sees that Carl has had to restore what he took from us."

"Ah, but the letters have been delivered to their proper addressees."

"Yes, but Mr. Hamlyn doesn't yet know why Carl passed himself off as me, and—"

"And he doesn't need to know," Carl said, coming up behind him and dropping his hand onto Trevor's shoulder. "We had an agreement, remember?"

Trevor knocked Carl's hand away. "An agreement I was forced into!"

"Ah, that word again, *forced*." Dr. Tenney made a final adjustment to the wire-bound globe of air and metal, leaving it balanced on the spring at a precarious angle. "Let us discuss the implications of force. Shall we?"

With a hand on the shoulder of each, Dr. Tenney steered Trevor and Carl to the chairs. Although tempted to resist, Trevor thought better of it. He seemed to have a chance to get the discussion he'd wanted.

"I assume when you speak of force, Mr. Blake, you do not refer to physical force but to a use, or perhaps I should say abuse, of power."

Being addressed formally made Trevor uneasy. "He used both, sir. What's more, he swore he'd hurt or kill us if we didn't cooperate, and since Les has no power, he's defenseless against someone like Carl."

Dr. Tenney pointed the stem of his unlit pipe at Trevor. "You, however, have power. You are not defenseless."

He turned to Carl. "Mr. Holdt, you seem to have gone to a great deal of effort to gain entrance into the Community. How did you expect to profit?"

Carl leaned forward. "How did you know my full name? I never told you."

Dr. Tenney smiled. "It's my business to know things. Now answer *my* question."

A PERILOUS POWER

173

Carl scowled. "Why shouldn't I want to get in?" he asked in a surly voice. "I'm gifted."

"So you are," Dr. Tenney agreed pleasantly. "Your sister, however, has the greater gifts. Yet you did not seek entrance for her."

"I would have, once I got in. She's shy and wouldn't apply on her own. I always have to do things for her."

"You are indeed a solicitous brother. Oh, but I should say 'half brother,' shouldn't I?"

"What difference does that make?" Carl was defensive. "And how do you know?"

"Let us say that I have been watching your career for some time." Dr. Tenney paused to fill and light his pipe. "I know much about you—and your sister. Your half sister, that is. I know that your mother was forced to marry your father against her will and despite the fact that she loved another man. That three years after you were born, she ran away with the man she loved, abandoning you, which, I daresay, you have always resented. For two years they hid successfully from your father. During those two years, Miryam was born. She bears her father's surname, Vedreaux, though he and her mother were not wed."

Carl grew progressively more nervous and angry as Dr. Tenney proceeded. "You have no right—" he said. "You've been spying."

"In a sense. I make it my business to know all I can about the gifted. Your mother was highly gifted. It was through her that you and your half sister inherited your talents. Your father tracked down your mother and her lover, shot him, and brought her back. She stayed with him to protect her daughter, because your father threatened to kill the child if her mother tried to leave again.

"It is sad but no surprise that your mother died young, leaving her little daughter to the tender mercies of you and your father. You had by that time discovered that Miryam had power and that you could not only draw on it but link it to yours tightly enough to make her your slave. The poor girl has not had an easy life."

"Neither did I," Carl snapped. "Not with a mother who hated me."

"As *your* father hated Miryam," Dr. Tenney said. "Your sister, though, has come out of that sad childhood less damaged than you."

"What is that supposed to mean?" Carl sat as though poised to leap from his chair and attack Dr. Tenney.

Trevor watched closely, resolved to go to the doctor's defense, if necessary. The doctor seemed unworried, however, and could undoubtedly defend himself. Trevor was delighted at the way Dr. Tenney had exposed Carl's true nature. He waited for the doctor to pronounce judgment and exact a punishment—one that Trevor was sure would include barring Carl from entrance into the Community as well as restoring all that Carl had stolen from him and Les.

Dr. Tenney merely smiled and said, "It means that while your ambition is laudable, your unworthy motivation has blinded you to the possibilities that attend your rare talent."

Trevor could restrain himself no longer. "Rare talent! He's a thief and a con man. Is that what you call talent?"

"He is also a leech. It is that talent to which I refer." The doctor paused to expel smoke from his mouth and watch it form a perfect ring and float to hover like a halo over Carl's head. "It is not an approved talent, and it has become exceedingly rare. Yet it has undeniable advantages."

A PERILOUS POWER

"I was told I'd never be admitted into the Community with that gift," Carl said.

"That's true, I'm afraid." Dr. Tenney sent another smoke ring to follow the first. "At least, under ordinary circumstances."

"Look, I don't get this," Trevor broke in, outraged. "The way you're talking, it sounds like you'd approve of his being in the Community. Even though you obviously understand what he's done and what he *is*."

"Oh, yes. I do fully understand," Dr. Tenney said with a slow smile. "It is you who fail to understand.

"Young man, I am an Adept. No one in the Community has more power than I. Several in the Community object to the ways I use my power, and, I must confess, some have proposed that I be ejected from the Community. That's of no consequence, since no one has the power to do it."

He chuckled and sent several smoke rings spiraling toward the ceiling before continuing. "I am fully aware of Mr. Holdt's devious nature. His treatment of his half sister has been appalling. But as it happens, his talent is one I would find useful. I would soon have sought him out, if he had not kindly saved me the trouble by showing up on my doorstep. And I will have no difficulty keeping Mr. Holdt controlled. I have, in fact, been exercising that control since his arrival. You may have noted the times he has lapsed into a semiconscious state in which he could obey orders but not initiate any action."

Carl jumped to his feet and confronted the doctor with raised fists. "What right do you—"

His fists unclenched; his hands went to his throat and clawed at it as though trying to remove an invisible noose.

E. Rose Sabin

Choking, face turning crimson, he backed to his seat and sank into it.

His color returned to normal. His hands fell to his lap. He glared at Dr. Tenney but said nothing.

"You see?" Dr. Tenney addressed Trevor. "Another demonstration. When he learns to accept instruction, he will be a convenient tool."

Trevor was horrorstruck. Les had been right about this man: He intended to bring Les and Miryam back here. They would all be in his power.

But no, he was letting Les's paranoia influence him. Dr. Tenney had done nothing to threaten him and had agreed to uncover Les's talent. Carl was getting no more than what he deserved. Trevor decided to withhold judgment until he knew more specifically what the doctor planned.

"Will you have Carl give back the money he stole?" Trevor asked.

"I doubt that he has much of it left. Don't worry; far greater riches can be yours when you discover the full extent of your talent."

The doctor's response intrigued Trevor. He had not thought of his power as the key to wealth, but of course it could be. Carl had spoken of the great wealth of Doss Hamlyn. Undoubtedly it had been gained through a judicious application of his talents.

Dr. Tenney puffed placidly on his pipe, and Carl sat in sullen silence, leaving Trevor to his thoughts. His imagination conjured up schemes for gaining control of businesses, making power-guided investments, accumulating a vast financial empire. He licked his lips.

Uncle Matt and Aunt Ellen had not put their talents to such use. They lived comfortably, though, without the hard labor that had been his father's lot. They simply weren't ambitious.

But *he* was.

And Les was not. He would have been content to remain on the farm, to inherit it one day from his father, and to spend his life slopping hogs and raising beans and carrots and turnips and corn and cabbage. Les was lucky that Trevor had led him away from all that to a better, more exciting, and more rewarding life. He might throw away his opportunities and return to the farm if Dr. Tenney did not find him and bring him back here. Or if he was brought back but refused to let the doctor test him. With all that Les's friendship had meant to him through the years, he could not let Les make a tragic mistake; he had to keep him here and help him develop his gift.

A whirring sound intruded on his thoughts. He followed the doctor's suddenly intent gaze and saw the wire and brass sphere the doctor had so carefully adjusted spinning and bobbing on its spring like a top. Dr. Tenney rose and rushed toward it, setting his pipe on the first table he passed.

A scream from Carl stopped him short of his goal.

"No! She can't!" Carl shouted, tearing at his head. "Stop her!"

Dr. Tenney left the globe to its wild gyrations and hurried back to Carl, who was writhing and flopping about in his chair. The doctor placed his hands on Carl and tried to quiet him.

"Come here, boy," he shouted to Trevor. "Help me."

Trevor got up and moved warily to the doctor's side, uneasy about helping his enemy.

"Grab his hands," the doctor ordered.

Carl's hands were clawing at his face and scalp. Trevor

had to use all his strength to pry them away and hold them still. Carl fought insanely, screaming, spittle flying from his mouth, his eyes rolled back in his head. His struggles knocked over his chair and tossed him onto the floor. Trevor and Dr. Tenney both lost their grip on him and had to throw themselves onto him to subdue him again. He beat his head against the floor. Both hands gripping Carl's, Trevor placed a knee against his forehead to keep his head still. The doctor held his legs to stop his kicking and rolling.

The seizure went on and on. Dr. Tenney panted, his face red from unaccustomed exertion. Trevor's hands grew slick with sweat, and he knew he couldn't hang on to Carl much longer.

Abruptly Carl went limp. In the ensuing silence Trevor heard a loud clunk. The odd sphere of wire and brass had tumbled from its spring pedestal and was rolling toward them.

Dr. Tenney let go of Carl and gathered up the sphere. He peered through the wire strands into its empty interior. "Well. I might have known," he fumed. "It's that meddlesome witch interfering again. Think she's won, but she's dead wrong. I still have the tool I need to drain power from the members of the Community and appropriate it for my own use."

He held the sphere over Carl's head and plunged his hand between the loosely wrapped wires. Trevor could hear his fingers tapping the interior of the brass hemisphere. After a few seconds, he withdrew his hand. Trevor was sitting on the floor beside Carl. The doctor placed the hand that had been in the sphere on Carl's forehead for a moment, then raised it to Trevor's.

The doctor's fingers felt cool against his sweaty brow. He

relaxed beneath the soothing touch. "Good boy," the doctor murmured.

Trevor heard Carl stir beside him, but he didn't bother turning his head to see whether the seizure was recurring. His eyes had closed; no need to open them so long as Dr. Tenney's comforting hand remained in place.

"What are you doing?" he heard Carl ask in a shaky but sane voice.

"You know that your tie to your sister has been broken," the doctor responded. "You'll need another partner. I'm preparing one for you."

Dazed, Trevor only partially grasped the meaning of the doctor's words. He should object; he knew that, but he couldn't raise the energy.

The doctor's hand pressed harder, guiding Trevor's body back to lie flat on the floor. "Sleep," said the doctor softly.

He fell at once into a dream from which he could not wake. In the dream, he saw a snake slide its sinuous body between the wires over the brass hemisphere. Green and glittering like those that had chased him in the forest, it glided toward him. He lay helpless, unable to move as it slithered onto his body, stretched over his face, raised its head, and struck, sinking its fangs into his forehead.

Trevor moaned with pain but could not move to shake the serpent off. It did not retract its fangs from his brow, but seemed to pass through the incision it had made and pull itself slowly into his brain. He felt it winding through his head, threading itself through his thoughts, binding his will.

The pain ceased when the snake settled in, its entire length inside him. He felt fingers press the spot where it had entered. "It's done," a voice announced. "His power is yours. And *you* are mine."

E. ROSE SABIN

15

CROSSTHREADS

The Community was not at all what Trevor had expected. He had been picturing it as a place: a fenced compound with massive iron gates behind which the members lived in splendid security and isolation.

It was not a place; it was people. Ordinary people, as diverse as a cross section of any large city would be. Thirty or forty of them crowded into the patio of the pleasant but unpretentious home of a Community member, a meeting place chosen at random, Trevor learned, its location transmitted by code to the members. The Community functioned as a secret society, exchanging passwords and arcane handshakes, sending encrypted messages, holding clandestine meetings. Trevor was reminded of a secret club he and Les had organized when they were about nine years old. Its sole purpose had been to exclude those classmates who were not among their privileged friends.

Like that club, this group cast suspicious glances at one another as though wondering who might be a traitor. All spoke in guarded tones, and, despite the crowding, all kept a careful distance from the initiates in case they might be informers and spies.

Dr. Tenney alone of the group maintained an air of cheerful equanimity. He'd gotten over his anger at the failure of his servant to return with Les and Miryam and dedicated himself with great enthusiasm to arranging Carl's and Trevor's presentation to the Community. That occasion had arrived, and he radiated confidence and good cheer.

He stood with his two initiates beneath a potted plum tree hung with lanterns. Most of the company was standing, though Doss Hamlyn sat on a stone bench in the center of the patio. A young woman sat beside him, and a tall, muscular man stood directly behind them. His protective stance made Trevor suspect he was a bodyguard. Dr. Tenney paid the man no notice but identified the pretty, dark-haired woman beside Hamlyn as Hamlyn's daughter, Leila. She gazed with frank interest at the two young men, but her father scowled when he looked their way.

Hamlyn knew that Carl had pretended to be Trevor on the visit to his house. What explanation the doctor had given for that deception, Trevor didn't know. Dr. Tenney didn't seem to feel that it would spoil their chances for admission to the Community.

After spending the past four days a prisoner, along with Carl, in Dr. Tenney's house, Trevor no longer wanted to be admitted. Dr. Tenney had given him no choice. Their admission, he'd explained, would tip the balance of power in his favor and away from Doss Hamlyn.

Trevor hoped that when they each demonstrated their gifts, some of the gifted would sense that Carl was drawing on Trevor's power to perform his feats. Trevor performed a jump too high to be possible without the use of power, and he also picked up a rock from the garden and made it fly around a tree, then brought it back to his hand. Carl picked up a lawn chair and floated it to him, and then leaped over a tall bush. Trevor expected someone to notice the similarity in what they did.

Apparently no one did. Dr. Tenney had explained beforehand that the demonstration did not need to be impressive; it merely had to prove that the applicants *were* gifted. None of the members ever displayed the full range of his talent to the others. It was common for the members to conceal their most important gifts.

"Then what use is the Community?" Trevor had asked.

"It provides protection for its members," Dr. Tenney had stated. "And for some of us it offers opportunities to explore creative uses of our power." He winked at Carl.

With the demonstration completed, it was time for speeches on behalf of the candidates or in opposition to them. Dr. Tenney had introduced them to the group before the demonstration, praising them in glowing terms. Now he made only a brief statement recommending their acceptance, and the chairman opened the floor to any other members who wished to speak for or against the candidates.

Doss Hamlyn rose to his feet, and the murmur of conversation faded into silence. He addressed the group in a low voice that nevertheless carried easily. "I wish to go on record as opposing the entry of these two young men into the Community. The letter of introduction sent me by Matthew Blake is not sufficient to convince me that his nephew, Trevor Blake, would be a trustworthy and valuable addition to our Community. The letter was, in fact, first presented to me not by Mr. Blake but by Mr. Holdt, purporting to be Mr. Blake. The explanation that this deception was merely an attempt to assure the entry of both young men does not satisfy me. I do not question the validity of their gifts, but they are untrained and lacking in self-discipline. Despite the letter from my friend, I am inclined to withhold membership from Trevor Blake. And since for Carl Holdt we have only Dr. Tenney's dubious recommendation, I strongly advise rejection of his application."

He resumed his seat as the crowd reacted to his statement with a rustle of whispers that died away when Dr. Tenney stepped forward and signaled his desire to be heard.

"I regret that my esteemed colleague places so little faith in my recommendations," he said with a slight bow to Hamlyn. "He is entitled to his opinion. I will venture to suggest that his opposition to these candidates is a reflection of his animosity toward me and not an objective consideration of their talents and worth to the Community. If someone other than I had sponsored them, I daresay Mr. Hamlyn would not have raised the same objection. Has he not said frequently that we need to train new blood?

"Their little indiscretion in misidentifying the bearer of the letter of introduction was not intended maliciously but done in a misguided but well-meaning attempt by one friend to assure the other's favorable reception. I ask you to view it as a sign of their eagerness to become a productive part of this Community."

Trevor glanced at Doss Hamlyn in time to see him shake his head with a look of resignation. His daughter patted his hand consolingly. Their reaction astonished Trevor. Doss Hamlyn clearly occupied a prestigious position within the Community. He'd been sure that Hamlyn's opposition would sound the death knell to his and Carl's aspirations. But Hamlyn seemed to anticipate defeat.

Dr. Tenney stepped back beneath the plum tree and smiled at Trevor and Carl while the rush of conversation

E. Rose Sabin

resumed. "I doubt that anyone else will ask to make a statement," he said. "The vote will be called for in another minute or two. We'll have to leave while it's taken. They'll call us back to announce the results."

As the doctor predicted, the chairman approached and asked them to leave while the community voted. They threaded their way through the crowd, entered the house, and passed through it and out onto the front porch, where the doctor plopped himself down on a porch swing and motioned to Trevor and Carl to sit on the steps. Carl sat, but Trevor leaned against the front railing and gazed out into the night.

No matter what happened, no matter how the vote went, all his hopes had been dashed. Dr. Tenney had made Carl his tool; Trevor's linkage with Carl made him nothing more than an extension of that tool. He'd never be able to achieve his own ambitions; he was nothing more than a slave, as Miryam had been.

The odor of pipe smoke wafted around him, a smell he had come to hate. He glanced at Dr. Tenney and turned away, sickened by the contentment on the man's face as he puffed on his pipe.

The voting didn't take long. To Trevor's surprise, it was Hamlyn's daughter who came to fetch them. She stepped back to let them precede her into the house and through it to the patio. As Trevor passed her, she pressed a piece of paper into his hand.

A lantern hung over the door to the patio. Trevor fell back behind Carl and the doctor and paused beneath the light to uncrumple and read the note.

If you need help, nod once in my direction. I'll do what I can. It was signed *Doss Hamlyn.*

Hastily Trevor balled up the paper and concealed it within his palm. He hurried to catch up with his companions. When he stepped up beside Dr. Tenney, the Adept grasped his closed hand and with a powerful grip forced the fingers open and removed the note.

"Tch-tch," the doctor chided. "Can't have you consorting with the enemy."

Tenney held the note in his own hand. Trevor didn't see him read it, but he must somehow have known its contents. Trevor gazed at Doss Hamlyn and tried to nod; he couldn't bend his neck.

His muscles tensed, sweat broke out on his face, but his neck remained stiff, his head unmovable. He saw Hamlyn glance at him several times and look away with pursed lips and an angry shake of his head. The big man behind him also looked angry. Leila had returned to her place beside her father. Her eyes met Trevor's gaze, her nose wrinkled as if in disgust, and she, too, turned away. Trevor felt abandoned.

The chairman announced the results of the vote. Trevor heard, but only when applause and cries of welcome rose from the crowd did the impact hit him. They'd been admitted to the Community.

Les awakened to the certainty that he'd been asleep for a very long time. His body felt flabby, his skin clammy. He stank of sweat and sickness. His mouth was dry and foul-tasting, his lips cracked and sore. His eyelids seemed to be glued shut, and when he tried to lift his hand to his eyes to wipe them, the weakness in his muscles made the effort impossible.

He tried to remember what had happened to him, but his mind seemed as helpless as his body. He searched lethargically for something his thoughts could grasp, some contact with the exterior world that would allow him to make sense of his plight.

He lay on downy softness. Something soft and warm and silky covered his body. Something like fur.

He remembered the furs. They'd covered the whole floor of . . . of Veronica's home.

Veronica. She'd done something to him. And to Miryam. He remembered Miryam. Remembered her saying, "I'm free." That was the last thing he recalled. He had known what it meant. He struggled to recapture the meaning.

Soft footfalls broke his chain of thought. He heard the splash of water, felt a damp cloth touch his face, smooth gently over his brow and cheeks, move down to his neck. It cooled his skin, eased the dryness of his lips. He found he could open his eyes.

Miryam crouched above him, bathing his shoulders and chest. He tried to speak, could only croak.

She started at the sound, set down the basin she held. "Les! Thank the Power-Giver! You're awake."

He tried again to speak. His lips formed her name, but he couldn't get out the sound.

"Wait," she said. "I'll get water."

She moved away, was back in seconds. Lifting his head, she placed a cup of water against his lips and helped him drink. The water relieved the dryness and the stiffness in his vocal cords.

"What happened?" His voice was hoarse, but the words came out.

"We aren't sure," she said. "You reacted badly to the power thread being drawn through you. Veronica said it was because of something Dr. Tenney was doing at the same time, but she doesn't yet know what. She said that until she found out, it could be dangerous to use power to heal you."

Her voice faltered and he saw tears fill her eyes. "I've wondered if I should do it no matter what she said. I've wanted to so badly."

"How . . . how long?" He couldn't complete the question.

"It's been four days. I've been so afraid for you." A tear splashed onto his chest, leaving a warm trail on his bare skin. She wiped at her eyes. On her hand was a ring she hadn't worn before. Its semitransparent orange gem gleamed with an inner light.

He remembered the stone Veronica had placed on Miryam's forehead, remembered how it had been transformed into a window of fiery light, remembered what he'd seen through that window.

"You're free. From Carl."

She nodded. "For the first time since I was a child. But I haven't been able to enjoy it, seeing you so near death. If I'd lost you, it would have been too high a price."

"No," he said. "Worth it. You're more important." He wanted to say more, wanted to remind her of all that she could accomplish with her gifts, talented as she was. Without power he was no match for her, would only hold her back.

She bent and pressed her lips against his cheek. "I don't think so," she said.

Her tenderness moved him so that he did not trust himself to speak for several moments. Helpless to respond in kind, he shifted to safer ground, asked, "Where's Veronica?"

"She's here. Working on something. I'll tell her you're awake."

Miryam stood but had not stepped away when Veronica appeared beside her.

"I heard you talking," the Adept said. "I'll make you some soup. You need to get your strength back. Miryam, I'll need your help."

Veronica picked up the basin and cloth Miryam had been using and carried them away. Miryam smiled sadly at Les and trailed after the Adept.

Les could not see them from where he lay, but he listened to the familiar sounds of clanging pans and bubbling water, breathed in the mingled odors of boiling meat and herbs. It reminded him of home.

His weakness gave him an excuse to think of nothing but how hungry he was and how good the food would taste. He slipped into a dream state halfway between waking and sleeping. The sounds and scents receded into the background, and an odor of pipe smoke blended with them. He could feel the thick, soft fur beneath him and the warmth of the fur tucked over his body. Yet at the same time he felt a cold breeze blowing against him, ruffling through his hair as he walked—walked!—along a dark street and climbed into a waiting carriage.

The horse's clomping hooves, the jounce of the carriage over rutted roads, the press of the other passengers against him as he was squeezed between two other people on a seat not designed for three—all these were as real to him as the clinking of Veronica's spoon against the metal pot and the whistle of steam in the teakettle. He was only vaguely curious about this odd phenomenon, assuming it was a dream, until next to him a voice said, "Well, Trevor Blake, how does it feel to have attained your goal?"

Les recognized the voice. Dr. Tenney. A chill of fear crept through him. This was more than a dream.

"It's not what he expected," said the person wedged

A PERILOUS POWER

189

against his right arm. "Not what I expected either, exactly. But I'm not displeased. They're all afraid of you, aren't they?"

That voice was Carl's, and it held an awe and respect that Les was suprised to hear.

"Oh, no, not all." A chuckle accompanied the doctor's answer. "I have enemies. You heard Doss Hamlyn's opposition. But so long as I can control a majority, Doss can't do much."

"I'd like to learn how you exert that control." Greed made Carl's voice eager.

Les thought he saw a brief flare of light. Pipe smoke poured into his nostrils, choking him. Dr. Tenney's deep inhalations were clearly audible. "You'll learn." The Adept's voice was garbled as though his words were spoken around the pipe stem. "You'll learn much, both of you. As long as you both remember who controls *you*."

The shudder that coursed through Les might have been his own or Trevor's; he couldn't tell, and it made little difference. Somehow he was in Trevor's mind; nothing else could explain what he heard and felt. Could he make Trevor aware of his presence? If only he knew how to send.

But if he was in Trevor's mind, he shouldn't *have* to send. Maybe he only needed to speak.

He couldn't. Not aloud. His throat refused to form sounds, his tongue and lips refused to move.

All right, form the words mentally. Clearly and distinctly, as though you were speaking. Like this: Trevor, it's Les. I'm here. What kind of trouble are you in? Where are you?

His lips moved. Trevor's voice mumbled, "Les?"

He'd done it! He'd gotten through.

The carriage shook; a wheel must have jolted into a pot-hole. His head banged against the carriage roof. The three bodies crushed closer as the carriage swayed dangerously. Dr. Tenney swore. Burning ash fell onto Les/Trevor's arm. Les heard the doctor's pipe shatter on the carriage floor.

"Here's your soup." Veronica's cheery voice and the steamy scent of beef and vegetables replaced the sensations of his dream vision. "Come on. I'll help you sit up."

His hunger had gone. "Trevor," he gasped. "I was in Trevor's mind. I heard them talking—Carl and Dr. Tenney. Trevor's in trouble. We've got to find him."

She forced the hot bowl into his hands. It burned his fingers; it was all he could do to hold on to it. She steadied him and supported his head and shoulders so that he could sit. "Eat," she ordered.

"I can't. Didn't you hear what I said?" he asked, balancing the bowl gingerly in unsteady hands. "I was with Trevor. It wasn't a dream. I was really in his mind. I know I was."

"Eat your soup. Then we'll talk about it." She dipped a spoon into the thick soup and lifted it to his mouth.

He turned his head away. "How did I do it?" he persisted. "Am I finding my talent?"

She shook her head and jabbed the spoon into his mouth before he could dodge again. The hot liquid scalded his tongue. "It means that what I did when I used you for a channel created a link between you."

He tried to set down the soup bowl. She took it from his hands and continued feeding him. "I'll explain it after you finish the soup. You need to build back your strength. The link increases the danger to you, but it gives you a chance to help your friend. But you can't help him while you're too weak to sit up on your own."

That, of course, was true. He stopped protesting and ate the soup, even let her bring him a second bowl. All the while, he repeated mentally, *Hang on, Trev. I'm coming.*

If Trevor had sent such a message to *him*, he would have received it. But with no talent he had little hope that Trevor would receive it. Yet he couldn't stop his mind from repeating it again and again: *I'm coming, Trev. Hang on, I'm coming.*

16

NIGHT JOURNEYS

The buggy rocked to a halt. Trevor swiped at the burning pipe ash, flicked it from his hands and clothing.

He flattened himself against the seat back to allow Dr. Tenney to lean forward, gather the shattered remnants of his pipe, and stuff them into his pocket with a rueful sigh. Carl swore and straightened his jacket. The driver came to the side and peered in at them.

"Ever'body all right?"

"Just shaken up a bit," Dr. Tenney replied. "Is the buggy damaged?"

"Not so's I can't fix it. But being jerked that way's sprung the horse's shoulder and lamed 'er bad. She can't pull this hack. Don't know what we'll do. 'Twon't be easy to find another out this time o' night."

The man's voice was husky with fear and sorrow. Trevor knew the injury he described would be slow to heal. If the mare was his only horse, he faced several weeks of lost income.

"More like impossible, I'd say," the doctor answered. "But let me look at the horse. It's possible the injury looks worse than it is."

"No, sir. Wish that were the case, but I can see the separation, and the poor horse is suffering bad."

Despite this affirmation, the doctor hopped from the cab and hurried to inspect the horse. In a moment he shouted for Trevor and Carl to join him. Trevor scrambled down and picked his way over the rutted street. The coach lantern spread its light over the horse standing with her head down, her flanks trembling.

"Boy, can you heal?" Dr. Tenney whispered into Trevor's ear. At Trevor's whispered negative he turned to Carl. "You?"

Carl shook his head. "Miryam could, but since I no longer share her power . . ."

"All right. We'll have to fake it." The doctor glanced quickly at the driver, who stood back, watching with a disapproving scowl. "My good man," Dr. Tenney said, "I have considerable knowledge of medical matters. I am, in fact, a doctor. With the assistance of my young companions, I can adjust the horse's shoulder so that it falls back into place and her pain is eased. She'll be able to complete the route with no discomfort."

The driver shook his head dubiously. "Wouldn't want no harm to come to the horse," he said.

"None will. I know what I'm doing, I assure you." Giving the man no chance to object, Dr. Tenney placed his hands on the injury. "A blocking spell, so she can't feel pain," the doctor whispered to Carl.

Trevor felt power being drawn from him. The horse lifted her head and gave a surprised snort. The doctor pressed the horse's shoulder. When he drew his hand away, no sign of injury remained.

It was a deception, Trevor knew. Dr. Tenney had not healed the mare. He'd only masked her pain and hidden the injury beneath a cloak of illusion. The driver was convinced. He hooked the carriage to the horse's harness, and his passengers crowded back inside.

Trevor despised himself for not speaking up. He knew too well what would happen to the horse. By the time the blocking spell wore off, the injury would be compounded beyond repair. The horse would have to be put down. So that he could complete his comfortable ride home, the Adept had condemned the mare to agony and death and her owner to poverty.

Les, you were right. I wish I'd listened to you.

Les haunted his thoughts. Les would not have kept silent about the horse. Les had seen Dr. Tenney for what he was, had escaped, and the doctor's ghoulish servant hadn't yet been able to find him. Veronica must be protecting him, but Trevor could not count on her help after being rude, questioning her power, and ignoring her advice. He got into this mess by himself, and he'd have to get himself out of it. He spent the rest of the ride home pondering how to do this.

In the days since Dr. Tenney had bound him to Carl, Trevor had tested every talent he had or thought he might have, but he could find no gift of his free from Carl's domination and therefore from Dr. Tenney's. He had to escape, but he could see only one way to do that. He would have to kill the doctor. Not by power; that would be impossible. He'd have to find a way to do it using normal subterfuge and superior physical strength.

He'd observed that the doctor's self-indulgent lifestyle left him weak and easily winded. If he could take him by surprise and strike quickly before the Adept could summon his power, he might succeed. Dr. Tenney's insistence on keeping Carl and Trevor with him, forcing them to stay in his home, would work to Trevor's advantage, increasing the opportunities for such an attack.

Trevor dreamed of killing Carl as well, but he knew that the link between them would not permit it. To kill Carl would be suicide. With Dr. Tenney out of the way, though, he could engage in a power struggle with Carl that might place *him* in the dominant position.

When the carriage delivered them to Dr. Tenney's house of horrors, Trevor had not developed a specific plan for killing the doctor, but he had convinced himself that he could and must do it at the earliest opportunity, before the doctor sapped his will.

Miryam insisted that she should go with Veronica to scout out Dr. Tenney's home. Les declared that if she went, he would go. He'd regained strength in the past three days, but neither Veronica nor Miryam felt he was well enough for the planned foray. So Miryam yielded and agreed to stay behind with him, while Veronica reconnoitered on her own. The Adept, after all, was able to conceal and protect herself.

"I don't work the way he does," she said. "Wouldn't be caught dead using those contraptions of his. He's no match for me, in spite of them. You two stay locked in here, and you'll be safe enough while I'm gone. No need to worry about me."

She left, and Les felt suddenly awkward and ill at ease. Miryam was close to being an Adept, he felt sure. He couldn't let himself care for her, yet he knew he did care, very much.

She smiled, and her smile drove out his fears. "Miryam," he said. "Miryam, I shouldn't love you, but I do."

She stiffened. "What do you mean, you shouldn't love me?"

"I have no talent. I'll hold you back."

"Is that all?" Relief was evident in her soft laugh. She gave him a quick kiss on his forehead. "Les, it's only *because* you don't have power that I can love you. For so many years Carl's used my power to do terrible things to other people. It's made me despise power."

"But you weren't to blame for what he did," Les said, taking her hand in his.

"The power was mine. That made me a part of it. I always felt guilty and unclean. But you—without using power, you have strength." She swallowed hard before continuing. "I . . . I want to be like you. I mean to set aside my power and be strong without it."

"But you have so much. It would be a waste—"

"Shhh!" She pressed the tips of her fingers against his mouth.

His hand closed over hers, and he felt her ring with its fiery gem. "This ring—doesn't it represent your freedom to use your gifts?"

She looked surprised. "Or to *not* use them. But it's more than a symbol. Veronica made it for me. She says it's for protection and that while I have it on, neither Carl nor anyone else can draw on my power. No one will control me again."

"Then promise me to wear it always." He gazed into the soft brown depths of her eyes. They'd lost that wounded look; he saw his own love reflected in them.

He couldn't believe his fortune: that she could love him, that she was glad he wasn't gifted, or couldn't use whatever gift he might possess. After all that had happened in Port-of-Lords, he no longer wanted to find his talent. For her sake

A PERILOUS POWER

he would have been willing to pursue it, but he was relieved to know he needn't do so.

He slipped his arms around her and pressed his lips against her cheek.

In that instant the room faded away, and her face receded into fog.

Instead of kneeling on thick fur, he seemed to be walking cautiously across a wood floor. In the dim light he could barely make out the outspread hands with which he picked his way through a forest of small tables. Not Veronica's tables. These held twisted shapes of metal and wire and glass. He was in Dr. Tenney's laboratory.

Yet he was not. Hands patted his face, shook his shoulders. A voice called his name.

He couldn't respond. His body, his own body, hadn't moved, and he retained a faint awareness of it. Yet his mind was captive somewhere else, seeing through someone else's eyes. *Trevor's.*

He was sure of it, though this time no one spoke in his vision, and he could not read the intentions that directed his host's movements.

Veronica had explained his previous experience as being due to a link created when she'd routed Carl's power through him as she separated it from Miryam. Dr. Tenney must have been with Carl when Veronica freed Miryam. The doctor would have known what was happening and must have replaced Carl's link to Miryam with a link to Trevor. In some way Les had been drawn briefly into that link.

Veronica hadn't expected the phenomenon to recur. It was, she'd explained, something like an afterimage, a fading shadow. But she had been wrong. He was back in Trevor's mind, accompanying him on some mysterious errand.

E. ROSE SABIN

Trevor stopped at a table and unwound and detached a long, thin wire from the odd assemblage on it. Les could see him testing the wire's strength, wrapping several lengths of the wire around one hand, wrapping the other end of the wire around the other hand so that the middle section of the wire stretched tautly between them. Thus equipped, he moved stealthily from the hall out into the corridor.

It was clear to Les that Trevor intended to garrote someone.

Trevor, no! Be careful! Les's thoughts screamed the warning, but Trevor continued resolutely forward with not the slightest hesitation to indicate that he'd heard.

Les cursed his helplessness.

Trevor turned and passed through a doorway into what seemed to be a study. Through Trevor's eyes Les saw the gleam of Dr. Tenney's bald head visible over the back of a chair. The doctor was seated at a desk; Les couldn't see what he was doing—whether reading, writing, or perhaps dozing in his chair. Slowly Trevor drew nearer. Again Les attempted a mental warning, but again it went unheeded.

Trevor stood directly behind the chair. He raised his hands to bring the wire over the doctor's head. Les, looking out through Trevor's eyes, spied what held the doctor's attention.

On the desk directly in front of him sat a lidded gallon jar. Inside, a white moth beat its wings against the imprisoning glass.

Trevor's hands paused in their downward motion. Dr. Tenney leaned forward. The wire flamed, crisped, shriveled to nothing. A scream tore from Trevor's throat.

The chair and its occupant vanished, Miryam appearing in their place. She was shaking Les, patting his cheeks, call-

A PERILOUS POWER

ing his name. They were both kneeling on the furs.

He jumped to his feet, pulling her up with him. "Dr. Tenney has Veronica," he panted. "He might be killing Trevor. We've got to get to his house. Right away."

He raced for the door, had it open by the time she caught up with him.

"How do you know these things?" she asked, holding his arm. "Veronica said we weren't to leave here."

"I was with Trevor. I saw. We've got to go, no matter what she said." He pulled free and ran toward the dark street, looked back, and saw her shut the door and hurry after him.

"It's the middle of the night," she said. "How are we going to get there?"

"I don't know." He looked up and down the street. "We've got to find a way. Steal bicycles if we have to. Or a horse, if there's one anywhere close."

She nodded. "We might find a cycle. Some of these buildings have courtyards, and that's where their residents might keep bicycles. I don't like the idea of stealing, but I've done worse things for Carl, so if you're sure it's necessary . . ."

"I'm sure. Let's go."

Hiking up her skirt, she ran with him.

They crossed a street lit by a flickering gaslight. Beyond the reach of that feeble light the night seemed darker. Miryam pulled him to a stop at an archway past which he could see nothing but blackness. "Here," she whispered. "I think this passage leads to a courtyard."

"We need light," he said.

She cupped her hands. A tiny flame, like the glow of a match, hung suspended above her palms. Small as the light was, it allowed them to see the brick walls of the passage and set their course between them. It did not allow them to see more than a few paces ahead or to know whether any barrier blocked their way.

Torn between the need for haste and the need for caution, Les entered the passage at a pace that kept him at the edge of the light.

Something stirred in the shadows. Les slowed; Miryam held the light high. A cowled figure barred their way. Hands emerged from its long sleeves, metal hands with steel fingers that locked around their arms. Miryam's light went out. From within the creature's hood a toneless voice said, "Dr. Tenney is waiting for you."

It was the doctor's servant. The metal hand was icy; Les's arm grew numb. He struggled against the viselike grip, his battle conducted in total darkness. He struck the creature with his free hand, used his feet and knees to pummel it. The blows could have fallen on rock. They jarred Les, brought tears of pain to his eyes, and had no effect on his captor. Les's arm was bloody, his fist and knees bruised and bleeding. Not being able to see Miryam added to his desperation. He remembered the ring she wore. It was supposed to protect her.

A brilliant light shattered the darkness. A captive lightning bolt blazed down, striking and severing the arm that held Les.

Les stood stunned and blinded. "Run, Les," Miryam's voice urged.

He blinked, saw through a red haze. The servant's robe was burning. By the light of that fire Les saw that Miryam remained a prisoner. She had used power to send the lightning, freeing him instead of herself.

"Go!" she urged again.

But he could not leave her. The servant stomped around,

its movements erratic. It dragged Miryam with it as a child carelessly drags a doll. Les had to save her.

As its robe burned, the thing's body grew visible: a construction of metal and twisted wire, like the devices in the doctor's laboratory.

Les lunged for the arm that gripped Miryam. It swung away from him. The last remnants of its robe crumbling from it, the metal servant turned and ran from the passage, dragging Miryam with it. Les followed, the metal hand still clamped around his wrist, the severed arm clanging against the brick wall as he ran.

Les emerged from the passage only a fraction of a second after the servant. The street was empty. He peered into the darkness, straining to see, to hear.

The night was silent. The whole thing could have been no more than a dream, except for the twisted metal shackled to his arm. He wrenched the thing off. It clattered to the pavement.

"Miryam!" he shouted. "Miryam, where are you?"

"Quiet down there," a gruff male voice called from a window above his head.

He ran down the road, staring into the darkness, hoping to catch a glimpse of his quarry. Hearing a yowl and a thud behind him, he whirled to race in the opposite direction.

A scrawny cat bounded across the road and leaped over a stone wall. Nothing else.

Dispiritedly he walked back to the passage. The servant would take Miryam to Dr. Tenney's house. Not knowing what else to do, Les groped his way through the passage into the courtyard. Straining to make sense of shadows, he stumbled about until he ran into one of the bicycles Miryam had predicted they'd find. By touch alone he found the front of the cycle, gripped the handlebars, and pushed the two-wheeler back to the passage, which somehow he located in the dark.

The cycle clanked and clattered, and he was sure the building's residents would hear and chase him. A high-pitched query came from a window overlooking the court-yard, but no one challenged him. He scarcely breathed as he wheeled the cycle through the passage. Not until he reached the street did he dare to swing onto the seat, balance precariously, and finally pedal off.

He had only a vague idea of where Dr. Tenney's house was located; he knew that it was on the outskirts of the city, far from his present location. His body ached from his exertions against the servant. He rode poorly; he'd been on a cycle no more than two or three times before. The front wheel wobbled, making the bicycle veer from side to side like a foundering ship. He reached a section lit by streetlights where, sweating and shaky, he stopped to get his bearings and to think what to do.

He knew little of Port-of-Lords, but by the soft illumination he spied a landmark he recognized: the Maritime Museum. Carl had pointed it out to them when he conducted them from the train station en route to the place where he had drugged and robbed them. It had stuck in Les's mind because of its odd construction, its front built like the prow of a ship. He had seen it again the day he and Carl had gone to visit Doss Hamlyn.

He thought he could find Hamlyn's mansion from here. It wasn't too far; he could make it. Hamlyn could direct him to Dr. Tenney's house. With luck he could be persuaded to help.

17

NIGHT TERRORS

Les climbed off the bicycle and staggered to Doss Hamlyn's front door. He grasped the heavy bronze knocker and dropped it into its cradle several times, then pounded on the door with his fists.

"Who is it?" The words boomed out from no discernible source. He thought he recognized Doss Hamlyn's voice.

"It's Les Simonton. I need help."

Several minutes passed during which Les wondered whether he'd been heard. He lifted his hand to knock again, when the door swung open, apparently of its own accord. Les saw no one in the lighted foyer, but he stepped inside anyway. The door swung shut behind him.

"This is a most irregular time to pay a visit," said the disembodied voice. "Please state your errand. Be brief."

How could he be brief when he had so much to explain? "I need help for my friend Trevor Blake. And for a girl named Miryam Vedreaux. Dr. Tenney has them, and they're in terrible danger."

Again he waited. Needing to sit, to rest, he looked longingly at the antique chair, shook his head, and stayed on his feet.

"Follow the light, please," said the voice, startling him out of the numbness of exhaustion.

A globe of silvery light danced in front of him and bobbed away. He trailed after it, this time taking no note of the rooms through which it led him. He expected to be conducted to the study where Hamlyn had talked with him and Carl. Instead he was guided into a large bedchamber with a bed wide enough to accommodate eight sleepers. The light globe burst like a bubble. It was no longer needed; a rich golden light streamed from the ornate gas chandelier above the bed.

Doss Hamlyn, wearing a brown velvet robe, sat in a straight-backed armchair near a curtained window. He hadn't bothered to comb his hair or wash the sleep from his face. He looked much older than he had when Les had seen him before. He motioned to a second chair. "This had better be important," he said.

"It is, sir." Les launched into the tale, speaking rapidly and holding nothing back.

Hamlyn interrupted occasionally with a pertinent question, frowned when Les spoke of Veronica, but neither his questions nor his expression gave Les any hint of his reaction to the story until the telling was complete.

Then he said, "Carl Holdt deceived me, with your help. I offered assistance to your friend Trevor when he and Carl were voted into the Community, and he spurned my offer. I see no reason to help him now. As for Veronica, that witch can take care of herself."

"But, sir," Les argued, "Tenney is holding Trevor a prisoner and probably prevented him from accepting your help. Please believe me, the situation is desperate. You and Trevor's uncle were good friends; his Uncle Matt sent us to you because of that friendship and because he believed that the

Community stood for something good. Was he wrong about the Community and about you? Will you turn your back on the nephew of your good friend?"

"Humph! Matthew Blake and I *were* good friends, but that was many years ago. And the Community is not what it was when I wrote Matt about it." Hamlyn stopped and stared at the curtained window for a few moments, then said, "Well, I suppose for Matthew Blake's sake I should do something about young Trevor."

He rose and came to stand in front of Les. "I'd like to see Tenney brought back into line. He's a brilliant fellow, really. Probably has more talent than all the rest of the Community combined. What it was that twisted him, I don't know, but three or four years ago, about the time he moved into that ugly old house on the edge of town, he started using his power to manipulate people and gain undue influence in the Community. I warned several of the members. So far, I've prevented him from taking over, but now he's shifted the balance in his favor by bringing Carl and your friend into the Community. He'll turn the whole Community to a direction it was never meant to take, and I doubt that I'm strong enough to stop it." He wiped the sleeve of his robe across his forehead.

"He can't do that if we rescue Trevor and Miryam," Les said.

Hamlyn nodded. "We'll need help." He stared at the door to the room as if he expected that help to walk in unannounced. "I'll get on it right away, but it will be some time before we can move against Tenney. You might as well get some sleep. I'll take you to the guest room."

More delay. Les's heart sank. "I don't think it's safe to wait," he said.

"It's certainly not safe to jump into this thing unprepared," Hamlyn answered. "I know far more about Tenney than you do. You came to me for help, and I've agreed to give it. You'll have to trust my judgment. Besides, you look in no shape to go anywhere at present."

Les had to admit that he wasn't. He let Hamlyn lead him to a nearby room where an inviting bed conquered his resistance. Under a cloud-soft quilt the clean, smooth sheets smelled of lavender. He lay down, vowing to take only a short nap, and fell into a restless sleep full of troubling dreams: dreams of Trevor, of pain, of strangulation.

An invisible band tightened around Trevor's neck, choking him, cutting into his flesh. He gagged, fought for breath, clawed at his throat.

"That's a taste of your own medicine, Trevor, my boy. Don't like it much, do you?" Dr. Tenney stood facing him, desk chair shoved aside.

Trevor backed against the wall. He needed its support. The band dug into his neck, and his fingers couldn't get hold of it to loosen it. Black spots danced before his eyes; he felt himself losing consciousness.

Dr. Tenney regarded him calmly. "I'm disappointed in you, my boy. After all I've done for you, I can't think why you would turn against me. Perhaps you thought you no longer needed me, now that you're a member of the Community?"

Trevor couldn't answer. His knees buckled, he slid down the wall. Dr. Tenney grasped his arms, hauled him up, thrust him into the desk chair. The pressure on his throat diminished enough to keep him from passing out, but not enough to relieve his pain and fear.

E. ROSE SABIN

"Foolish, foolish boy, to think you could harm an Adept. No one can sneak up on me. *No one*—not even another Adept." He waved his hand at the jar on his desk. The moth had settled on the bottom of the jar, and only an occasional weak flutter of its wings assured Trevor that it lived.

Dr. Tenney gazed down at Trevor with a sorrowful look. "Such betrayal, when I had wonderful plans for you. How could you have thrown away the opportunity I offered you?

"Ah, you seem unable to answer. Struck dumb, no doubt, by the heinousness of your deed. Tch, such a pity."

Trevor yearned to leap up and wrap his hands around the doctor's neck, or at least to lunge forward and ram his fist into the fat belly that presented such a tempting target. But he couldn't move. The Adept's power held him both motionless and speechless.

"I can't bestow blessings on a traitor, can I?" He shook his head sadly. "No, I'm afraid you've forfeited the power and wealth that could have been yours. Carl, I think, will not be so foolish or so ungrateful.

"I've been protecting you from him, you know. Allowing him to draw only the merest bit of your power. Enough to perform the parlor tricks required by the Community, enough to be sure the injured horse could get us home. Nothing that would cause you discomfort or shame."

He stopped and turned, opened the drawer of his desk, fumbled inside, drew out a pipe pouch, extracted a briar pipe, and gazed at it lovingly. His fingers stroked the carved bowl; he held the cherry stem up to the light. "My favorite pipe," he said.

He made a production out of filling and lighting it, puffed on it, and blew the smoke into Trevor's face. Trevor's eyes watered. The tightness in his throat wouldn't let him cough; he could scarcely breathe.

The doctor smiled, enjoying Trevor's agony. "Carl is intelligent, you know. Devious, yes, he is that. But sensible enough to know how to realize his ambitions. He would not make the foolish mistake you've made.

"I intend to remove the restrictions I have placed on him. He will follow my orders; he will have no choice about that. But so long as he acknowledges his dependence on me, he may do what he wishes with you. I will permit him to draw all the power he wants and to send you on whatever private errands may suit his fancy." He paused to blow several smoke rings, then continued, "Do you feel an unpleasant tightness about your neck? Yes, I see that you do. I'm afraid, though, that you will have to endure it as a reminder of your folly. It will not prevent your drinking or eating a little soft food. It will not allow you to speak, and you will never again be free of pain."

He set his pipe down beside the jar on his desk. "Come, I have work to do. I'll turn you over to Carl. He's probably asleep, but I'm sure he'll forgive my waking him when he understands the gift I'm giving him."

Carrying a lighted candle, the Adept forced Trevor to follow him meekly to Carl's bedroom. Trevor's muscles were no longer under his own command; he was helpless to do anything other than what the doctor willed.

He stood in utter misery while Dr. Tenney shook Carl awake, explained that Trevor had tried to kill him, and that as punishment he was henceforth wholly under Carl's control. "Do what you want with him," the doctor said. "He's your toy."

Carl stared stupidly as though he thought he might be

dreaming. But the Adept's words gradually penetrated. He broke into a broad grin.

"Enjoy yourself," Dr. Tenney said and left the room.

"I will," Carl called after him, laughing. He beckoned Trevor nearer. "Oh, yes, I will," he said, his gleaming eyes reflecting the flame of the candle Dr. Tenney had left in the candlestick on his nightstand.

Trevor raged against his helplessness. His attempts to use his power were futile. He raised his hand to his throat and tried to loosen the band, but there was nothing to touch or pull, and rubbing only made the pain worse. He wished the band would tighten and end his misery. That wouldn't happen either. Dr. Tenney's power kept the tightness at just the level needed to cause great pain without preventing shallow breathing.

He became aware of Carl's gaze fixed on him, gloating. His hands fell to his sides; he tried to conceal his discomfort. Carl's amusement told him how badly he failed.

"Take off your shirt," Carl ordered abruptly.

Trevor tried to utter a refusal, forgetting he could not speak. Carl laughed at his soundless mouthings and repeated the command.

Trevor tried to cross his arms in front of him, found himself unbuttoning his shirt instead. His hands moved independently of his will. In a moment his shirt lay on the floor, and he stood bare to the waist.

"Come here, country boy," Carl said, beckoning. "Dr. Tenney said you're to be my toy. So. We're going to play some games. Lucky for me you won't be able to cry out when they get a little rough. Take off your belt."

Again Trevor had no choice but to comply. His shaking hands fumbled with the belt buckle, got it open, and pulled

A PERILOUS POWER

the belt off. He felt himself wrapping one end around his hand and letting the other end, the end with the metal buckle, dangle.

"Now, let's see how hard you can strike with that." Carl spun him around as he gave the order.

Trevor was forced to lift his arm and fling the buckle hard against his own bare back. Hard, but not hard enough to please his tormentor. "You'll have to do better than that," Carl said. "Try again."

He did. And again. And again, on and on, until his back was raw and bleeding and his arm was aching from the exertion. When at last Carl allowed him to let his arm drop to his side, he thought it was over, but after only a few seconds' respite, Carl had him raise the belt again, this time to strike his chest.

The night lasted forever. It left his body bruised, bleeding, turned into an alien thing, a false friend that surrendered itself to the bizarre whims of another. The horrors in his mind crowded it to the verge of insanity. When the physical pain and the mental anguish of having his own power turned against him sickened him so that the power band around his neck could not prevent his stomach from spewing out its contents, Carl beat him and made him clean up the vomit while tears streamed down his face.

Finally he was allowed to collapse onto the cold floor and lie there while Carl stretched out on his warm bed and mused aloud of new torments he intended to employ.

"The more broken you are, the more unimpeded the flow of power," he said cheerfully. "I learned that with Miryam, you know. The power sluices through you, and I absorb it all. There's nothing left in you to stop it."

Trevor heard but didn't care. Power. What good was it?

E. ROSE SABIN

It hadn't protected him. He felt torn into tiny fragments and scattered past all reclaiming. He remembered the outrage he'd felt when Carl had stolen his money and documents. Now Carl had shredded not only his flesh but the pride that let him feel anger. He was numb, incapable of feeling anything except a wish for death.

A light tap on the door raised not the slightest flicker of interest or fear on his part. He lay unmoving while Carl stepped over him to pad to the door.

Dr. Tenney's voice drifted through the fog. "Sorry to arouse you so early. I expect you had a busy night. But I thought you'd want to see who's come back into the fold. No, no. I said *see*. She's not yours anymore. I've given you a new toy to take her place. Her arrival is most timely; I have plans for her. I merely felt I should extend you the courtesy of informing you that your sister is no longer among the missing."

Carl's sister. Miryam. Trevor turned his back to the door and curled into a fetal position. Maybe Miryam hadn't seen him. He didn't want to be seen like this. Perhaps, after all, a scrap of pride remained.

He heard Miryam's voice but made no attempt to distinguish the words. Carl's mocking tones erased everything else.

"Let me at least heal his wounds." That was Miryam.

Heal his wounds. Whose wounds? His? So she *had* seen him and witnessed his disgrace.

Heal his wounds. Some wounds were too deep for any healing. Miryam of all people must know that.

Carl laughed again, and the rest of the conversation was lost in his laughter.

Go away, Trevor thought. *Go away and leave me alone.*

The door closed. Someone had heeded his mental plea.

A PERILOUS POWER

Not Carl. Carl stepped over him and sat on the bed. He nudged Trevor with his foot. "Get up, my pretty toy. Not so pretty anymore, but that can't be helped, can it? Get up. We have time for a few more games."

Trevor's traitorous body staggered to its feet and picked up the discarded belt, while his mind fled away and hid in a dusty corner.

18

$\int$HATTERED GLASS

Les awoke to the mouthwatering aroma of fried fish and fresh fruit. A cheery voice sang out, "I've brought breakfast. Father said you'd be famished."

He got his eyes open and his mind functioning enough to recall the previous night. Breakfast! No time. He had to find Miryam, had to rescue Trevor. He sat up and glared at the woman who stood beside the bed holding a tray.

The glare faded in the light of her friendly smile. He let her place the tray on his lap. Slivers of white fish fried in a thin batter were arranged like a fan in the center of the plate, slices of several kinds of fruit spread around them in a colorful wreath. Milk in a tall, frosted glass completed the meal.

"I can't . . . Need to get moving. Too much time's gone by already." He heard the lack of conviction in his voice.

"Father isn't quite ready. You have time to eat, and you'll need your strength. I'm Leila Hamlyn, by the way." Her smile put dimples into her cheeks. Her short dark hair framed a heart-shaped face.

Hamlyn's daughter. Rich. Probably spoiled. She had a pretty face, but she wouldn't have the character Miryam had.

Miryam! He had to get to her. He put down the fork he

had picked up without realizing it. He couldn't eat. He had to find her.

Leila placed a hand on his shoulder. "I know, it's hard to wait, and you feel guilty about sitting here eating a big breakfast. But really, you can do nothing right now. If you go rushing out and get a cab to Dr. Tenney's, what are you going to do when you arrive? What do you think you can accomplish by yourself against a powerful Adept?"

He scowled. "You read my mind, didn't you?"

A rush of color only added to her beauty. "I'm good at reading people," she said. "Your expression, your posture, your movements all show what's in your mind."

"All right, I'll eat," he said, yielding grudgingly. "But if your father isn't ready after that, I *will* go on my own."

"And add one more to the number to be rescued," she said with a touch of anger. "I'll try to hurry Dad. But he does have a lot of preparations to make, if we're to have any hope of success." She turned and left the room.

He *did* feel guilty about eating; she'd been right about that. She'd also been right in saying that he needed his strength. He took a bite of the succulent fish. Snared by the moist, rich flavor, he didn't rest his fork until the plate was empty.

After draining the glass of milk, he set the tray of empty dishes on the floor, got up, and stretched. He regarded himself in the mirror. He needed a shave, his hair was a tangled mess, his clothes were sweat-stained and wrinkled.

A bathroom opened off the guest room. In it he found shaving materials, hairbrushes, combs. He decided to give Doss Hamlyn as much more time as it took him to wash and shave. He could make himself somewhat more presentable, though he could do little about his clothes.

He emerged from the guest room feeling refreshed and

ready for action. He glanced about to get his bearings and locate Doss Hamlyn's room. A door opened and Leila emerged into the hallway.

"Father's driver is bringing the carriage to the front door. We'll be leaving in about ten minutes."

"*We?*" Les frowned. "You aren't going."

"I insisted on it," she said, dimpling. "My gifts may be helpful."

"It's not safe," he said. "You could get killed."

"The decision's made. Come on." With a toss of her head she brushed past him and led him through the corridors and downstairs to the front entrance. A carriage trimmed in gold and ebony waited, drawn by a pair of spirited black horses, impeccably groomed, a liveried driver in the seat behind them.

What was Doss Hamlyn thinking of? Les had thought Hamlyn realized what they were getting into, but he couldn't be taking this rescue attempt seriously if he allowed his daughter to go with them. This was worse than the delay. Les wished he had left last night when it was clear that Hamlyn was not going to take immediate action. He'd been lulled into sleeping late and eating a luxurious breakfast, and now here they were; taking a woman and setting off in a showy carriage as though embarking on a pleasure jaunt.

"Go on. Get into the carriage. Dad will be along any minute." Leila prodded him lightly, her hand on his upper arm.

He moved toward the carriage as if plodding against a stiff wind. This expedition was all wrong. He needed to stop it, to find another way to reach Dr. Tenney's house and rescue Trevor and Miryam. But he could think of no way to undo the harm he'd done, no way to avoid the disaster he'd set in motion.

A PERILOUS POWER

The driver, a tall man with broad shoulders and muscles that strained the seams of his braid-trimmed jacket, had leaped to the ground and opened the carriage door. With Leila behind him, Les could not bolt and run. He could only climb into the carriage, sink down onto the plush seat, and think about the doom that lay ahead for them all.

Leila climbed in and gathered up her full blue silk skirt to make room beside him. "You're worried." It was a matter-of-fact statement. "You think we're going about this in the wrong way."

He couldn't deny it, couldn't think of anything to say that wouldn't sound surly and ill-tempered.

"I understand your anxiety for your friends. But really, Father knows what he's doing. I can't promise that his plan will work; Dr. Tenney is clever and strong. But I *can* promise that if anything can defeat Tenney, it will be Father's plan."

"You are reading me again."

"I sense what you're feeling—your emotions."

"Look, I'm sorry. I don't mean to insult you or your father. But, yes, I think it's a great mistake to drive up to Dr. Tenney's front door in this rig. I think it's a mistake for you to go with us." He threw his arms wide. "I think this whole trip is a mistake."

She nodded. "I don't know how to convince you that it isn't. You'll have to wait and see. Oh, here comes Father."

Doss Hamlyn strode toward the carriage, attired in striped morning coat, silk top hat, white satin necktie, and perfectly fitted black trousers. He carried a walking stick of highly polished wood with a gold handle and tip. Les's spirits sank lower. The man was dressed for a formal dinner or an appointment with some dignitary, not for bursting into Dr. Tenney's house of horrors and confronting the Adept.

E. Rose Sabin

He could only mumble a dismal, "Hello," in response to Hamlyn's hearty greeting.

The driver shut the carriage door when Hamlyn was seated, and moments later the carriage was rolling smoothly over the brick roads.

They rode in silence. Les wanted to ask Hamlyn his plan, but couldn't speak without revealing his deep distress. Hamlyn volunteered no information, and Leila sat in confident ease, apparently feeling that no more needed to be said.

Hamlyn had promised to call on other members of the Community to assist in the rescue, and Les wondered where these others were. He refrained from asking. Perhaps they were planning to meet at Dr. Tenney's house.

Hamlyn sat erect, his walking stick upright between his legs, his hands resting on its handle, his eyes closed. The hairs on Les's arms prickled as though with static electricity. Hamlyn was doing something, working some spell.

Les glanced at Leila. She smiled encouragingly but did not speak. Undoubtedly she understood what her father was doing, but neither bothered to explain. After all, to them he was nothing but a normal, a no-talent.

The carriage stopped. Leila sat up. Her father opened his eyes. "It begins," he murmured.

The driver opened the door and helped them descend. When Les emerged from the carriage, the driver stuck out his hand. "I'm Peter Loftman," he said. "I work for Mr. Hamlyn, but I'm also a member of the Community."

So at least one other gifted *was* present. Les saw no others and hoped that Hamlyn, Leila, and this Peter would be enough. He doubted that they would be, but it was too late to say anything about it.

To Les's surprise, Leila took the lead in marching toward

A PERILOUS POWER

the stairs. Her father fell into place behind her, Les followed, and Peter took his place at the rear of the procession. Les welcomed the man's presence. Built like a prizefighter, he would be a help in whatever was to come. They proceeded single file up the clattertrap steps and across the porch to Dr. Tenney's front door.

Leila knocked on the door. *As though we've come to pay a social call,* Les thought. Whatever he'd expected, it had not been this direct approach.

The door swung open. Dr. Tenney's cloaked metal servant stood in the doorway. Its missing arm had been replaced.

"We wish to see your master," Leila said quietly.

The creature did not move. It continued to block the entranceway, though it made no threatening movement. Fearing for Leila, Les pushed past Hamlyn, stepped up beside her, and stretched an arm in front of her.

"Stand back!" she hissed.

At the same time, Hamlyn grabbed him from behind and pulled him back, away from Leila. "Wait!" He whispered the command in Les's ear.

The servant lurched forward, then swayed back and forth, pivoted, and trundled into the house.

Hamlyn leaned close to Les and said in a low voice, "Be ready to act on my signal. While Leila and I distract Tenney, you and Peter," he indicated the carriage driver, "get inside. You won't have long to find your friends; you'll have to run."

"What about Carl?" Les asked.

"Peter will be able to handle him. No more talk—Tenney's coming."

A cloud of odorous pipe smoke preceded the Adept. Leila stepped back and wedged herself between her father and Les. Peter stepped forward so that the four conspirators stood abreast, with Leila and Hamlyn in the center, Les and Peter at either end.

Dr. Tenney appeared in the doorway. He surveyed his visitors, his face registering no surprise, only mild amusement. "Well, well. This is quite a delegation. I wonder to what I owe such an honor." He peered through the haze of smoke, thickening it as he did so by rapid puffs on his pipe.

"Ah, I see!" he crowed delightedly. "You've brought back young Mr. Simonton so that I can proceed with his testing. How kind of you."

Hamlyn said, "Mr. Simonton is concerned about his friend, Trevor Blake. He's here to see him."

"But, Doss, you must have assured him that he has no cause for concern." Dr. Tenney paused to blow out a fresh cloud of smoke. "Now that Mr. Blake has been inducted into the Community along with his friend, Mr. Holdt, they are under my tutelage. These two fine young men will be a credit to the Community, I might add. Last evening I kept them up quite late practicing honing the focus of their power. I was rather hard on them, so I encouraged the two lads to sleep in this morning. They are not yet ready to receive visitors."

Hamlyn responded with a courtly nod. "In that case, perhaps you would be so good as to deliver an invitation from me to Mr. Blake. In honor of my friendship with his uncle and to celebrate his entrance into the Community, I would like him to dine with my daughter and me tonight." He reached into his waistcoat pocket and extracted an envelope sealed with green wax. He held it out to Dr. Tenney. "If you have no objection, we'll wait here for Mr. Blake's answer."

The Adept frowned but reached out and grasped the envelope. His thumb rested over the wax seal. Hamlyn did not

A PERILOUS POWER

release his hold; the two men stood linked, neither moving. Tenney seemed unable to break the link; a look of surprise flitted across his face.

Explosive cracks sounded throughout the house. Shards of glass rained down onto the porch roof and fell to the ground as every window burst. The house quivered; splits appeared in the walls.

"Go!" shouted Hamlyn.

Peter darted forward, through the doorway. Les followed on his heels. They raced through the hallway and up the quaking stairs. The house seemed to be tumbling down around them. Hoping Hamlyn would be able to keep the doctor immobilized, Les threw open the first door they reached on the second floor. The room was empty; he ran on, as Peter emerged from checking a room on the opposite side.

When they reached the door to Dr. Tenney's laboratory, the metal servant blocked their way. Les stopped, but Peter lunged at the thing, shoved it backward, toppled it to the ground, and jumped on top of it. His heavy boots crumpled the metal skeleton. He jumped off, and the thing tried to rise. Peter stood back and clapped his hands. A globe of green fire sprang up from his palms. He hurled it at the servant. Like lightning it danced over the twisted frame. The servant fell, twitched, and lay still.

Les made a quick circuit of the room, though he was sure it was empty except for the servant. Peter gestured, and the green fire swept up from the metal creature, gathered itself into a sphere the size of a handball, and returned to him. He hurled it toward the nearest table with its assemblage of wire and metal. It flared around the object, reduced it to slag, and sped to the item on the next table.

E. Rose Sabin

"Come on," Peter called, heading out the door. "Not much more time."

Les tore his gaze from the destroying fire and ran to help Peter search the remaining rooms. Most were bedrooms, all were empty, and in every room the mirrors had shattered and sprinkled shards of glass across the floor.

The last room they entered was the doctor's study. It was empty like the rest, but on the desk sat the jar with the captive moth inside it.

Les grabbed up the jar. The moth slid along the bottom as though dead. He grappled with the lid. The building shook.

"We have to get downstairs," Peter said. "No one's up here."

Les abandoned his attempt to open the jar and carried it with him as he raced after Peter. They descended the stairs, clutching the banister and testing each step as the wood crumbled beneath their feet. With a shout Peter jumped as the last few steps collapsed. Hugging the jar to his chest, Les leaped beside him.

They split up to search the downstairs rooms. Bits of ceiling were falling; walls gaped open where doors were locked. The rooms were empty.

Les heard Peter give a loud cry. He plunged toward the sound. In the kitchen Peter held a struggling Carl in a choke hold.

"The others?" Les asked.

"He's all I found," Peter said.

"Where are they? Trevor and Miryam?"

Carl spat. Peter tightened his grip.

"Don't strangle him. Let him speak," Les cautioned.

The house tipped and sent them skidding across the floor-

A PERILOUS POWER

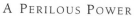

boards. It slammed them into the wall by the cast-iron stove. Then slowly the house righted itself and the sounds of disintegration ceased. They pushed away from the wall. Peter had kept his grip on Carl, and Les clutched the jar.

The cracked walls began to heal themselves. Rents in the floor closed; gaps in the ceiling melded together.

"Tenney's free," Peter said.

Carl grinned.

Had he not recognized the approaching footsteps, the reek of pipe smoke would have told Les who was coming. He could think of only one thing to do. He smashed the jar against the iron stove.

The white moth drifted to the floor amid the broken glass. Slowly, very slowly, it flexed its wings.

E. ROSE SABIN

19

TRAPS

Trevor's body was suspended in nothingness. Thick smoke filled his nostrils, reducing his breathing to short, desperate gasps.

The Adept had said only that company was coming, and as part of his cleaning to prepare for the guests he was placing Trevor and Miryam where they could not be seen. Dr. Tenney had blown pipe smoke through an odd device from his laboratory. Vibrating wires and rotating metal points had woven the smoke into a kind of cocoon into which Trevor had been drawn. He seemed to be suspended outside normal time and space, yet dimly as through a thick haze he could see persons and objects in the doctor's house.

He could also see the similar smoke shroud in which Miryam floated, though her figure was no more than a dark shadow within a gray cloud. He could do nothing to help her—he could not even help himself—so he let her slip from his mind.

Wherever he was, he had one constant point of reference: the red glow from Dr. Tenney's pipe. That point was not stationary; it moved about, and he seemed to float along with it wherever it went. It seemed that he hovered somewhere above it so that it glared up at him like a baleful red eye. Occasionally a small flame flared from it, the smoke thickened, and Trevor fell into a kind of stupor.

Shapes, vague and indefinite, moved beyond the blanket of smoke. Muted bits of color and distant murmurs of sound came to him like echoes of a dream but failed to arouse his interest.

Something jolted his cocoon, left it rocking like a rowboat in rapids. The smoke thinned, but only for a few seconds. He had a momentary vision of Doss Hamlyn and his daughter, Leila, standing face to face with Dr. Tenney. The Adept, pipe in mouth, glared at Hamlyn. Leila glanced upward, and her blue eyes seemed to linger on his face. He thought she saw him, but the smoke thickened, choking him, the vision faded, and he doubted that he'd seen anything but a hallucination.

In the hallucination someone ran. On the periphery of his vision he saw, or thought he saw, a figure dash away from Leila and Hamlyn, and he thought the runner was Les.

Les. Good old Les. If I'd only listened to you, I wouldn't be here, wouldn't have . . . Les mustn't know what happened with Carl, how he can control me. No, can't think about that. Can't think . . .

The image of Les refused to be banished. In his semiconscious state, Les's face floated with him in the void. He thought he heard Les calling his name. He tried to summon strength to answer, until he remembered he had no voice.

Another jolt followed, and, as before, a violent rocking made Trevor strain to see through the smoke. He made out the glow of Dr. Tenney's pipe; nothing else.

Not quite nothing. A vague blur swam into his line of vision. It had to be the cocoon of smoke that held Miryam.

Her shadow inside it was moving: twisting as though she was trying to escape. The blur shifted nearer.

What would happen if the two smoke prisons came together? Miryam was a healer. If he could he touch her, she could relieve the pain that still afflicted his throat.

He wriggled about, finding motion difficult, like trying to swim in gelatin. Still he persisted, and the blur filled his view. The shape within it became more clearly defined. It moved with slow, erratic waves of arms or legs.

He duplicated those motions, and the blur melded with his cocoon. He thrust his arm out, pushing against the resisting smoke, and touched something—an arm. He found the wrist, tightened his fingers around it, and pulled the body toward him.

Miryam's face became visible. Her brown hair swirled as if she were submerged in water. Her eyes were wide, frightened.

Her other hand clutched his shoulder. "Les," she whispered. "He's here. In danger. Got to help him."

She put Trevor to shame: Her first thought was for Les, not for herself. He'd been about to say—or try to say, *Heal me*. Instead he forced what he hoped was a reassuring smile, focused carefully, and attempted a sending.

If we get out of this binding, grab Les. Take him to that other place—the woods—that only you can get to.

She nodded, seemed to calm. Her grip on his shoulder relaxed into a more normal hold. She'd heard!

But he might have also increased their danger. Unless the smoke blocked the outward flow of power, Carl would have received the sending.

Trevor was considering what to do about that when, before he was prepared for it, the cocoon of smoke dissipated

A PERILOUS POWER

and he and Miryam tumbled to the floor. His arm braced to try to break the fall; his hand jammed down onto a piece of glass.

The hard landing and the pain lancing his hand distracted him. He saw where he was, but several moments passed before he could react. Miryam recovered more quickly. She jumped to her feet.

They were in the kitchen. They had fallen beside Dr. Tenney, who stood facing Les and Carl. The big man who had stood behind Doss Hamlyn and his daughter at the Community gathering now had Carl in a choke hold. Miryam ran toward Les. He halted her at arm's length and pointed to the floor between them, at something Trevor could not see.

Carl's struggles ceased and Trevor's throat tightened; the pain encircled his neck with greater force. He couldn't rise, couldn't breathe. Carl had transferred *his* pain to him.

He could manage no more than a feeble wave to Miryam to urge her to hurry, to escape with Les. He saw her crouch instead and scoop something off the floor.

"I'll thank you for that insect," Dr. Tenney said, stepping past Trevor and holding an open palm toward Miryam. "It's part of my collection."

Choking, unable to breathe, Trevor couldn't understand, couldn't see what was happening. His head swam, his lungs labored for breath. The sudden drain of power brought extreme dizziness but a removal of the added pressure on his throat. He sucked in air and willed the room to stop spinning.

Carl was free. The man who had held him lay on his back, his head against the iron stove. Blood trickled from the side of his mouth. Trevor couldn't tell whether the man was alive or dead.

Carl lunged forward, shoved Les aside, and seized Miryam. She threw up her hands, and a white moth flew toward the ceiling. Dr. Tenney grabbed for it, missed, grabbed again.

Miryam struggled in Carl's grasp. Les fought to free her. Dr. Tenney fashioned a net of smoke and cast it at the moth. No one was watching Trevor.

He spotted the large shard of glass that had cut his palm. He sat up and, with his good hand, grasped the glass. He stood slowly, unsteadily.

Dr. Tenney, his back to Trevor, flung the smoke net over the fluttering moth and with a cry of triumph reeled it in.

Trevor lunged for Dr. Tenney and drove the shard deep into the Adept's back, feeling the glass cut into his own palm. Tenney dropped the net and fell forward. He lay sprawled on the floor; a red stain spread out from the tip of glass poking through his shirt. Trevor wiped his bloody palm on his trousers and leaped at Carl, who had grabbed Miryam's wrist.

Les kicked Carl's groin. Carl yelled and doubled over, releasing Miryam.

Run, both of you! Trevor sent desperately. But again Miryam bent and found the moth, flapping feebly in the dissolving remnants of the smoke net. She placed her hand in front of it and with the other hand waved it onto her palm.

A blast of pain struck Trevor. He collapsed, groaning. Carl had again transferred his hurt. As Trevor watched helplessly, unable to move, Carl straightened and kicked Miryam's hand so that she dropped the moth. It drifted to the floor. Carl headed for it, but Les tackled him, shoved him away. Trevor felt again the drain of power, and Les collapsed into a heap on the floor.

With Carl's power concentrated on Les, Trevor could

move again. He crawled toward the moth. As he reached for it, a mouse scampered in front of him, distracting him for a fatal instant. A booted foot stomped down on the moth and ground the delicate creature into the floor. Miryam screamed.

Trevor looked up into the face of the man who had fallen against the stove. The blood on his face had dried; his face was pale, slack. Only the eyes looked alive. They glittered with a terrible triumph.

Carl stared into that face as though hypnotized. "Dr. Tenney?" he whispered.

Trevor staggered to his feet and hauled Les up. "We've got to get away," he rasped.

Miryam caught hold of Les's hand and tugged him toward the door. Trevor followed. He was right behind Les as Miryam led them into the next room. But the muscles in his legs locked, halting him. The pressure on his throat tightened so that he couldn't call out. He could only watch helplessly as Les and Miryam ran down the corridor toward the front door.

Trevor was no longer with them. Les realized it as he and Miryam raced through the front door. He turned, saw Trevor standing frozen at the far end of the hall, hands tearing at his throat. He started back, but Miryam's outcry stopped him. He stepped out onto the porch.

Doss Hamlyn lay stretched out, unconscious. Leila knelt beside him, weeping and stroking his hand. Miryam dropped down beside her, felt for a pulse in the man's neck. "He's alive," she said. "I can help him. I'm a healer." She pushed Leila out of the way and bent over Hamlyn.

Les helped Leila to her feet. "Are you all right?" he asked.

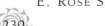

She didn't answer. Her blue eyes gazed at him with a vacant, childish stare.

"Miryam, something's wrong with Leila, too," Les said. "We've got to get her and her father out of here. If we can make it to the carriage . . ."

The carriage stood at the curb, the horses waiting patiently, flicking flies with their tails.

Hamlyn groaned and sat up.

Miryam slipped her arm beneath Hamlyn's shoulders and helped him to his feet. "He needs more healing," she said. "I don't have the time or the strength right now."

Les guided Leila and did what he could to help Miryam with Hamlyn. They reached the carriage, got the door open, pushed Leila inside, and lifted Hamlyn in after her.

"I'll drive. I can manage horses," Les said.

Miryam got into the carriage, and Les clambered up onto the driver's seat and took the reins. He urged the horses into motion.

They pranced ahead a few steps, whinnied, tossed their heads, and stopped. Les looked toward the house. The big man stood on the porch, Carl beside him, supporting Trevor, who seemed to be unconscious.

The horses reared and screamed with fear but refused to move forward.

Miryam called to him from the other side of the carriage. "It's no use, Les. Climb down here. Hurry."

He jumped down beside her. She pulled Leila from the carriage, held her by the hand. "Hold her other hand and don't let go," Miryam instructed. "I'll try to take us through to the secret woods."

"What about Hamlyn?"

"We'll have to leave him."

A PERILOUS POWER

Leila began a mournful keening. Miryam clamped a hand over her mouth. "Hush, dear. Quiet," she cautioned.

Leading Leila and Les, Miryam set out at a slow, deliberate pace across the road and into the empty field on the other side, walking in a straight line from the carriage so the vehicle would shield them from the view of the watchers on the porch.

One of those watchers gave a shout. The horses whinnied and broke into a wild run. The carriage clattered and rocked along the rough stone street, bearing Doss Hamlyn with it.

Behind him Les heard someone running toward them. The steps drew near, then grew more distant, though they did not seem to slow and Miryam did not quicken her pace.

They walked into a cold, gray mist and out of it onto a tree-shaded path. A soft sense of peace settled about them. It was near dusk, and birds sang sleepy melodies from the woods. Miryam led them on until she reached the clearing where they had paused before.

"We made it," she said. "I don't think they can follow us here." Dropping Leila's hand, she sank wearily to the ground beside a large tree root.

Leila gazed about in bewilderment. "Where . . . ?"

"It's another place, another world," Miryam answered.

Leila gave her an uncomprehending look.

"Dr. Tenney's done something to her mind," Miryam said. "I don't know if I can heal her. I'll try, but I have to rest first. Don't let her wander off." She leaned her head against the tree root and closed her eyes.

Les felt tired and shaky, too, but he dared not follow Miryam's example. He held on to Leila and walked around the clearing. His mind was in turmoil. He kept seeing that thick-soled boot smashing the moth, grinding it to nothing.

E. ROSE SABIN

How could Veronica have let herself be trapped and killed?

And Trevor. Dark shadows had ringed Trevor's eyes; a nasty red gash circled his neck. He'd been shirtless, his chest and back bathed in blood. He'd looked half dead. Yet he'd found the courage and strength to drive that glass into Tenney's back.

Peter would not have crushed the moth, nor would he have gone to Carl's aid. The real Peter must be dead; Tenney must have been badly injured and had overcome that injury by transferring his consciousness into Peter's body.

If Tenney could save himself in that way, Veronica might have avoided death. She was as strong as Tenney; stronger, maybe.

He remembered that a mouse had scampered across the floor just before Trevor could rescue the moth. He recalled Veronica telling him that her consciousness rode in the moth. It was possible that she had transferred it to the mouse in that fateful moment.

His grip on Leila's hand loosened.

"Veronica," he said softly. Then louder, "Veronica. If you're alive, hear me, please. We need your help more than ever."

From deep within the woods an owl hooted. Leila pulled her hand from his and dashed into the woods. Les sped after her, but she leaped and dodged like a frightened foal. He ran into a spiderweb, brushed its sticky strands from his face and hair, and rushed on. A branch caught his hair; he paused to disentangle it.

He could no longer see Leila in the closeness of the woods and the gathering darkness. Bushes rustled to his right. He made his way in that direction, shouting her name.

A chorus of night insects snapped on as if cued by an

A PERILOUS POWER

invisible conductor. No other sound answered his frantic cries. He kept going, kept calling, refusing to abandon the search.

He heard a splash. The creek! He remembered seeing it before. Leila might have fallen in. He ran toward the sound, tripped over a tree root, fell, picked himself up, and limped forward a few more steps.

The gurgle of the creek alerted him in time to keep himself from toppling in. Anxiously he scanned the dark water for Leila's blue skirt. Seeing nothing, he lifted his gaze to the far bank.

Moonlight fell on a grassy strip that sloped up toward another stand of trees. Leila was seated on the grass; in front of her stood a large white owl.

The owl's head swiveled to meet Les's astonished gaze. "Who-ooo," it said.

Leila giggled.

"Veronica?" Les breathed the question.

20

Plots and Counterplots

With a suddenness that nearly toppled him, Trevor could move again. More important, freed from the paralysis that had descended not only on his body but on his mind as well, he could think.

Leila *had* been here. And her father. They had come to help him, though he hadn't responded to the note they'd given him when Tenney had presented him and Carl to the Community. Les must have brought them. Because he had been here, too—and had escaped again.

With no power, Les had done what Trevor with all his power could not do. But Les had Miryam's help, while his own power was bound to Carl.

Trevor's throat tightened from the pain that Carl was sending to compensate for his hurt pride and for his mistreatment by Les and the man whose body Dr. Tenney had taken.

In that body, Dr. Tenney paced back and forth in the empty downstairs room to which he'd taken them when it became clear that Les, Miryam, and Leila had evaded him.

"Clever they were, too clever," he muttered, stopping to pick up a pipe and fill it. "Almost had me. Shouldn't have been able to do that. Left me too weak to stop 'em from getting away. Not used to this body, have to learn to manipulate it."

He lit the pipe, drew in, and was struck with a fit of coughing. "Damnably annoying," the Adept muttered when the coughing subsided. "Should have remembered that Peter never smoked. It'll take some getting used to before I can enjoy my pipe again. Another thing to hold against him and his friends."

He resumed pacing, wearing a clear trail through the dust that covered the floor. As he passed Trevor, he glared. "Lucky for you young Peter was handy. It was a simple matter for me to slip into his body and take it over. Otherwise I would have grabbed yours. No chance of them actually killing me, though they did a good bit of harm. This body is younger and healthier, but I prefer my own. More used to it."

Unable to speak, Trevor could only turn his head to show his contempt. Against his will, his head turned back so that his gaze again met the Adept's.

Tenney continued, "When I find Carl's sister, I'll force her to heal my body so I can get back into it. Then they'll pay for what they've done, and so will you. Second time you've tried to kill me. Thought you'd learned your lesson after that first time. You'll learn this time, no question about it." He headed for the stairs. "Come with me," he called over his shoulder.

In spite of his difficulty breathing, Trevor had to respond to Tenney's command. He marched after the Adept like an automaton. Carl stalked beside him, sending him furious glances along with stabs of pain throughout his body.

Dr. Tenney led them into his laboratory. In front of the

doctor lay the twisted and partially melted remains of his metal servant. Beyond that ruined figure lay overturned tables, the devices that had been on them scattered, broken, and burned.

Tenney shook his head sadly. "This will have been Peter's work," he said. "He was always creative with his manipulation of fire." He stepped over the crushed servant and picked his way through the debris, stopped to pick up a strip of metal and a mangled length of wire. "Well, he's paying for it."

Carl looked startled. "You mean that guy you took over wasn't dead after I slammed him against the stove?"

"No, of course not," the doctor answered impatiently while righting tables and placing on them the ruined remnants of his machines. "It would have done me no good to go from an injured body to a dead one. You know I'm not a healer. Peter was only unconscious."

"So what happened to him when you took over his body?" Carl persisted. "Didn't that kill him?"

"No, he'll survive as long as his body does. His essence exists in a diffuse state, only semiconscious, but able, I trust, to suffer. Tch! Look at this!" He interrupted his explanation to pick up the cylindrical device he'd used to transport Trevor and Miryam to this laboratory. The cylinder was crushed flat and disconnected from the base, which was still relatively intact.

The Adept examined it intently. "It will take a good deal of work, but this might be reparable." His gaze roved over the other debris, and he shook his head. "I'm afraid there's little else that is."

Trevor was not interested in the condition of the doctor's machinery. He was fascinated by the information Dr. Tenney

A PERILOUS POWER

had imparted about the man whose body the Adept had taken over. It might be possible to save that man and drive the doctor out of his body.

It might, but not by any power of Trevor's.

Dr. Tenney kicked a piece of broken glass, sent it scudding across the floor. Trevor glanced at it and was reminded of the moth, freed from the jar only to be so callously crushed. Veronica might have had the ability to dispossess the doctor, if she had survived.

Dr. Tenney returned from his walk through the wreckage and confronted Trevor and Carl. "All my enhancers, destroyed," he said angrily. "So much work, gone in seconds. I wonder if they think that will stop me. If so, they've made a fatal error."

He rubbed his hands together and gazed intently first into Trevor's eyes, then into Carl's. "These mechanical power enhancers were efficient but not the best. No, the best enhancers are the human variety." His twisted smile turned Peter's handsome face into a demon's visage. "That's a secret Carl knows well, don't you, my friend?"

Carl didn't answer.

Dr. Tenney chuckled. "Human enhancers, all under my control, all contributing their diverse gifts to the power pool that *I* alone may draw from. That's far better than anything my enemies have destroyed here." With a broad wave of his hand, he dismissed the ruined laboratory.

"Come." He beckoned, and Carl and Trevor fell into step behind him as he strode from the laboratory and went down the hall to his study. "I'll call a meeting of the Community. It's time I put those dilettantes to good use."

He sat down at his desk and took out paper and pen. While Trevor stood behind his chair, helpless to move except

at the Adept's command, and Carl watched from a distance, Dr. Tenney penned one letter after another. "Think of it," he said cheerfully as he wrote. "A whole crowd of gifted, ready to do my bidding. I can transform them all into my personal enhancers. There's nothing I can't do, nothing I can't have, when I control the Community. And you, my young friends, will have the privilege of facilitating that control."

He paused, blotted the ink on his latest note, and turned to look at the two young men, the terrible smile again distorting Peter's face. "Hamlyn has headed up the opposition to me, he and that gifted daughter of his. But they're out of the way. Their attack on me left them open to my counterattack. I doubt Leila has much of a mind left, and Hamlyn is in no condition to attend a meeting. He may recover, but I don't intend to wait for that. I'll act before my enemies have a chance to regroup."

He carefully folded the letters he'd written and set himself to writing more. "These will go to every member of the Community," he explained. "I'm requesting a meeting tomorrow at noon at a home where we often meet because it has a garden large enough to accommodate us all. Of course, 'I' will be unable to attend, and I trust that Doss Hamlyn will be similarly indisposed. However, his friend and employee, Peter Loftman, will attend in his place. And you, Carl, will be Dr. Tenney's representative. You do excel at deception; you should have no difficulty in convincing my partisans to accede to my request."

Carl perked up, peeled himself away from the wall he'd been leaning against, and stepped forward. "What request is that?" he asked.

"To spare you some of their power for a struggle against forces that would destroy the Community," Dr. Tenney ex-

A PERILOUS POWER

plained as he continued to write his invitations.

"And if they ask what forces those are?" Carl was asking the questions Trevor would have asked, had he been able to speak.

"Forces led by that witch, Veronica. It's well known that she opposes the Community as it is now, though she was a leading part of it at one time."

Yes, Trevor thought bitterly, *and if I'd believed what she told me about it, I wouldn't be in this mess.*

"You may say that both Doss Hamlyn's illness and my indisposition are due to her machinations," Dr. Tenney continued. He chuckled and added, looking disgustingly pleased, "That's true in a sense. If she had not interfered, none of this would have come about. She's done me a great favor; pity she'll never know it."

That reminder of the crushing of the moth turned Trevor's stomach.

"What's his part in this?" Carl asked, jerking his thumb toward Trevor.

"Ah, yes, we mustn't forget him, must we?" Dr. Tenney smirked at Trevor. "He plays a very important part—a dual role. First, his power will be at your disposal, enabling you to exercise your gift to the fullest. As each person opens himself to allow you to take a portion of power, you will draw on Trevor for the strength you need to take it all. You cannot keep that power, which brings us to our friend's secondary role. Even an Adept cannot be everywhere and see everything at once, so our Mr. Blake will be the link between us, preventing you, with your own thirst for power, from holding back some of what you take. He will serve as a conduit, the power draining from you, and immediately flowing through him to me. That will take place because of the link

I created between you and because I control you both. However, I do not mean to leave you powerless, my boy. When you have completed your task, you may drain all that remains of Trevor's power; it will be my gift to you, a reward for doing a good job."

Carl grinned at that prospect. Trevor was helpless to protest, not that a protest would have been of any use. He'd been reduced to nothing more than an instrument to aid Dr. Tenney in achieving his purpose.

The Adept left no doubt as to what that purpose was. "By tomorrow night," he said, "the entire Community will be under my control, and all its combined power will be mine. With that power there is nothing I cannot accomplish. I can rule the country if I so desire."

By now he had a sizable stack of folded papers. He rose from his desk chair. "Now, Carl, be a good boy and go fetch us a carriage," he said. "Then you will both accompany me and help deliver these invitations."

He's got to be stopped, Trevor thought as they awaited Carl's return. *I can't kill him directly, but if Carl and I died suddenly while he's linked to us by the power channeled through us, I think it would weaken him—maybe kill him.*

I've got to try it. Carl will kill me anyway when he's taken all my power. I'd rather die in a way that will stop Tenney.

It was a weak plan, but he could think of no other. Nor could he think of a way to accomplish it, with Tenney allowing him no freedom of movement and Carl controlling his power.

He had to find something, some talent that lay outside Carl's ability to control.

Carl returned and announced the arrival of the carriage. Dr. Tenney escorted Trevor from the house, dickered with

A PERILOUS POWER

the driver, and settled himself and his two companions into the carriage for the ride into town.

As the horse clopped along, Trevor reviewed every way in which he'd ever used his power. Summoning Les to his side had been his most frequent use, but Carl had a firm lock on his sending ability. Equally bound was his gift of drawing objects to him or throwing them at a distant target. Likewise, he was blocked from bending metal as he had bent the pistol in the first mate's hands to escape being kidnapped and from augmenting his physical strength as he had done when he leaped from the ship to the dock.

Dr. Tenney leaned out the side of the carriage and shouted, "Hurry, driver. It looks like rain." A clap of thunder emphasized his words.

"Horse be going fast as it can, sir," the driver shouted back.

Dr. Tenney scowled, and Trevor feared the Adept was about to endanger another horse. But the doctor merely sat and chewed savagely on the stem of his unlit pipe.

A second thunderclap made Carl swear and peer out at the darkening sky.

Trevor remembered the storm he'd helped Aunt Ellen call the night the townspeople tried to attack them. The talent had been mostly Aunt Ellen's, but she'd said she wouldn't have been able to bring it without his help. He remembered how he'd pictured rain, how he'd imaged a hard, driving, crop-breaking rain. And the rain had come and saved them.

He thought rain. Thought a sudden clothes-soaking, street-flooding shower.

Rain fell in a wild, drenching burst. He couldn't tell whether he had brought it. The weather had already been threatening; the thunderclaps had heralded the nearness of the storm. It could be only coincidence that the rain had begun when it had. Certainly neither Carl nor Dr. Tenney acted as though the rain was unexpected or unusual—only annoying, since it meant that they must deliver the invitations in the rain.

He might have had nothing to do with the downpour, but Trevor had to think that he had, and that he could do it again; that when they attended the meeting Dr. Tenney had called, he could bring a lightning strike on Dr. Tenney, and on Carl and himself, too, if need be. Death would be a small price to pay to defeat the evil Adept.

Les called out, but after that single "who-ooo," neither the owl nor Leila paid him any attention. Yet he remained convinced that the owl was no ordinary bird.

"Les!"

He jumped and turned to see Miryam come through the woods. She ran to his arms. "Oh, Les, I had the most awful dream, and when I woke and you were gone, I thought . . ." She sobbed and bent her head to hide her face against his shoulder.

He held her close. "Shhh. It's all right. I'm safe and so are you."

Gradually her sobs subsided. She looked up. "I'm sorry. I feel foolish, but the dream was so vivid . . ."

"It was only a dream. Look, over there. It's Leila, but I don't know how she got across the stream. And that owl. I wonder if it could be Veronica."

Miryam's gaze followed his pointing finger. She smiled through her tears. "That's certainly no ordinary owl. Come with me. The brook is deep here, but I know a place where we can ford it."

A PERILOUS POWER

"Leila, stay where you are, please," Les called, hoping that she could understand. "Miryam and I are coming."

Miryam led him back into the woods and along a twisting path from which the brook was no longer visible. He feared that Leila and the owl would disappear before they reached them. They crossed the brook at a narrow spot where stones provided a slippery but passable bridge.

Once on the other side, they headed back at a fast trot to where they had seen Leila. To Les's relief, she was still sitting in front of the owl. The large white bird flapped its wings as they neared but did not fly away. He got onto his knees before it.

"Veronica?" Les asked hesitantly.

The bird's solemn regard was his only answer. Miryam hurried to Leila, sat beside her, and placed her hand on the girl's forehead. The girl shifted her gaze from the owl and regarded Miryam with a childlike trust. Les glanced at them, then turned his attention back to the owl.

"Veronica, if it is you, won't you give me some sign?" he pleaded. "Why are you in that form? Did Dr. Tenney do something to you? Can't you change to your human form?"

"Whoo-ooo-ooo," said the owl.

"You're not really an owl," Les persisted. "If you were, you would have flown away."

Again the bird flapped its wings and said, "Who-ooo-ooo."

"Can't you say anything else?"

The bird balanced on one foot and stretched the talons of the other, switched feet, and repeated the action.

"What's that supposed to mean?" Les said. "I asked for a sign, but I need something I can understand."

"Who-ooo?"

E. ROSE SABIN

"That sounds like a question. Maybe you've forgotten who you are. But how could that be? Please, Veronica, don't play games with us."

"That isn't Veronica," said a voice behind him.

He turned and saw Leila gazing at him with recognition and intelligence back in her eyes. She pressed one hand over the hand Miryam held clamped to her forehead.

"Who is it, then?" he asked.

"I'm not sure," Leila said. "I think—Did something happen to Peter?"

Les told her of the struggle in the kitchen, of how Trevor's attempt to kill Dr. Tenney had led the Adept to appropriate Peter's unconscious body. He told her of the crushing of the moth.

Leila shook her head. "So much happened, and I didn't know. But Veronica would not be easy to kill."

"I don't see how she could have survived. Unless . . . There was one thing," Les recalled, frowning. "I did see a mouse run past just before Tenney ground the moth into the floorboards."

"Aha!" Leila exclaimed. "That's just what she would do—transfer her consciousness to something else. No doubt she escaped and is now back in her own form."

"But where is she?" Les demanded. "And who is this owl?"

"I'm sure it's Peter. Veronica must have transferred his essence and brought him here to protect him from Dr. Tenney. But tell me everything that happened after Dr. Tenney shut down my mind. What about Trevor? Is he safe?"

"Tenney still has him," Les said, and told her how they'd escaped, but that Trevor had been unable to run with them and had urged them to go on without him.

"I wanted to go back for him." He fought to keep his voice

steady. "Miryam called me. She needed help with you and your father."

"My father! Is he alive?"

"He lives," Miryam put in before Les could answer. She sounded tired and weak; she must have used up her strength healing Leila. No wonder she'd been so quiet.

"Where is he?" Leila asked. "Not in Tenney's hands, is he?"

Miryam told her of leaving Doss Hamlyn in the carriage. "The horses ran with it. I don't think Tenney and Carl could have stopped it. They'd already used so much power that they couldn't do much. That wouldn't have lasted long, but it would have given time for your father to reach a place of safety. As it gave us time to get here." Her hand fell away from Leila's forehead. She leaned back, her eyes closed.

Les hurried to her, supported her in his arms. "You need to rest," he said. "And we have to find Veronica."

"I can't do anything until I regain my strength. Then I'll try to take us through to Veronica's house. That's where she's probably gone."

Leila clasped Miryam's hands. "You've exhausted yourself tending me. Let me help you. I'm not a healer, but I can lend you power." She glanced nervously at the surrounding woods. "I don't think it's safe to stay here at night."

"What about the owl—er, Peter?" Les asked. "Do we take him with us? An owl should be safe here."

"I think we should take him," Leila said. "Is that what you want, Peter?"

"Who-ooo," said the owl emphatically.

Miryam sat up. "Taking you all through won't be easy. But Leila and I can rest at Veronica's. I suppose we should go now."

She joined hands with Les and Leila. Leila stretched out her arm, and the owl flew onto it. They moved along the bank of the stream, the owl staying on Leila's arm. They had not gone far before entering the familiar grayness that obliterated sight and sound.

It seemed that the transfer from one world to another took longer than it had before, perhaps because Miryam was weaker. Les had begun to fear that they were lost in the nothingness between worlds when light burst around them.

They stood among small tables, while bundles of herbs hung from cords over their heads. Les felt the soft springiness of fur beneath his feet. A wonderful aroma of stewing vegetables made his mouth water.

"About time you got here!" Veronica bustled over to them wearing a white apron and brandishing a long spoon. "What took you so long?"

The owl flew up from Leila's arm and coasted to the floor on outspread wings. Leila dropped Les's hand and with a small sigh slipped to the floor beside the owl. Miryam remained standing but swayed with weariness.

"Wore yourselves out, did you? And at that you left Trevor, so I don't know what good your wild foray did." She shook the spoon in Les's face.

The owl's feathers bristled; it flapped its wings. "Who-ooo-ooo," it said in a menacing tone.

"Why have you brought that bird here? It was safe enough in the woods."

"It wanted to come with us," Les said, taken aback by her scolding. "We thought—it is Peter, isn't it?"

"So, figured that out, did you? Well, Peter's consciousness is in it, sharing the owl's mind and overriding its instincts. I suppose he might as well stay. We have to get his body back. Which means I have to take on Dr. Tenney. I expected that sooner or later." She turned and stalked to the stove, thrust the spoon into the bubbling pot.

Les followed her. "We did get Miryam, so it wasn't a useless attempt. We almost got Trevor, but Dr. Tenney did something to him so he couldn't move."

"Miryam would have been safe if you'd stayed here as I told you instead of traipsing off on your own," Veronica snapped, stirring the soup with a vigor that sent splatters of hot liquid flying about.

Les backed away and bumped into Miryam, who'd come up behind him. She put her hands on his shoulders and whispered into his ear, "She's not as angry as she sounds. She's worried."

"I'm worried, all right," Veronica said, taking out the spoon and again shaking it at Les and Miryam. "I've stayed away from the Community since it became an exclusive club with Berne Tenney wielding so much influence, but now I'll have to get involved. He has to be stopped.

"And you, Les. I keep warning you Trevor'll be the death of you. You won't listen." She sighed and turned to pick up bowls stacked on a nearby table. "No help for it," she said, ladling soup into the bowls. "Eat and rest while you can. Tomorrow will see this whole thing settled, one way or another."

21

Death Storm

The Community met at the house Dr. Tenney specified in the message Carl and Trevor had helped him deliver the previous evening. A gravel walkway led along the side of the host's home and through a gate in a stone wall. The wall and the row of poplar trees bordering the garden prevented any curious normals from observing the meeting.

More than twenty members were already gathered when Dr. Tenney ushered Carl and Trevor through the gate and along the paths winding through the neat flowerbeds and past sparkling fountains.

As still more members arrived, Dr. Tenney moved off, working the crowd—shaking hands, slapping backs, bowing over ladies' hands. Trevor could not hear the conversations; he could not tell whether the doctor was recognized. Most likely the Community merely accepted him as Peter, a fellow member and Hamlyn's friend.

Not a cloud marred the expanse of blue sky above them. It would be difficult to conjure storm clouds out of a clear sky, especially with Carl draining his power. Still, Trevor was determined to try. With no allies here, he would have to act alone, surrounded by gifted, who might easily detect his attempt. He could see no chance of success, yet he closed his eyes and concentrated on clouds, wind, rain. Lightning.

A sharp nudge in the ribs broke his concentration. "What are you doing?" Carl demanded.

Trevor feigned innocence and shrugged his shoulders to convey lack of understanding.

Carl scowled. "You can't use your power, you know that. You can't move or talk, either, so I don't know what you think you *can* do. But you're up to something. It's tickling my brain. And I don't intend to let you interfere with Dr. Tenney's plans."

Trevor continued his innocent act, though he didn't suppose Carl was deceived. Yet the fact that Carl knew he was doing *something* but couldn't seem to tell *what* gave Trevor reason to hope.

He waited until someone greeted them and Carl returned the greeting with a false smile and ingratiating manner. Taking advantage of Carl's momentary distraction, Trevor formed mental images of fast-moving clouds, white at first, but growing darker until they blackened and spawned lightning bolts and thunderclaps.

He didn't have to scan the sky to know his image was not becoming reality. Sunlight glistened in the water of the fountains and played over the flowers, bringing out the brilliance of their colors, providing an idyllic setting for Dr. Tenney's cruel plan.

In Doss Hamlyn's absence the opposition to Tenney seemed ready to accept the supposed Peter as their spokesman, judging by the nods and exchanged handshakes Trevor saw each time he glanced toward the doctor.

Carl gave Trevor a warning glare and moved off in the opposite direction from the Adept, working the crowd in much the same way. Trevor followed his role of nodding and forcing a smile when anyone spoke to him, then moving away as though needing to speak to someone else.

He didn't have much time; he must do what he could while Carl was busy elsewhere. Again he sent a mental probe skyward, searching, pleading for storm clouds. The sky remained cloudless.

Dr. Tenney headed toward him. Trevor steeled himself for the punishment he was certain was coming. But when Dr. Tenney reached his side, he said, "It's going well, my lad. I think it's time to put my plan into effect."

The Adept stepped up on a bench so that all could see him and raised his hands to signal a desire to address the assembly.

As the members ceased their conversations to listen, Trevor again stabbed a mental probe skyward, searching, pleading for a storm. Carl joined the doctor but said nothing to Trevor. Either he no longer sensed Trevor's efforts or he did not think them worthy of concern. He kept his attention fixed on Tenney.

Trevor also listened to the doctor's discourse, but at the same time he intensified his probe.

"My friends," the doctor began, "I am addressing you today on behalf of Dr. Tenney and of Doss Hamlyn."

Dr. Tenney must assume that they all accepted him as Peter.

"Neither the doctor nor my esteemed employer is able to be present," Dr. Tenney continued. "Both have suffered serious harm at the hands of one not of this company, one who has used the power of an Adept to meddle in affairs not hers and to stir up strife and dissension in these august ranks."

He's talking about Veronica, Trevor thought. *Veronica died when the moth was crushed—didn't she?* But these people didn't know that. The doctor was using Veronica as a rallying point, a means of getting the Community to act together against a perceived danger.

If Veronica *had* avoided destruction, Trevor could not expect her to help him. She'd protect Les and Miryam if she could, but she had no reason to do anything for him. He aimed another bolt of power at the unchanging blue sky.

Maybe I never really had the talent to do this. Maybe Aunt Ellen called the storm, and only let me think I helped. I'm fooling myself, clutching at straws, when I know it's impossible to stop Dr. Tenney.

His call for rain, his picture of a stormy sky, grew hazy, halfhearted. He heard Dr. Tenney say, "Doss Hamlyn and Dr. Tenney have put aside their personal differences and have asked me to request that you all do likewise. On their behalf, I ask you to pledge your assistance in combating this threat to our existence as a Community and possibly to our independent use of power, as well. You all know of Veronica Crowell's disdain for the Community; she's made no secret of it since her withdrawal from our ranks. But until recently she has been content to ignore us. Now, however, she has taken action against us. The woman is extremely dangerous. You can imagine what power she possesses to have been able to damage both Hamlyn and Tenney. Who among us has as much power as they? We can defeat her only by acting in concert." He let his solemn gaze wander over the audience.

He must have judged the reaction to be favorable; he motioned Carl to his side. "Carl Holdt, here, will move among you, and if you agree to help destroy this evil, you have only to clasp his hand as a token of your willingness to cooperate."

This was Trevor's last chance. He strengthened his storm image. A wisp of white cloud floated into sight above the treetops. No touch of rain about it, but it provided a focus for his desperate probes.

Carl moved off, while Dr. Tenney remained on the bench watching Carl's progress. Trevor expected someone to have enough talent to see through the deception. The Community must include truth readers. But they must not be exercising that talent. Convinced by the testimony of their eyes, they accepted the man who'd spoken to them as Peter and fell into the trap he'd set for them. One by one, each member offered a hand to Carl.

And each time Carl clasped a hand, a jolt shook Trevor. He felt first a surge of power and then a rapid drain that left him light-headed. He'd barely caught his breath after the first time when it happened again. And again.

Trevor glanced upward. The small cloud had drifted nearer the zenith, but it had not enlarged or darkened. But if he could grasp power as it surged through him . . .

Another jolt. Another surge. *Storm!* he thought, visualizing lightning and pounding rain.

Trevor did this no more than four times before Carl stopped his circuit of the members to go to Dr. Tenney and motion him to step off the bench. When the doctor did so, Carl whispered something to him.

Trevor staggered. The power band tightened, and he gasped for breath. A sensation crawled over him like that produced by Carl's hated touch. He opened his mouth, but pain gagged him, wouldn't let him make a sound.

All the shame, the agony, the hatred swarmed into the white cloud, turning it black, swelling it.

Pain drove Trevor to his knees. Carl and Dr. Tenney approached him, and Carl yanked him to his feet.

"Think you're clever, do you," he whispered into Trevor's ear. "Think I can't tell that you're grabbing power? You'll suffer for that."

"Fool!" was Dr. Tenney's single comment.

Pain twisted through Trevor, though Tenney's power held him upright, not letting him fall. He suffered again the indignity of Carl's forcing him to flog and then tear at himself. Held motionless, he sent a mental cry upward into the cloud.

A clap of thunder made eyes turn upward to cast worried looks at the sky.

"Come, hurry," Dr. Tenney urged, climbing back onto the bench. "We can complete this meeting before the rain begins."

Carl left Trevor and passed again among the group, shaking hands.

With each handshake, a great weakness swept over Trevor. The power drain was more than he could bear. Agony thrust into him, flame burst through him. His back arched; his head fell back; his eyes stared at a sky filling with black clouds.

A clap of thunder boomed from the clouds.

Dr. Tenney jumped off the bench and hurried to Trevor's side. Carl reached him only a moment later. "Kill him!" the doctor ordered.

The band around Trevor's throat tightened so that he could no longer breathe. His body felt aflame. He hurled his pain and desperation skyward.

A bolt of lightning set the sky ablaze. Its fire answered the fire in Trevor's body. Light blinded his eyes. He heard no thunder.

*   *   *

Veronica took her hands from the crystal she'd been staring into for what seemed hours. "It is time," she said.

Finally.

Miryam clasped Les's hand. Leila bent and placed her hands on the shoulders of the owl. They huddled together, and Veronica joined them.

"Remember," she said, her gaze boring into Les, "the gift of power is never lightly given. The recipient may use the gift, misuse it, or reject it. The Power-Giver bestows wisely, but we do not always receive wisely. Seek wisdom before you act."

He had no idea what she was trying to tell him. This was no time for lectures. "Let's go," he said.

Veronica's forefinger traced a large rectangle in the air in front of them. A door materialized. Veronica pushed it open and motioned them through.

They were on a city street, standing in front of a gate in a wall. Veronica pulled her door shut behind them. "Unlatch the gate and go in," she said.

Miryam opened the gate. The owl flew in, and they all followed.

Storm clouds gathered overhead. A peal of thunder rang out, startling the owl. It flapped its wings and said, "Who-ooo-ooo."

"Move forward," Veronica urged. "Hurry."

Les could hear a babble of voices farther in. He took the lead and followed a path that wound through poplars and issued out into an open area dotted with flowerbeds and fountains.

People milled about in confusion, taking no notice of the

new arrivals but blocking their path and their view. Les pushed his way through them, trusting the others to follow. Spatters of rain struck his face and arms.

Once through the crowd, he saw Dr. Tenney, in Peter's usurped body, standing under a large mulberry tree. Carl stood beside him, looking down. Les drew closer. Only then did he see Trevor lying on the ground between Carl and Dr. Tenney. Les hurried toward them. Miryam caught hold of Les's hand and ran with him.

Dr. Tenney looked at them and scowled. Les was halted, unable to move closer. Trevor's body arched and spasmed. Miryam released Les's hand and ran on. Shouting, "Stop that!" she hurled herself at Carl.

A massive lightning bolt streaked down and struck the ground with a force that knocked Les backward. An enormous clap of thunder deafened him, left shock waves vibrating through him.

He struggled to a sitting position, clapped his hands to his ears, and squinted to see through the afterglow.

The ground beneath the mulberry tree was littered with inert forms: Carl, Trevor, Dr. Tenney's usurped body. Miryam!

Les staggered to his feet. He lurched to Miryam's side, bent, searched for a pulse. Nothing.

He knelt beside Trevor; his friend was not breathing.

He stood and howled, "Why? Why did we wait so long? Why did we come too late?"

Inside his mind a voice whispered, *It is not too late if you use your gift.*

"Veronica!" he shouted.

The small woman hurried up to him.

"What's my gift?" he demanded. "Tell me."

"I think you know what it is," Veronica replied. "You have only to decide whether to use it. No one can make that decision for you."

22

GIFTED

Les knelt beside Miryam, lifted her lifeless body in his arms, and kissed her lips. Gently he lowered her and went to Trevor. "We swore we'd stand by each other, no matter what," he said to his friend's still form. "You promised to help me find my gift. I think you have."

He sat on the ground between Trevor and Miryam. Within his mind the lightning bolt had etched a picture framed in fire. Vividly he saw four figures climbing a long ramp. Miryam and Trevor walked together, while Carl and Dr. Tenney in Peter's body trudged along behind them as if forced to take each unwilling step. Trevor and Miryam climbed joyfully toward an immense being poised at the top of the ramp. Clothed in brilliant light, the being played a haunting air on a reed pipe. Its form seemed human to Les until he saw that its legs were hairy, shaped like goat's legs, and its feet were cloven hooves.

It ceased its piping, stood, and raised its arms as if to embrace the two who approached. But its golden eyes, terrible and beautiful, were fixed on Les. *Come if you will,* it seemed to say.

You will accept me in exchange for them? Les did not voice the question; the being had no need of spoken words.

You have that gift—the gift of trading death for life. You must act now, and for them all.

All? I have to restore Carl and Dr. Tenney along with Trevor and Miryam?

The being nodded gravely. *They come together; they must depart together.*

Trevor and Miryam drew near the top of the ramp.

The exchange, if it is to be made, must occur now, the being sent. *How do you choose?*

"Miryam, Trev," Les murmured. "I can't let you die."

The being smiled. *Death is not the most terrible fate. They have so much to offer in life.*

Then choose.

Les thrust his own image into the picture. He raced up the ramp, careened past Carl and the doctor, caught up with Trevor and Miryam, and dodged around them to stand between them and the welcoming being. They stared at him in amazement. He spread his arms to block their movement. "Go back!"

They opened their mouths as though they would have argued, and Miryam did cry out, "No, Les!" But the ramp dropped away abruptly, leaving Les standing on a flat surface, while the others slid down a sharp decline.

He watched them disappear into the distance below, turned, and entered the embrace of the glowing one.

Trevor's head throbbed. Light filled his eyes, so that he saw only a brilliant glow. The ground beneath him was wet and smelled of recent rain, though no rain was falling now.

Arms supported him and raised him to a sitting position, though he would have preferred to lie still. Hands encircled his neck, and he wondered whether the torture was about to begin again.

No! The power band was gone and he was breathing freely. Someone raised a glass of water to his lips, and he drank with an ease he had not known since Dr. Tenney had punished him.

Nearby a woman broke into loud sobs. He thought that strange, since it was clear that rescuers had arrived.

"Shut up, Miryam! Be glad you're alive."

That was Carl. The lightning had struck. He should be dead. He and Dr. Tenney. Trevor shook his head to clear it.

"Careful, Trevor. You're not yet fully healed." Veronica's voice.

He blinked, the light dimmed, and he was able to distinguish shapes through a golden haze.

Dr. Tenney wasn't dead! Trevor made out the tall form of the Adept's stolen body. Leila, Doss Hamlyn's pretty daughter, stood beside him. He had to warn her that the man in that body was not her father's trusted friend.

"Be still," Veronica ordered when he struggled to rise. She was behind him, supporting his back. "You can do nothing to help here. You need to rest and let your power come back. I must help the others. You will serve best by staying out of the way and letting Leila and me work, and Miryam, when she's able."

Miryam. That was who was crying. Trevor tried to turn, but Veronica prevented him. "Don't move, just rest," she said. "And don't worry about Carl. I've severed the bond between you. He can't touch you."

He remembered the cruel thoughts Carl had poured into him as Dr. Tenney readied a deathblow against him. *Carl wanted me to die with that hurt in my mind.* "He doesn't deserve to be alive," Trevor said aloud.

"Living is not just for those that deserve it, any more than dying is," Veronica said, bending toward him. "Now stay here; don't move."

"Veronica, look out!" Leila hurled herself between Veronica and the largest owl Trevor had ever seen.

The bird's curved beak jabbed into Leila's breast. Blood spurted from the wound, staining the owl's white feathers. Splashed with crimson, the bird flew upward.

Veronica jumped for it and missed. Its talons raked her hands. It circled once above their heads and vanished into the clouds.

The man who Trevor had thought was Dr. Tenney held Leila, while Veronica worked to stanch the flow of blood. "Fool girl, thinking I needed defending," Veronica muttered, then called, "Miryam, get over here. Leila needs your healing. I'm too drained from all the others."

Miryam came from behind Trevor and walked slowly to the injured girl. She seemed dazed. But when she placed her hands over the wound, color came back into Leila's ashen face.

"Thanks, Peter," Leila said to the man who held her. "I'm all right now." She embraced Miryam. "Thank you, Miryam. I wish I could heal *your* hurt."

The man whose body Dr. Tenney had stolen must be back in that body. His actions were not those of the Adept.

Yet Trevor did not think Dr. Tenney was dead. He and Carl were alive; Dr. Tenney must be, too. The strange presence of the owl and its attack on Leila made sense if Dr. Tenney had transformed himself or taken over the bird.

Trevor remembered then what must have been a dream— a dream of walking up a golden road, Miryam at his side, Carl and Dr. Tenney behind them. A strange being waited for them at the road's end, but before they could reach him, Les had come and—

A sudden dread gripped Trevor. Les!

He whirled around, heedless of the dizziness caused by the rapid motion.

Carl sat propped against the trunk of the mulberry tree. Only a short distance from him Les lay on his back, his body straight, his arms crossed over his chest. Trevor knew before he reached him that his friend was dead.

Numbly Trevor went along with the others to Doss Hamlyn's home. They found Hamlyn recovering in the care of his servants, the horses having pulled the carriage home. Fortunately, he needed no further healing. Veronica and Leila were exhausted. After forcing Tenney, weak from his near-death experience, out of Peter's body and transferring Peter's consciousness into it from the owl, they had restored power to many of those from whom Dr. Tenney had stolen it. The owl's attack and flight had prevented them from completing that work. Hamlyn offered to take into his home the members who had not yet been healed.

Peter, guarding Carl, whose manner still held a trace of defiance, asked, "What about this guy? What's to be done with him?"

The question roused Trevor from his stupor, and he listened for the response, willing the judgment to be death.

Doss Hamlyn said, "In a sense it's a good thing he became a member of the Community. As a member, he's subject to its rules, including some that have not been invoked in years. When a member has misused his power in as harmful a manner as Carl has done, we can strip him of that power and remand him to the civil authorities for trial and punishment. I believe he can be convicted of theft and assault, if Trevor is willing to testify." He looked at Trevor.

Trevor shrugged. "I'll do whatever it takes to get him put away for a while, but no punishment's enough for him."

"I think you underestimate the effect that being stripped of power will have," Veronica said.

"He may get out of prison, but the Community will continue to keep him under observation," Hamlyn said. "We will keep him honest."

Trevor wasn't satisfied, but the decision was not in his hands. He sank back into his despondent daze.

While the others made decisions, he followed directions: sat when they told him to, walked when they told him to, went where they took him.

It wasn't until he, along with Miryam and Leila and Veronica, wound up back in Veronica's home that he started to feel again. And what he felt was grief intermingled with rage.

Leila brought him a bowl of soup and urged him to eat. He pushed her hand away so roughly that the soup slopped over the bowl onto her hands. She set the bowl on the nearest table and mopped the hot soup off her burned fingers with the hem of her blouse. He should apologize for hurting her, but what did one more stupid act matter?

Leila gave him a pitying look and walked away to join Miryam on the opposite side of the room. They talked together in low tones, and Leila picked up Veronica's crystal globe and gazed into it.

Veronica walked over to Trevor. "Carl no longer controls you," she said. "I've seen to that. When I healed your throat, I traced that injury to its cause and severed the binding. The ties were not as complicated or deeply entwined as those that bound Miryam to him."

E. ROSE SABIN

He only nodded. He didn't want to talk to her. She should never have allowed Tenney to escape. She should have foreseen the danger and prevented it. She should have saved Les.

But he had no right to censure anyone. It was because of his folly that Les was dead. If he had listened when Les first warned him about Tenney, his friend would be alive.

"It should comfort you that Les found his gift," Veronica said.

"A gift of exchanging his life for mine and for the others—what sort of gift is that?"

"The greatest of gifts," Veronica insisted. "Of the few who possess it, most lack the courage and the love to exercise it. Your friend lacked neither; you should be proud of him."

"Proud? That Les threw away his life?" Trevor let his bitterness pour out.

Veronica's sharp voice cut through his anger. "You don't honor your friend by wallowing in grief. Make his death count for something. Go after Tenney. Clip his wings."

"How can I do that?"

"You'll find the way. You have power."

"Not like his." Trevor said. "He's an Adept, and he still has some of the power he drained from the members of the Community. How am I supposed to fight that kind of strength? *You* couldn't defeat him. How do you expect me to?"

"I *could* defeat him, but I'm needed here, and you need the confidence and self-respect that will come from vanquishing the one who did you so much harm. He's greatly limited by the owl's body. His own body has been destroyed; I saw to that."

"How do you know he hasn't already found another body to transfer into?"

"It isn't an easy thing to do. He's been using a lot of power, and he can transfer only if he finds a body handy and conveniently helpless. He hasn't done so; of that I can assure you. I wouldn't send you after him if I didn't feel you had a chance."

Trevor considered. "A chance. Not much of one." Everything he had attempted against Dr. Tenney had gone wrong. He didn't dare try again.

"Will you let Les's death be in vain?"

"So that's what this is all about? You didn't want Les to use his gift to save me, did you?"

"I hoped he wouldn't have to. Now I'm asking you to prove that you were worth it. You owe it to Les—and to yourself."

"And if I fail, I'll prove that I *wasn't* worth it."

Hands on her hips, she glared down at him. "You came here for training in the use of power. How do you think that training is accomplished? It's through practice. And you've had a lot of that recently. You've learned that your power has limits, and by calling down that storm you tested your strength and found it greater than you expected and more deadly. You still need to learn to focus. And the only way you can learn that is by doing it."

He looked away from her, rubbing his hand over the fur he was sitting on. "You talk as though going after Dr. Tenney is just a training exercise."

"In a sense everything is a training exercise," she said. "We learn by doing. Sometimes the lessons are terribly painful. Your Uncle Matthew sent you here for training because he knew that. He learned the hard way how deadly the careless use of power can be. I'd guess he hoped to spare you the kind of painful lesson he got when he caused the death of his sister. It was, I suspect, his way of redeeming himself.

"Except that his plan backfired, and Les is gone, and if you refuse to stop Tenney, your life will be a failure and so will your uncle's."

"That's not fair." His rage rekindled, Trevor met her gaze. "My Uncle Matt is no failure, and you have no right to bring him into this."

"No? He came to this Community for training, and he did learn what talents he had and how to use them to protect himself, but he was always too afraid of hurting anyone to develop them fully. He could have made a real difference if he'd dared to use them in a positive way, as a force for good. I'm guessing that he knows that and that he doesn't want you to make the mistake he made."

"And that means I have to go after Dr. Tenney?"

"You don't *have* to go after him, Trevor. You have the opportunity. You have the chance to prove to yourself and everyone else that you can."

He thought of Uncle Matt and the sacrifice he and Aunt Ellen had made to send him here. He thought of Les and the ultimate sacrifice he had made. Wearily he said, "Tell me where to find Dr. Tenney."

"He'll return to his house," Veronica answered, wiping her hands on her apron. "You'll have to lure him away from it. He stored power in those diabolical machines of his, and although Peter destroyed most of them, if any at all remain usable, he'll become more dangerous."

"I don't know how I could lure Tenney outside or what to do if I could." The whine Trevor heard in his own voice sickened him. He despised himself for being afraid.

A PERILOUS POWER

267

Veronica stood waiting, arms crossed.

He thought of Les, who had dared oppose the Adept with no power at all—or none that he knew he had.

He met Veronica's eyes. "I'll do it," he said in a sudden burst of resolve. "Tell me what to do."

She shook her head while her gaze continued to burn into him. "I can't tell you that. After you've lured him from the house, you'll have to find a way, not to kill him but to destroy his power."

His resolve melted. She was asking the impossible. He pulled up his knees, leaned his arms on them, and lowered his head onto his arms, hiding his face. He heard Veronica's footsteps march away from him.

A soft touch on his shoulder made him look up to see Leila smiling down at him.

"I'll help you, Trevor. I owe it to my father to see that Dr. Tenney is stopped. Together we can do it."

He shook his head, watched her smile fade.

Her gaze held no anger, only compassion. Again she touched his shoulder lightly. "It's all right," she said. "You've been badly hurt. We shouldn't ask this of you. I'll try on my own."

"No!" He scrambled to his feet. "It's too dangerous for you. I'll do it. Veronica's right. I owe it to Les."

Veronica returned. "Good for you. Have faith in yourself. You *can* do this. But remember, you have the power to call for help if you need it."

He said, "I'll remember," but he thought, *I won't call for help. I'll do this alone—for Les.*

You made a wise choice, Trev, spoke a voice in his mind. Les's voice. *You won't be alone. I'll be with you. We started this thing together, and we'll end it together—one way or another.*

E. ROSE SABIN

23

FRIENDS IN NEED

Trevor watched the hack bump and sway along the rough road, leaving him stranded outside Dr. Tenney's house. He searched for some sign of occupancy, beating his way through tall weeds to check the sides and back of the house. While he had been imprisoned in the house, he'd noted that the doctor kept candles and oil lamps burning in his laboratory and in his study throughout the day, but no lights were evident in those rooms now.

The owl had no need of light, Trevor reminded himself. It was a nocturnal creature.

He returned to the front of the house and stepped into the street to escape the clinging weeds and pick the burs off his trousers. His confidence was ebbing.

He moved farther from the house, into the noonday sunlight. From there he cupped his hands around his mouth and shouted, "Dr. Tenney, it's Trevor. I'm out here. Come and get me."

No one answered. If Dr. Tenney was affected by the owl's natural instincts, he would not willingly emerge at this hour. Trevor wished Veronica had suggested some plan instead of merely warning him not to go inside the house.

He regretted his hasty rejection of Leila's offer of help. Hamlyn's daughter had considerable power, he knew, though he did not know her specific talents.

But I'm not alone, he thought, recalling Les's voice. *Les, if you're here with me, show me what to do.*

He waited for some kind of response until a rustling in the weeds drew his attention and he caught a glimpse of a sinuous black form. A snake.

Owls ate snakes. And mice. The overgrown fields surrounding Dr. Tenney's house must be full of both. Would the Adept's diet be guided by the bird's hunger? It might be worth a try.

He closed his eyes and concentrated on sensing the small movements, the soft sounds of hiding creatures. Slowly, carefully, he drew them toward him. Opening his eyes, he saw the high stalks set in motion by the passage of small bodies.

I don't need so many. Five or six mice. Maybe a snake or two. He narrowed his summons. A gray mouse slipped out of cover and sat at the edge of the road, its nose twitching with fear. Another joined it; two others. A black snake slithered onto the dusty road.

He turned them, sent them toward the house. They seemed as reluctant as he to approach it. The mice crept forward in short bursts, followed by long quivering pauses. The snake reached the house's shadow, turned, and whipped away. Trevor could not call it back. The mice would have to serve.

He forced the creatures to climb up onto the rickety porch steps and to chase one another back and forth on the steps, making scrabbling noises that the sharp-eared owl would hear.

E. ROSE SABIN

A feathery white blur plummeted downward from an upper-story window and snatched a mouse in its talons. With squeaks of fright, the other mice dashed away. The owl perched on the porch roof and consumed its prey.

"Dr. Tenney!" Trevor stepped closer but remained in the street. "I know that's you. I have to talk to you. I can help you regain human form."

The owl cleaned its beak on its feathers and regarded Trevor. *Come into the house, my boy, and I'll listen to what you have to say.* There was no mistaking the oily voice in his mind.

"No, you come down here," Trevor shouted to the owl.

It is you who want to talk, not I, the voice came again. *It is not your place to dictate the terms.*

Trevor looked at the porch with its doorway yawning open into darkness like a hungry mouth. Even if Veronica had not warned against it, he could never bear to enter that place again.

He stared up at the owl, and the owl stared back at him, offering no further communication, merely waiting as though time meant nothing at all to it.

He had to do something. He glanced at the posts supporting the porch roof. The one on the corner to his right looked as though it would support his weight. If he climbed to the roof and met the owl there, it would not be as bad as going inside the house. He had no plan for dealing with the Adept once he reached the roof; he could only hope that something would present itself. He could not endure this inaction.

He raced to the corner of the porch, vaulted onto the porch railing, and shinnied up the post. Reaching up, he grasped the roof overhang and tried to haul himself onto the roof.

The owl spread its wings, flew upward at a sharp angle, and plunged toward Trevor. He dared not loosen his hold to fend off the bird. The powerful talons clamped around his arms, the wings flapped, and the great bird pulled Trevor up over the edge, dragged him along the roof, and dropped him facedown on the rough wooden shingles. The owl released his arms only to hop onto his back so that he could not rise.

He hurled his power at the bird, remembering to shield immediately. He felt the owl sway and dig its talons through his clothes and into his flesh. He lowered the shield to launch another bolt.

Fiery worms attacked his mind, boring into his brain, sending shock waves of pain through his head. He gasped, struggled against unconsciousness, and lost the battle, though only for a few moments.

He regained awareness when a voice spoke in his mind. *So kind of you, my boy, to come back and offer me a more appropriate host than this ridiculous fowl. I thank you.*

The talons pulled free, tearing his flesh. He felt the bird's weight lift off him, heard the swish of wings; the wind of the bird's passage swept over him. The owl, freed of its tenant, had flown away. Dr. Tenney had installed his consciousness in Trevor's mind!

It hovered over his own pain-disordered thoughts, a black-winged bird of death. He fought it with waning strength. He felt his body roll over, sit up, rise to balance precariously on shaky legs, all in obedience to no command he had given. His legs carried him unsteadily toward a

E. ROSE SABIN

second-story window that opened onto the porch roof. His arm lifted, poised to break the cracked window and allow entrance into the house.

Have to stop this. Trevor tried to pull his fragmenting thoughts together. *Need help. Les!*

His arm swung. The window shattered. Blood flowed from a jagged cut on his wrist. His booted foot kicked out the rest of the glass. Though he seemed powerless to stop it, Trevor knew he was lost if he entered the house.

Les! he sent again.

I'm here, Les's quiet voice said in his mind. *I'll do what I can, but it won't be enough. Tenney's too strong. Call for more help, quick, while you can.*

Trevor hesitated.

Les's voice grew faint, garbled. *No time for pride. Ask help. No shame. You wanted Community. Call.*

It might already be too late, but he tried to send. *Leila, Peter, Miryam, Veronica! Help me! I'm caught. I can't do this alone.*

He heard his own mouth utter an angry exclamation, the only indication that the feeble sending might have gotten through. A cottony blanket clamped over his thoughts, smothering further attempts to call. Dazed, losing himself, he could only mumble, "Les."

His hands grasped the window frame; his foot lifted to stand on the sill. From somewhere came the strength to stiffen his arms, dig his fingers into the rotting wood. He willed his muscles to obey *his* mind, not the alien commander's.

Power. In response to Les's faint whisper Trevor dredged up his fading power, channeled all he could find into the control of his own body. It wasn't enough. He could not move backward, away from the window. He could only refuse to move forward, and that not for long.

It's hopeless. Give up; you can't win. You're stupid to think you can defeat an Adept.

At first, he accepted the thought as his own. Only a faint echo of Les's voice cautioning, *Don't listen,* alerted him that Dr. Tenney had inserted the despairing thought into his mind.

Anger fueled his power; his will strengthened. The dampening blanket grew lighter.

Hang on, Trevor. We're coming. He recognized the sending as Leila's.

His muscles tensed. He pushed himself back, away from the window. His foot caught on a loose shingle. Unbalanced, he toppled backward, slid down the sloping roof.

Fool, I won't let you kill yourself. At Tenney's sharp voice, Trevor caught himself, hung on to the rough wood at the roof's edge. Turning onto his stomach, he inched back toward the window.

Again Leila's words penetrated the mind fog. *Keep fighting. Your friends are on their way.*

Hurry, he sent and twisted away from the window. Dr. Tenney's growl issued from Trevor's throat. Pain stabbed through his body, exploded in his brain. He couldn't see, couldn't hear, could feel nothing but all-consuming agony.

"You," he gasped. "You have to feel this, too."

He didn't know if that was true. He *wanted* it to be true, wanted to think that to make *him* suffer, Tenney had to suffer along with him.

He withdrew as he had from Carl's abuse, tightening himself into a tiny ball, rolling into a distant corner.

In his mental exile the pain lessened. He constructed a wall around himself, imaging bricks and mortar. The wall took form. As it grew higher, the pain receded to a memory. He allowed himself a small sense of triumph. Yet something nagged at him. A thought, perhaps his own, perhaps a sending from Les or from Leila. Something said, *Wall Tenney, not yourself.*

Wall Tenney? Surely that was impossible.

He added another row of bricks to the top of his wall, and as he came to the wall's corner, he curved it outward, away from himself. He added more rows of bricks, stretching their line outward, building frantically now, working from outside the wall rather than inside.

He visualized Tenney as he had been before his body was killed, pictured the round-cheeked, bearded face, the pudgy body. In the mouth he visualized the Adept's ever-present pipe. *That should please you,* he thought with a grim smile.

A portion of wall exploded outward. Bricks flew toward him. One struck his head, another his shoulder. He fell backward, fresh pain flowing through him.

No! This is my mind. I won't let you control it. Trevor hefted a brick that had fallen. He hurled it at the figure climbing out of the hole in the wall. Clamping his teeth against the pain that coursed through him, he gathered the rest of the bricks and replaced them before the Adept recovered from the blow that had toppled him back into the enclosure. As Trevor worked, the pain receded.

Hurriedly he built the wall higher until he could no longer reach its top. He visualized a ladder, leaned it against the bricks, and climbed it. His construction had become a tower with no windows or doors interrupting its solid walls. He gazed down into the interior. The Adept, shrunk to doll size, glared up at him.

I'll have to roof it over, he thought. *That should make it impossible for him to escape.*

He imaged planks of thick, hard wood and struggled to carry these up the ladder and lay them across the top of the tower until the opening was nearly covered.

Have mercy, my boy, came a plaintive voice from the dark recesses of the tower. *You can't leave me here alone in the darkness. Leave me at least a breathing hole.*

Trevor considered. Despite the vividness of the image in his mind, the Adept had only his consciousness, no body that needed light to see by or air to breathe.

I'll be able to help you if you leave me an opening, the imploring voice rose to him faintly as from a great distance. *Think of it: the power of an Adept at your command.*

I want no help from you, Trevor shouted into the last open space, creating echoes that swirled down the tower. He slammed the final board into place, clambered from the ladder onto the plank roof, and secured the boards with mortar, nails, and crosspieces, all furnished by his fertile imagination.

When the structure was complete, he climbed down from the ladder and walked around it, inspecting his handiwork.

"Trevor! Trevor, can you hear me?"

Leila's voice roused him from his fantasy. He became aware of the rough wooden shingles beneath his hands, the awkward angle of his body on the sloping porch roof. He realized that the pain Dr. Tenney had inflicted was entirely gone. He also realized that Leila's voice had not spoken in his mind; he had heard it normally, through his ears.

He opened his eyes and cautiously raised his head. Leila and Peter stood in the street, gazing up at the porch roof.

"Thank the Power-Giver! You're alive!" Leila called to him. "Where's Dr. Tenney?"

Trevor sat up, sent a tentative probe inward, and explored his own mind. He sensed a closed-off area, did not probe that spot too deeply.

"I'll explain later," he called back. "First I need help getting off this roof."

Only when they had all gathered in Veronica's house did Trevor describe his battle with Dr. Tenney. The tables were shoved together against the wall to clear a space in the center of the round room next to the stove and woodbin. The group sat on the furs, Trevor in the center, with Veronica, Leila, Miryam, Peter, and Doss Hamlyn encircling him. Hamlyn looked out of place in the eccentrically furnished room, but he had insisted on being present.

"As a friend of your uncle, I've been deeply concerned for you all along," he said. "I was injured attempting your rescue earlier, and I participated in the lending of strength in your contest with Tenney. I must know the outcome of the contest."

"So, you were all helping. I didn't do it on my own." At one time the revelation would have been a blow to his pride. Now he could smile about it. He wasn't really surprised; he'd felt the infusion of strength that came when he called for their help. He didn't know how much of his success was due to his own ingenuity and power and how much to the efforts of his friends.

Did it matter? *No,* he answered his own question. *I'm lucky to have these friends. No one gets through life on his own.*

A PERILOUS POWER

"We started channeling power to you as soon as we got your sending," Leila explained. "That was all we could do. We didn't know your situation, couldn't advise you. We tried to send to you, but Tenney was able to block our sending. So we were working blindly, focusing power and hoping you'd be able to use it."

Trevor nodded. "I had other help, too. Les was with me, I don't know how." He looked at Miryam. "I do know that I couldn't have done it without him."

The eager expression on her face made her look almost pretty. "Tell me about it, please."

He told them. Where he would have skimped on details, their questions drew out every particular. When he finished, Leila threw her arms around him and hugged him. "Trevor, that was brilliant. And it took real courage."

He felt his face flush with embarrassment. He could find no words to answer.

Hamlyn regarded him with a frown. "So Tenney's consciousness is alive in you. You realize, son, how dangerous that is? That mind tower you built—he'll find a way to tear it down. It may take him a while, but you won't be able to hold him forever."

The words sent a chill of fear through Trevor, but before he could speak, Veronica intervened. "I think he can," she said, her sharp-eyed gaze scanning the faces around her. "He can, *if* we are all willing to give up a portion of our power. If we each pass to Trevor a bit of our power—of ourselves— for the strengthening and binding of the tower, Tenney will never be able to escape. The question is: Will you each relinquish part of your power for that purpose? I will do so, but since I have more to give, the rest of you may be unwilling to follow my example. Your gift must be completely voluntary. And Trevor is not exempted. He will have to give up more than any of us. To keep Tenney imprisoned will require a large part of his power for the rest of his life."

"What are the alternatives?" Peter asked quietly. "For Trevor especially. Is there no way to release Dr. Tenney and deal with him?"

"No safe way," Veronica said. "His consciousness needs a place to go. If we could extract it from Trevor and prevent it from entering any of us, Tenney would be destroyed. That would be the simplest solution. The problem is that if Tenney were let out of his prison, before we could force him to abandon Trevor's body, he would certainly destroy Trevor. We must sacrifice Trevor if we are to do away with Dr. Tenney."

The chill that had invaded Trevor intensified, freezing his blood. He had wanted to die. Now he wanted to live. But only if Tenney could be kept imprisoned and helpless.

"Trevor's gone through enough," Leila said, her eyes sparking with anger. "He certainly isn't to be a sacrifice."

"I'll give all my power to keep Tenney bound," Trevor said. "Will that be enough?"

"Possibly, but I can't be sure," Veronica answered. "Even with all yours and part of mine, well . . . you know how great Tenney's power is."

"There's no need for Trevor to use all his power. I'll gladly give up part of mine," Leila said.

"I haven't wanted anything more to do with power," Miryam spoke up. "He can have all of mine, and gladly."

"A kind offer, but not one I'd allow Trevor to accept," Veronica said. "You may give him part of your power, but most you must reserve. Your life is not over. You have much to contribute, and you will need power to fulfill your potential."

Miryam started to object, but Doss Hamlyn cut off her words. "Here, here. Let's have no more talk of all these noble sacrifices. The entire Community owes much to Trevor. I will call on those who had their power restored after so nearly losing it all to Tenney and urge them to give a small portion of that power to Trevor. I'd be very surprised if anyone would refuse."

"I certainly would not," Peter said. "I'll gladly contribute."

Veronica nodded. "An excellent suggestion, Doss. Such an action will be the best thing the Community has done in a long while. Perhaps there is hope that it will, after all, return to the nurturing that was its original purpose."

"I'm sure there is," Hamlyn said, smiling. He rose and shook Trevor's hand. "I'll get on it right away—as soon as I've made my own power donation."

The others also rose and surrounded Trevor. Leila embraced him and the rest placed their hands on his shoulders and back. He felt an infusion of love and strength flow into him, melting the ice, filling him with warmth.

He sensed the separate strands: Veronica's, taut and sturdy as a steel cable; Miryam's, a braided rope of diverse talents; Peter's, supple and sharp like the tail of a dragon; Hamlyn's, a succession of businesslike darts aimed directly at their target; Leila's, soft yet strong, intertwining with his own. And another's, all-embracing, joining with the other friends. Les.

Trevor laughed with joy and let his power mingle with that of all of his friends.

Deep into his mind the power poured, circling that dark space where the tower hid. He saw the brick wall thicken, the roof grow sturdier. From within he thought he heard a despairing groan.

Epilogue

Veronica set a cup of tea on the fur next to Miryam. "You drink that," she ordered.

"I don't—"

"I know, I know," Veronica interrupted. "You don't want anything to drink, and you can't eat anything, you're so wrapped up in your grief. Well, it's time you stopped moping. You need that tea, and you *are* going to drink it."

She watched closely while Miryam reluctantly picked up the cup and sipped the amber liquid. When the girl set the cup down, Veronica shook her head.

"Don't think I can't see how little of that you drank." She sniffed. "You're not taking enough to keep a moth alive."

Miryam smiled wanly and said, "I'm not a moth."

"No, you certainly aren't. You are a lovely and talented young woman with her life ahead of her."

The smile vanished. "A life that doesn't mean anything without Les," she said tiredly.

"A life that Les *gave* you and certainly doesn't want you to throw away. You have every right to grieve, but you also have much to be thankful for. You are alive, free from Carl, your gift is yours alone to use—"

"Or not to use," Miryam broke in. "The only gift I want is one that will let me join Les."

"Perhaps someday that gift will be yours. Now it is not. And I don't intend to let you starve yourself to death. You drink the rest of that tea while I fix you a proper meal."

"I'm not hungry. Food just sticks in my throat."

Veronica walked toward her stove. With her back to Miryam, she said, "You need a purpose in life." She slammed an iron pot onto the stove and yanked an assortment of vegetables out of mesh bags hanging from the ubiquitous strings. "You've made it clear that you don't want to use your gift, but you need to decide what you do want to do with your life."

Saying nothing, Miryam picked up her teacup and studied it as though she could read her future there.

Veronica, too, did not speak but busied herself peeling vegetables and tossing them into the pot.

Finally Miryam sighed and set down the cup. "I don't know what I want to do," she said. "I only know that I'd like to leave Port-of-Lords—go as far from it as I can."

"Well, that's something, at least," Veronica said as she poured a pitcher of water into her pot and stirred vigorously. "This is a big country. You could go across it to the east coast. But what will you do when you get there?"

Miryam's shoulders slumped. "I have no idea," she said dully.

"Well, I *do* have an idea." Veronica turned to her. "I've been thinking. The Community here in Port-of-Lords has taken a turn for the better, no question about that, but I still don't have much love for it. When Kyla established the Community, it was intended to be a place for training people new to their gift. Young people, especially."

E. ROSE SABIN

"You knew the Lady Kyla?" Miryam showed the first spark of interest Veronica had heard in her voice for a long time.

"Of course I knew her. She practically raised me."

"Lady Kyla did? The one who brought magic back to Arucadi? You can't be that old!"

Veronica chuckled at the undiplomatic statement. "I'm older than I look. But my age is beside the point. I was telling you that the Community here lost sight of Kyla's purpose. It's regained that, for now anyway. But I see a great need for a school that trains the gifted in the use of their powers. If Trevor and Les had had something like that, things might have turned out very differently."

"I suppose so," Miryam said, falling back into her lethargy.

"You could start such a school, Miryam." Veronica shook her spoon at her protégée. "Even though you don't want to use your own power, is there any reason why you couldn't train other people to use theirs responsibly?"

"I wouldn't know how to do that."

"Oh yes, you would. You wouldn't have to do it alone. You'd find others to help—gifted teachers who would be delighted to guide students not only in subject matter but in the wise use of power."

With her forefinger Miryam traced a pattern on the fur she sat on. "It would be an awfully big job."

"It would be a life's work. Would anything less important be worthy of a life Les died to save?"

"I suppose not, but . . . would *you* help?"

Veronica turned back to the stove and gave her soup a vigorous stirring. "I could," she said after a time. "But it would have to be your project, not mine. You'd head it up; I'd stay in the background."

"So long as I know you're there to advise me." Miryam

A PERILOUS POWER

stood and picked up her teacup. "And I'd be doing it for Les. I'd name the school for him."

"Now you're thinking," Veronica said. "You can call it the Lesley Simonton School for the Magically Gifted. That has a fine ring to it."

"It does, doesn't it?" Miryam came to stand beside her and put an arm around her. "What's for supper? Suddenly I feel hungry."